"I've read it three time<u> </u>...nd love it more and more each time. On tra<u> </u>к to being my top read this year. It's gonna be hard to beat"
Abigail, Bookstagrammer

"OMG, wow. I loved it so much. I'm gutted it's finished. Honestly, I'm buzzing - it was amazing!"
Heidi H, Book Lover

"I can't express how much I love this book. You are truly an amazing author"
Claire, Bookstagrammer

"Loved the twists & turns throughout this one that made for a tense psychological read at times"
Sandra, Book Lover

"Oh my, I loved it! I read it yesterday and couldn't go to bed until I had finished it. You are a beautiful writer"
Naomi, Bookstagrammer

"I've cried, I've laughed, I couldn't put it down. That just sums up a typical T.A. Rosewood book"
Jess, Bookstagrammer

"What a rollercoaster this book has taken me on!
If you're into psychological thrillers and want to be
kept on your toes, this is the book for you!"
Melissa, Bookstagrammer

"I always worry with follow-ons that they won't match
up but with these, you got it spot on!
I LOVE everything about your books!
They will all stay with me forever"
Alice, Bookstagrammer

"She's done it again!! Written a masterpiece that I flew
through and didn't want to put down. I absolutely love
all the books by this author. Intense twists and turns
that just made for a gripping read"
Chloe J, Bookstagrammer

"Think this is the best one yet!
Stayed up late to finish it. I Loved it!"
Kayleigh, Book Lover

"This has kept me up until the early hours. I just
needed to know what was going to happen next.
Just brilliant!"
Polly, eBook Lover

"I am SOBBING!!! What a storyline!
It kept me guessing right to the end"
KML Books, Author & Book Blogger

Telling *Lies*

Dear Sophie,

Merry Christmas

Best Wishes

Telling Lies

T.A. ROSEWOOD

ISBN 978-1-80068-498-0

For Billy & Anni. xx

Prologue

As she slowly turned back round, her face stinging with pain, she knew this had to be the last time he ever struck her frail, bruised body making her feel so worthless and insignificant. He had taken his last swing at her now and she was determined she wasn't going to take anymore. She just couldn't. Mustering as much faltering energy as she could, a rapid fire inside her lit up and she suddenly thrust her pained, battered body towards him. Grabbing his head hard in her tiny hands, screaming as loud as she possibly could straight into his now, shocked face. She could feel her entire body trembling with anger, the adrenaline scaring through her chest cavity, kicking in and giving her the strength and the power she needed to finally fight back. This was it, she had to stop him for good this time.

Stumbling backwards with shock at her sudden attack, he fell, hitting his head on the edge of the kitchen table. Her chest heaving, breathing rapidly, she watched as this person who she had once thought so much of, once loved more than anyone ever before, sat up, his evil eyes glaring at her with blood trickling down the side of his sweaty face. Scared for her life, she turned slightly, wrenched open the kitchen drawer and grabbed the biggest knife she could find as he gradually began pulling himself back up.

"No more. I tell you. I'm not taking this anymore, don't come any closer, I mean it," she cried out, tears now streaming down her reddened face. She was shaking like never before, like someone else was shaking her body ferociously. She began taking steps backwards to escape his clutches, as she watched him try and stand. Her hand still wielding the knife in front of her pointing it at him with the full intent on using it if she really had to. She knew he wasn't going to leave it; he would never just stop there, especially as she had fought back this time too. Knowing this wouldn't end well, she had to do whatever it took. She had to get away, this had to stop today.

"Now come on, you know you won't do anything with that thing, give it here, let's sort this out," he said, stumbling again.

His voice always calmed a little after every time he had hit out, maybe knowing that he'd gone too far but wanted her forgiveness, wanted her to love him and forget his ways. He still had to be the one in charge though, he loved being in control of her and any situation thinking she was too weak to leave him or do anything to protect herself.

But this time was different, something had changed her mind about him for good. She just glared back at her husband, locking into his dark, angry eyes and shook her head, "No, I don't want to sort it out, don't come near me or I swear, I…I will kill you."

He laughed sarcastically, wiping the warm blood from his face, smearing it across his brutal hand that had struck her so many times before. She used to love those hands touching her, making her feel so loved at the start of the relationship. What had made him change so much, why had she put up with this for so long. Why and how had he become such a horrid person to be around and why did he always take it out on her?

Her thoughts were broken as he suddenly launched himself and grabbed her tightly around her wrist, "don't be stupid," he bellowed as they battled against each other, scrambling across the kitchen floor. So many times, he had hit her so hard, she'd passed out and by the time she came to, everything had been neatly put back in place. He would be there when she woke, towering over her to make sure she didn't leave, apologising profusely, crying for sympathy and forgiveness from her, telling her how much he loved her and needed her in his life, saying he wouldn't do anything like that again, but she wasn't going to let him win this time.

The fire inside her was raging and nothing was going to put it out today. Not this time. With an almighty thrust, and all the power she could muster, she yanked her arm away, out of his clutches, and then returned it swiftly toward his body, ramming the knife into his stomach without thinking, "I told you to leave me alone," she shouted, thrusting again and again, "I told you; I told you; I told you!" she shrieked as he reached out grabbing her arms, then losing grip again.

After what seemed like ten minutes, he became silent and lost his tight grip on her. He fell to the floor once more. As he hit the ground, smashing his head on the ceramic tiles, blood gushed from his wounds. Now, he remained down, stunned and bleeding heavily.

Gasping for breath, wheezing slightly; her chest felt heavy and in pain, her tears blurring her vision as she looked down at her blood stained, shaking hand. As she lifted her hand up, grasping tightly around the knife, she watched the dripping red fluid dropping down at her feet.

Everything seemed to be deathly silenced in the moment, her small but frantic movements seemed in slow motion, and she couldn't hear a thing apart from the thumping of her heart and his slight groaning and moaning as he lay there unable to sit or stand. Unable to get hold of her for once in his life, for once in their relationship, he wasn't in charge.

Glancing down at him curled up holding his stomach in agony, his eyes now closed tightly seething with the pain of the injuries she had just endured on him, she knew she had to go, and it had to be quickly. She was pretty sure enough damage had been done by the way he was staying on the ground and not coming at her again.

She dropped the knife, the noise twanging in her ears as it bounced onto the tiles. Her hand was free of the weapon and all she wanted to do was run away and never return. Spinning on her feet, stumbling out of the kitchen and into the hallway, she ran to the front door frantically unlocking it and swinging it open to the outside world. Bare feet, clothes ripped and tears filling her eyes, she was outside.

Running into the middle of the street, her face filled with sadness, her clothes splattered with both their blood, she stood there motionless, frightened, shocked, and alone.

Her mind was in complete turmoil fretting with questions as to what she was going to do, what she would say to people, who could she turn to. How could this have happened, why had she let it go this far, was he badly injured or could he be dead, could she have killed her husband, and more importantly, what would become of her and her innocent son?

Her son, the only good thing to come out of this relationship. The only thing she lived for in her cruel marriage for so many years. This thought just by itself, filled her heart with dread, filled her eyes with the biggest tears she had ever felt. Her son, her boy, her only child.

In that very moment, and just in the nick of time to give her the strength she needed, her beautiful, brave little boy appeared. He reached up and just held her hand as tightly as his trembling hand could do so. It was the two of them now, united. They were both safe from that man, she had saved them and would do everything to protect their life from now on.

Chapter One

Kate…

When you think about your future, what comes to mind? What do you really want out of this crazy world and everything that life can throw at you? How will your future turn out or evolve from this day forward, and how can you or could you, improve it along the way? Will you choose to study more, work up the career ladder you're already in, build a fantastic new life or be your own boss and have an amazing business? Do you dream of having lots of or more children than you have already, an extended family, a big house, fancy cars, and a great partner to spend the rest of your years with?

Most of these thoughts were something that played on Kate's mind so often, daydreaming about her future and how it would be. Sometimes it would take her off on a tangent to another world of creativity and adventures that she wanted to experience. She really had no idea how it was all going to eventually pan out but, she had fun dreaming. She was a big-time dreamer, but a determined one at that. The biggest dream she had was making her mum proud, which she never faltered to do during their years together.

Kate, a twenty-four-year-old waitress from Hertfordshire, England just getting by each month with her petty wages from two waitress jobs. She often thought to herself, was this all she had aspired to be when she left college? No, she hadn't but things just work out that way sometimes, well for some people anyway.

From a young age, she had always had big plans, dreams of running her own fancy, city restaurant. Following the likes of famous chefs, down to earth, Jamie Oliver or the more controversial style of Gordon Ramsay to help drive her into chef celebrity status success. She loved Jamie Oliver and his traditional home style of cooking and had even met him once at a food festival in Essex. Her signed cookbook was a treasured memory of that day aged just nineteen at the time, meeting someone she admired so much. After that, she had always hoped they would spot her food creations and talents on social media, tagging them in every post. Maybe they'd offer her a job at one of their places and believe in her to give her a step up the chef career ladder. But alas, this hadn't happened for her, but it was still alright to dream right? Being the optimist, she always clung to the idea that maybe they would spot her one day. 'What's the point in just pretending this is all that will become of my future when you can dream it to happen?', she used to say to her auntie.

She loved cooking and baking and had always spent hours in the kitchen with her mum creating new flavours of cookies, cakes and sometimes even bread. This was one baking mission that they never mastered to the standard they had hoped for although it always tasted okay to them. 'Bread is bread,' her mum used to say to encourage her daughter and keep her spirits up.

But after her mum, Fiona, died, that cooking spark in Kate died too. Her vision for dreamy cakes and special ingredient biscuits got lost and put away to the back of her mind. She just couldn't face it without her cooking buddy by her side, so she just opted for working in the industry instead. Waitressing at two local restaurants serving food instead of creating it kept her food cravings satisfied.

Kate had grown up in a loving home to her single parent mum, Fiona who had not been able to have children herself. She had fostered around five babies and had been on the adoption waiting list for seven years, patiently awaiting that all important phone call to say that she could finally adopt and be granted with her special bundle of joy. She loved fostering and specifically enjoyed fostering babies, but it was for such a short time. Usually having them leave to be adopted when they'd reach around twelve to eighteen months of age. After many discussions with her sister and researching like crazy, she decided she wanted to go down the adoption route, settle down with a child 'of her own'. She wanted to be able to give an unwanted child the life they needed and deserved.

The day finally came, and Kate arrived at just the right time in Fiona's life. Her online business was thriving selling handmade jewellery and she had a nice new apartment in the outskirts of town overlooking the marina near Hemel Hempstead. Kate had been born to a teenager, whose family had decided that the baby should be given up for adoption. The young girl had had a complicated life already and so her aunt had taken care of her throughout the pregnancy and made all the arrangements. The baby would be adopted as soon as possible after the birth.

Kate was the perfect match for Fiona, and she instantly fell in love, the moment she saw her laying in her hospital crib with a pink, woolly knitted bonnet on. She had practically run all the way to the hospital after they had rung her to say the baby had arrived and was ready to go to her new home the next morning.

It was mid-September when Kate had been born. Two weeks early, weighing in at six pounds exactly, looking ultra-cute with her scrawny little pouty face and super sweet, button nose. Her thick dark head of hair was adorable with one little curl at the front. She had been in the hospital for just over twenty-four hours after the birth, spending the evening with her natural mother. With all the documents signed, the mother didn't ask for any more information on where the baby was going.

All Fiona knew was the mother's name, that she was from the Cambridge area, and the fact that she had only been sixteen when she'd given birth to Kate. Her full name was going to be Katie-Jane Ellington and Fiona couldn't wait to get her new daughter back home.

There were various documents to sign and paperwork for Fiona to sort out and pick up when she arrived, but she knew exactly what she had to do. She had spent the past year or so learning the whole adoption process. All she wanted to do now was hold her little baby, her gorgeous new 'daughter' and give her all the love she needed.

That afternoon, her dream came true and as she placed her in the car, she smiled down at Kate and just gently kissed her little head as she slept peacefully sucking on her dummy, without a care in the world.

Kate began to sleep through the night by nine

months and on her first birthday, she took her first steps while they visited the beach in Dorset. Fiona felt so lucky to have Kate sharing her life, but time moved so quickly and before they knew it, Kate was approaching the dreaded teenage years and all the ups and downs that would bring along with it.

"Can you believe she's going to be a teenager already? Where has the time gone sis?" said Sally as they wrapped Kate's presents the night before her thirteenth birthday. Fiona's sister, Sally had been so supportive of the whole adoption. She had been as excited as Fiona and had been finishing off the decorating of the nursery while her husband and sister collected the baby from the hospital all those years back. She had even insisted on helping with the night feeds during the first few months. She adored her new niece and spoiled her at every opportunity.

"I know," replied Fiona, "it's crazy how fast the time has gone. I still remember the first day I saw her in the hospital," she said glancing over to the first ever photograph of Kate above the fireplace, in her new cot, "she looked so tiny when we collected her that day, and I couldn't wait to get her snuggled back at home," she continued, sealing the present with some sticky tape and tying some pink ribbon around the package, "I just wish I was going to see more years with her…"

"Hey, sister," Sally interrupted, "you know I'll take good care of her; I promise, she will have the life you had all planned out for her," she held her sister's arm tightly but gently at the same time reassuring her all would be ok.

Fiona had been suffering with constant stomach pains and back ache for the past eight months and she had tried to ignore them as much as possible. She hoped that her search on the internet about the symptoms she had, would not turn out to be true, but, after Sally's constant nagging to get to the doctors and a vast array of tests and scans at the hospital, her fears were proven right. And it was now too late to treat so they'd had to come to terms with it quickly.

It didn't help the shock they had felt, to learn that she had pancreatic cancer and it had spread too far to other organs. She was given a diagnosis of a matter of a few more months to live, that it could be weeks even. So, without thinking negatively she had to make plans quickly so that she knew Kate would be taken care of, financially and with the right people bringing her up.

As soon as Fiona had learnt that the cancer was inoperable and had bravely come to terms with the fact that she was terminally ill, she had asked her sister, Sally to take care of Kate, now just thirteen years old. Without any persuasion needed, Sally agreed and had moved the two of them into her penthouse apartment on the outskirts of Hertfordshire for two reasons. One, to take care of

Fiona for the last few weeks she had left in more comfort than her little place and two, so that Kate could get used to living with her and her husband, Rob.

Sally was the obvious option. Their parents were no longer around, and she knew that her sister would make a great stand-in mum when she had gone. She had a great marriage to Rob, of five years and was moving into a three-bed house in the next few months so Kate would be well looked after until such times as she could get her own place when she was old enough.

The three-month prognosis became just four weeks as her condition deteriorated rapidly. The last few weeks for Fiona and the whole family were very tough. Kate didn't attend school during that time, wanting to be with her mum as much as possible before she passed away. They would lay together talking about the adventures they'd had and watch Disney movies that they'd enjoyed together when Kate was much younger. Fiona had stopped making her jewellery and sold the remaining stock online apart from one particular necklace that she had worn for the past year. A dragonfly with a pink gemstone in the middle which she had given to Kate to wear, telling her that she only had to touch it when she felt alone, that it would represent her, and she would be there for Kate in spirit.

"You make sure you behave yourself for your aunt

and uncle okay darling?" she had whispered a few days before.

"I will mum, I promise," Kate had answered, trying her utmost to hold back the flood of tears that were waiting to cascade down her face.

"Hold my hand Katie darling," Fiona asked as she turned her fragile and cold hand over.

Kate held it with both of her hands, trying to keep her warm but as the hours went on, Fiona gradually said less, became even more cold and then silently drifted into a deep sleep.

"Katie, sweetheart, it's time," Sally said quietly as she sat beside her and wrapped her arm across Kate's shoulders. She had been there for the entire night, resting her head on the bed and not letting go of her mum's hand.

As Kate wearily lifted her head up, she looked at Fiona lying motionless and silent, "Mum…" she whispered. But as no sign came back, Kate knew. She had gone to sleep and was not going to wake up now. Her pain was over, but they felt thankful that she had gone peacefully with her daughter by her side.

The teenage years flew by and were not without the occasional argument, but Kate had made a promise to her mum, and she tried hard to keep it. Sally and Rob adored bringing her up and felt so proud of how well she had coped with everything and then going on to live by herself too.

When Kate turned twenty, she started a new waitressing job in Cambridge, commuting every day on the train. It wasn't ideal but she did enjoy the buzz of the city. The other staff members had become good friends and they'd often meet up after work and at weekends. Sometimes, they'd even go on short holidays together. Kate loved her job and when she had to help in the kitchen, it brought back great memories of cooking times with Fiona.

Her one-bedroom terraced house was a great little discovery. It was only rented but Fiona had left enough money in a trust fund for her that it was paying for it nicely. She had enjoyed decorating it, with Sally creating the Feng-shui balance thing that she loved doing. They'd even come up with a memory wall to put photos and ornamental flowers up to remember Fiona by. The necklace hung in the middle on a little heart hook whenever Kate wasn't wearing it. She worried that she would lose it at work and never be able to forgive herself so made it part of the display instead.

Everything was going in the right direction, and she had gradually begun to delve back into baking again, searching out the recipes she had created with her mum when she was around eight or nine years old. Her funny, scrawled writing on a notepad which had cake mixture encrusted on their favourite pages. The old thing was so special though and they both loved flicking through it to see what crazy creations they had made during that time. Sally thought it hilarious that they would come up with such crazy names for biscuits too.

With Kate's twenty-first birthday coming up, plans were already being discussed. Various celebratory options were put on the table to choose from. Such as spa days, Ibiza long weekender and meals out at some fancy restaurants in London and there was even a suggestion of jetting off to Paris for a special French dinner and show. With all the options available, Kate had decided she didn't want anything wild or fancy, so, they decided that Sally would throw her a slightly lavish dinner party with a few of her close friends back at their place. It was a night that Kate would always remember for more than one reason.

Chapter Two

Daniel...

Sally was laughing hysterically at her feeble attempts in the kitchen trying her hardest to create amazing and luxurious tasting food for the guests. In the end, she had let Kate take charge of the food decorating and instead, homed in her skills making exotic cocktails to finish the evening off.

"So, now you've reached the big twenty-one hey? What's next for our budding little chef?" asked Sally as the guests finished their food nibbles and retreated into the lounge to wait for their fancy cocktails to be prepared.

"Chef? Ha, I wish," Kate replied shrugging her shoulders, "I can't seem to get anywhere with my cooking lately. All I seem to do is serve food, then sleep, then serve food, sleep, serve, sleep, etc." she chuckled as she finished decorating the espresso martinis with three coffee beans on the top of each perfectly straight martini, "it's never ending with the two waitressing jobs I have now. It's just not the same cooking without mum, I've not felt confident about it for years really. I guess I just don't feel as passionate about cooking to be honest," she said, as Sally met her eyes, "Like I said, I just serve the food instead these days," she laughed, trying to perk the atmosphere up a little bit. She didn't want to upset Sally or seem down about cooking when she had gone to all this trouble to arrange this evening, "I have been dabbling with some of the cookie recipes that we made," she said trying to change the subject swiftly, "but…well, it just doesn't feel the same, you know? They never seem to turn out right."

"Aww, darling, I know it must be hard but, Fi, your mum, loved baking with you so much. She used to ring me when you'd gone to bed and tell me about the funny ingredients you used to like putting in," she nudged Kate's arm, "Hey, you know what you need to get you inspired?" pausing and now prodding Kate in the ribs, "A man. You need a nice young man in your life sweetie, someone to take care of you while you launch your cooking career," she joked, smiling widely and rather cheekily at Kate who was already shaking her head, "be a kept woman like me, it's fabulous darling," raising her cocktail glass and chinking their glasses together, laughing, she then continued, "Rob has always been a gem like that, maybe he could set you up with one of the lads from his rugby team. He's coaching the local team now you know, but they are around your age," she raised her eyebrows, thinking if she had spotted anyone suitable the last time she went to watch a match, "do you want me to ask him if there's anyone suitable?"

"Oh god no, auntie. Seriously, I'm ok by myself at the minute. I just need my big break at work, someone to spot me on Instagram or something," she pointed towards her phone, "I keep posting about food and stuff and tagging the well-known chefs and some of the local celebrities. I'm going to apply to some more up market restaurants, see if I can get something in London maybe? Jamie Oliver and Gordon Ramsey have places there. It's where the magic can happen apparently."

"I'm sure it does sweetie, but, hey, how about getting a bit of action away from work for a change? The guys in the team are really fit. Hey, I'll tell you what, if I wasn't past my due date, and not been so head over heels in love with my Rob, well, I may have tried my luck," her eyes lit up and she winked at Kate, sniggering a cheeky laugh.

"Auntie. Really, behave yourself," Kate laughed at her aunt's humour, she'd always been funny and loved being a bit cheeky.

Her husband Rob had always been 'in the money'

inheriting his grandfather's stately home in the Cotswolds. He had sold it a few years afterwards when he met Sally as they had decided to settle in Hertfordshire instead, starting up his own website company. It had built up so quickly and he now had around a hundred and fifty people working for him creating, selling, and managing websites to all types of businesses. And as most of it was done remotely, there was no need for offices, so the overheads and outgoings were minimal, meaning more profit for them in the long run. Any staff meetings were usually done either via video meetings or at a local hotel venue, with just the main team including Rob's new business partners. He went into partnership with them so that he could step back a bit and take some of the pressure off himself and Sally.

The two of them often flew off to their villa in the Italian alps where they would spend the week skiing and snowboarding together. Sally had suggested to Kate that she come along, and they would pay for her to have lessons. They'd offered to buy her everything she needed for it, all the clothing and boots for her, but it wasn't on Kate's agenda. Skiing or snowboarding wasn't something she had ever thought about trying and didn't really intend on doing so any time soon either. She much preferred sunshine beach holidays to chill out and never turned them down if they happened to have a trip like that. Kate appreciated everything that her aunt and uncle did for her and repaid them by being an amazing niece.

"Seriously though, lovely," Sally said as she sipped back her last bit of martini, "if you need any help in the love department, I'm your lady," she said, nodding her head towards her now rather embarrassed and red-faced niece, "why don't you come along to the next team meeting, just have a gander at the talent and see where it goes from there? You never know, the man of your dreams may be waiting for you on that rugby pitch."

"Maybe," Kate replied, with no intention of doing so, "anyway, let's get this mess cleared up, shall we?" she pointed to the array of dishes, pans and utensils that now adorned the kitchen worktops ready for a mammoth washing up task and dishwasher filling session.

"No, no," Sally shook her head and started ushering Kate out of the kitchen, "It's your special birthday, your night to relax and enjoy the evening. You're not to do any of it my darling, you've done too much already. Get in that lounge and have a bit of fun, I think they are getting the cards out for a game of poker or something?" Sally then donned her favourite pair of fluffy hemmed rubber gloves and began filling the sink with water for the bits that couldn't go in the dishwasher.

She may have been a kept woman, not having to go out and get a job for the past twenty years, but she was a workaholic indoors and would always keep her house clean. She edged more on the immaculate side than just tidy. Kate couldn't remember the last time she saw this place in a mess for any longer than half an hour or something out of place. It was always perfect, and Kate loved it.

Sally regularly joked about being a 'kept woman', but she had taken care of Kate and Rob was always well looked after. She never failed to have his dinner waiting for him after he finished his work from the home office in the garden. Their home was their palace and he spoiled her so much, as she deserved. The gifts and parcels that would be delivered every other day, the constant renewal of furniture and ornaments to keep everything up to date and modern looking. It was a show home year on year and at Christmas, it could be mistaken for being Lapland with the number of decorations and sparkle that would engulf the house and outside.

Kate eventually gave in, knowing full well, she would just be in the way now so, made her way into the lounge, but before she went through, the doorbell chimed, "I'll get it," she called out.

"Thanks sweetie, Rob, the door. Kate's not our maid you know," Sally called back in the hope her husband would hear her over all the laughing and chatting in the other room. He hadn't heard her calls, so Kate continued walking up the hallway.

On opening the door, she was met by a young guy

in a grey Superdry, hoody and dark blue jeans looking a little dishevelled.

She thought he must have been out on a run or something and she noticed that there was a large holdall at his feet, "Can I help you?" she asked cautiously, keeping the door firmly in her hand in case she had to shut it suddenly. There was always something on the news about cold callers using their skills and tactics to get into people's homes, especially in the more affluent areas. She didn't have a clue who he was and why he was here, so she held her stance firmly.

"Hi, sorry to bother you this late in the evening," his voice was smooth and gentle, "but, well, is Rob in? I'm from his rugby team," he asked, pulling down his hood and revealing a lush mane of jet-black hair that he quickly shuffled his fingers through to try and tidy it.

"Oh," Kate answered, taken aback by the friendliness tones of his voice, "Sure, come in, I'll go get him for you," Kate then opened the door wide and ushered him inside. It was bitterly cold outside now.

His manly scent wafted past her as he made his way into the hallway. It was strong and woody, but she quite liked it.

"I'm Daniel. You can call me Dan," he said, reaching out his hand to shake hers, after placing the bag on the floor again, "And you must be... Kate?"

He was now smiling sweetly at her, pulling her hand to his lips as she reciprocated with what she thought would be just a handshake.

Blushing slightly from the random kissing of the back of her hand, she felt hot and flushed. She'd not had that happen before. Immediately she felt shy and hated the fact that she knew her cheeks were rosy, red with embarrassment.

"Erm, yes, that's me, how did you know?" her face reddening even more as she took back control of her hand.

"Rob said he was having a birthday dinner party for his niece tonight and wondered if I'd like to pop over and meet you," he began taking off his hoodie as the warmth of the house must have hit him. His crisp white t-shirt underneath, lifted as the top went over his head, revealing a bronzed and obvious six pack, "Phew, warm in here isn't it?" he threw the hoody onto the holdall which he'd kicked towards the staircase.

"Erm," she stuttered, "Yes, I guess so. How did you know I was Kate though; I could've been anyone opening the door?" she asked him, trying her hardest to move her eyes away from his torso as his face met hers again.

"Well," he replied, straightening his clothing up, "The birthday badge and the crown thing on your head sort of gave the game away," he pointed to her over-sized and very pink, birthday badge attached to her sparkly top and the adorning tiara with 'birthday girl' lighting up in silver twinkly lights.

"Oh," she said, totally embarrassed yet again, with a slight giggle this time, "Auntie's idea all of this birthday paraphernalia." And rolled her eyes.

He smiled back at her and winked as Rob came into the hallway, "Dan, the man, you made it." They embraced each other doing the normal aggressive man-hug thing that men do. It always seemed such a rough thing to do, she never understood it no matter how many times she had witnessed it. Why so rough, why hit each other's shoulders so hard?

"So…" Rob said as he finished the hug and stood next to Dan, "you've met the girl of the moment I see?" he kept his arm around Dan's shoulders as he glanced across to see Kate smiling shyly, twiddling with her cocktail glass, which she'd quickly slurped up.

"Yes, we have met," Dan winked at her again, she blushed again, tilting her head down, twiddling with the glass nervously in her hand.

"Great. Come on then, let's get the beers in, we're just about to start another game of cards if you want to join mate?" Rob waved his empty bottle of beer and directed them both into the lounge as he went to the kitchen to let Sally know that Dan had come over, "Anyone else need a re-fill while I'm going this way?" he called as he raided the fridge for cooled bottles of alcohol, "Dan has come over darling," he shut the fridge and kissed his wife on the cheek.

"What's he doing here?" she asked as she placed the last plate into the dishwasher, glancing into the lounge area.

"I thought he could meet Kate, you know, try and set them up like?" he tapped her bottom as he walked past her, "Is that not a good idea? I thought you wanted her to meet someone?" he whispered back as he noticed that her tone of voice seemed a little hesitant and she was bending her neck to see into the other room, "where's the bottle opener gone sweetheart?" he asked.

"Yes, I do want her to meet someone, but..."

"Well what darling?' Rob replied, rubbing her lower back as he passed by, "He's had issues, yes but he's a nice lad deep down."

"I just wonder if he's not quite right for her, you know with losing his own dad like that and his illness. She's had enough sadness to deal with losing Fiona, don't you think?" she nudged his arm as he waded through the kitchen drawer, "Here…" she passed him the bottle opener from the windowsill where he'd left it earlier and forgot about.

"She's a tough cookie, our niece. I'm sure she will be fine. She can handle him and besides, you said it was about time she got together with someone and what better time than on her twenty first birthday?" he gave her a curt nod, "come on darling, she'll be alright, and she has old Aunt Sally to help her along the way too." Grabbing as many bottles of beer as he could, he walked back into the lounge leaving Sally feeling a little bemused at her husband's random behaviour and choice. He'd never got involved like this before. Why had he thought it was his place to play matchmaker and why Dan?

She decided she would leave it for now, maybe this was the right time and maybe she was just over-reacting about it all. Maybe she just wanted to be the one choosing the right man for her niece, she had promised Fiona she would take care of her and just because Kate was now old enough to take care of herself, she still felt responsible for her future. She never wanted to let her sister down and do everything possible right for her beloved niece.

Chapter Three

Falling...

The male guests had set up the cards ready for a game of poker while the ladies had moved over to the two sets of plush, grey suede sofas with cocktail glasses in hands, chatting about the latest celebrity gossip, recipes to try out from the restaurant that Kate worked at and of course, home décor ideas ready for Christmas in a few months' time.

Sally finished up in the kitchen, grabbed her new glass of wine that she had poured herself and joined them, sitting next to Kate on the arm of the sofa, "I'm sorry about that sweetie, honestly, I didn't know he'd invited one of the rugby guys round tonight," she whispered as she poured a little bit more sparkling cava into Kate's glass.

"It's ok auntie, really. He seems nice enough and it's sweet of Rob to think of me. He's a good uncle and you're a very lucky lady to have him," she held Sally's hand giving it a gentle squeeze and looked over to Dan who was checking out his hand of cards.

He must've sensed she was looking at him because after a few seconds, he glanced across and winked at her once again with a gorgeous smile on his face. She noticed that his teeth were perfect and so white, and his cheeks were now glowing from coming in from the cold outside. His hair was still a bit unkempt but sort of stylish with it in some way.

"Yes, I am lucky but, well, he should have asked me first really, I don't want you set up with just anyone do I? I mean..."

Kate interrupted, "Auntie, it's fine really, don't worry, I'm a big girl now, and like you said earlier, maybe it's time I had a man in my life," she said reassuring her with a look, "Let's just enjoy the rest of the evening, you never know, we might get along?"

By half eleven, all the guests had left leaving just Sally, Rob, Kate, and Dan who had moved back into the dining room where they'd put out more snacks on the table and drank through two more bottles of wine.

"I'm shattered," commented Sally as she gulped the last dregs of her wine, "think it's time to hit the sack my darlings," she pushed her chair back and yawned, "I'll just rinse these few glasses and then it's off to noddy land for us oldies."

"Yeah me too," agreed Kate, "Thanks for a great party you two, it was really nice to see everyone together for a change, and the cocktails were amazing as usual," Kate stood up and hugged Sally.

"Well, I know it was your birthday party, but I couldn't have got all that food done without your skills in the kitchen, you really do have a talent darling, well done," she gave her a big kiss on her cheek, "now, you are staying here tonight yeah? In your old room?"

"If that's ok, or I can get a taxi, it's not a problem, I've got the Uber app now, a car will be literally five minutes," she retrieved her phone from her dress pocket.

"No, that's fine, you know where your room is sweetie, it's all made up for you anyway so…"

"I've actually just ordered a cab if you wanted to jump in with me?" piped up Dan gulping down the last of his beer and placing the glass on the side as he stood up.

"Oh, maybe I could do that," replied Kate, "I have got work tomorrow evening so could do with getting a good night's rest in my own bed. Yes, if that's ok with you?" she smiled back at Dan and then across at Sally, "you don't mind do you auntie?"

"Of course not sweetheart. You make sure she gets home okay Dan," she nudged his arm as they walked past her, "Kate, text me when you get in please? You know how I worry until I know you are home, especially this late at night."

"I always text you, don't I?" Kate said as she grabbed her jacket.

After giving her aunt and uncle another big hug at the front door, she got into the taxi that had arrived within minutes, with Dan following behind, closing the door for her, and getting in round the other side.

For a few moments, in the cab, there was an awkward silence, then they both suddenly began to speak at the same time, then laughed.

"Sorry, you go first, it is your birthday," he gestured to her head once again where the birthday tiara still sat twinkling away.

She pulled it from her hair and switched it off, "Oh blimey, didn't even realise I still had this thing on. My auntie, she loves a sparkly dress up item, no matter how small, bless her," giggling nervously again, "thanks for letting me share the cab, we can go halves?" she began to reach for her purse.

"It's fine, no worries. You can pay next time," he answered, touching her hand to stop her opening the purse up.

"Next time, you're confident?" she replied a little shocked at her own confident reply, albeit a bit happy about it too.

He laughed again, "Well, a guy gotta try, hey?" he glanced out the window behind her, moving his head closer to her so that she could almost feel his breath on her skin, "you can see the rugby club from here, never realised it was so close to Rob's house," he commented pointing.

Kate looked at the floodlights in the distance briefly and then realised that it was nearly her road, "just up here on the left please?" she tapped the back of the driver's seat, then answered, "Yes, I hear the matches sometimes from my place, I've only been there a few times, rugby isn't really my thing to be honest."

"Really, even with your uncle coaching a team, that's terrible, what an awful niece you are," he nudged her arm with his, "I'm joking…not too many girls I've met like it to be fair. Maybe you'll have to come and watch me playing one afternoon? You never know, you may grow to like the sport?" He gently moved a strand of her hair away from her face and she felt a flickering of something in her stomach as his hand touched her face.

She hadn't even known him for more than a few hours but there was something about him that she couldn't work out. Was she liking to him, could there even be a next time? She thought about how he must look on the rugby field. All the men she had seen before were massive, muscular, and broad with rugged faces, some with bits of their ears missing from the countless scrums that they'd had over the years in the team.

"Maybe…look, thanks again for the taxi share. Are you sure I don't owe you anything?" she reached for her purse again.

"Nope. Honestly. It's fine. Next time, it's your shout ok?" he replied, winking at her as she closed the door.

She felt his eyes peering into her back as she walked up to her front door. He now knew where she lived. Would there be a next time, she wondered again as she plunged the key in the lock and opened the door. How was he so confident she'd want to see him again anyway? But, funnily enough, she did want to see him. She hadn't felt so sure about anything in a long while, but she liked him, and she didn't really know why.

She turned to see the cab driving away as she closed the front door and leant against it wondering if she would see him soon. Why had she taken to him so quickly, she'd never felt that way before? Never one for falling for someone so quickly, she shook her head as if to shake the thoughts from her brain. Throwing her jacket on the banister, she quickly sent a 'home safe' text to Sally who returned immediately with a big X.

She felt relieved that Sally hadn't asked any further questions about the journey home, what would she have said to her anyway if she had? There wasn't anything to tell really. She just had a funny feeling in the pit of her stomach about this guy. And she felt a little timid, at twenty-one now, a grown woman, this felt weird.

Morning came quicker than she had hoped for. Kate's head felt slightly cloudy from the amount of wine and cocktails she had managed to throw down her neck at the dinner party.

As she picked up her clothes from the previous evening, she smelt a waft of a vaguely familiar male aftershave – where had that come from? And then she realised, it was his smell, it was Dan's scent wafting up her nostrils. They must've got closer than she thought in the taxi. She raised it closer to her nose and inhaled it for a few seconds, smiling to herself at the thought of seeing him again. Her tummy fluttered once more, like hundreds of little butterflies flying around in there. For now, she would leave her top on the bed, maybe the smell would linger for a bit more and she could smell it again later.

'What on earth am I thinking?' she thought to herself. Why was she being so silly smelling a top because it reminded her of him? Why was she acting like some sort of teenager in love – she clearly wasn't either a teenager or in love for that matter. She'd only just met the guy for goodness' sake.

Her dress that she'd worn to the party was laying over the dressing table chair and as she rummaged for her lipstick in the pocket, she found a note with a number on it folded once. As she opened it, it read, *'Me again, Dan…Call me'*

Her mouth opened and she gasped at the cheek of

this guy. He must have slipped the note into her pocket while they were in the car at some point, and she hadn't even noticed. As slightly shocked as she felt, she also thought to herself that, actually, it was kind of cute. She placed it on the side next to her bed to call him later. For now, she needed a shower and hair wash ready for work tonight.

The nice hot shower was over and as she towel-dried her hair, she heard her phone ringing. Chucking the towel over the chair and jumping onto the bed to reach it, she managed to answer it in time. It was Sally.

"Hi Auntie, you ok?" asked Kate, turning to lay on her back. Her skin was hot and still a bit wet.

"Yes, I'm good my darling, how are you feeling after all that wine last night? Are you alright?"

"Oh yes, I'm fine, a little bit of a fuzzy head when I woke up, but nothing serious, I don't think I drank as much as everyone else anyway, did you need something?"

"Well, not really. It's just what with all the celebrations last night, I forgot to give you something. Would you be able to pop over later tonight?"

"Oh, I can't tonight, I'm working till ten thirty, so it'll be a bit late by the time I get out of there," she sat up on the side of the bed, patting her legs dry with the earlier dis-guarded hair towel, "I've got a day off tomorrow though, shall I come over around eleven, have a bit of brunch with you?"

"Perfect, yes that would be great. I'll see you then…oh, hang on sweetie, was the journey home alright, did you, well, you know, invite him in for a nightcap?" Kate could hear the smile on her aunt's face through the phone.

"God no, he's nice but, well, I've only just met him Auntie, I was too knackered for nightcaps anyway," they both laughed.

"Haha, ok darling. As long as you were okay and got home safe. Have a good evening at work, be careful and I'll see you tomorrow." she replied, blowing a kiss before hanging up.

As Kate placed her phone on the bed, she thought about what Sally had asked. Should she have invited him in? Maybe but maybe not. After all, she had his number now, so the ball was in her court, and she preferred it that way. She continued to get ready for work, pulling on her skinny black jeggings and white fitted blouse with the restaurant's embroidered logo on the right and 'staff' in bold print on the back. She didn't mind this work uniform; it was smart, casual but comfortable and they kept the half aprons there to put on when she arrived. Just as she pulled her socks on, the doorbell rang.

"Grrr" she grimaced, "what now?" and ran down the stairs to see who was at the door. On opening, she was taken aback as she faced a massive bunch of red roses staring right at her with a small blonde lady behind them.

"Kate Ellington?" the little voice asked politely from somewhere behind the blooms.

"Erm, yes, that's me," Kate replied as the lady passed the flowers to her.

"Lucky lady," she said, "enjoy," and turned on the step leaving Kate standing there with the biggest bunch of flowers she had ever seen. Even the wrapping looked expensive, and they were in a beautiful yellow box with silver butterflies on.

Closing the door behind her, she went to the kitchen, and laid the beautiful bouquet on the table. There was no information with them, no card to say who they were from. Nothing, just a little information leaflet stapled to the clear cellophane. She felt like running back out to catch the lady who had bought them, but she hadn't hung around and she was too busy admiring them along with the scent that was now filling the kitchen.

'Who would've sent these?' she thought. They were truly stunning and smelt amazing. She didn't think she had a vase big enough, if she had a vase at all if she was honest – she didn't get flowers regularly. Certainly nothing like this either. The odd small bunch of daffodils during the spring to lighten up the windowsill, that was about as flowery as she got. Not having the time to cut and display them properly, she didn't bother buying flowers for herself. Not like Auntie, she had fresh flowers delivered weekly without fail. And then Rob would buy her some for birthdays and anniversaries so there had always been the floral smells in the house but not something Kate had taken on when she had moved into her own place.

She ran back upstairs to collect her phone, and then coming back down, she took a quick photo of them and sent a picture to Sally, saying; *'look what just arrived for me'*

A text came back around a minute later, *'Oohhh, lucky girl, who are they from I wonder?'*

Kate typed back, *'no idea, no card or anything'*.

She searched around the bunch again in case she'd missed it, but nothing.

Another ping on her phone came through from Sally, *'I have a hunch it could be Dan???'*

Blushing immediately, Kate texted back, *'Really, you think so? Oh well, I'll have to wait and see. Gotta go work now. They'll have to spend the evening in the sink, I don't think I even own a vase that big auntie. Lol, speak soon, love you. X'*

After doing a small amount of housework and getting a wash on, it was time to head off for work. On the train journey, she scrolled through the pictures of last night and then came to the photo of the flowers again. If they were from Dan, he was certainly playing Mr. Keen and obviously trying to make a good impression. She had no idea for now but secretly hoped it might be him, surely it had to be. Maybe she would text him later? Just to say hi and see if he mentions the flowers? Her mind was wandering into some kind of nowhere land, and she nearly missed her stop. Collecting her bag and jacket quickly off the seat next to her, she hurried along the carriage, pushed the train door button, and made her way to the restaurant.

Chapter Four

The Messages…

The shift seemed to go quicker than usual for Kate and the team tonight. Mainly due to the fact there was a party of fifteen women in, for a hen-do. Kate always dreaded these types of parties. One would always get too drunk and throw up in the ladies' loo, there would usually be one that got too emotional because they'd recently broken up from a relationship and then that one who would get angry on too much Vodka. And the noise they would make. Cackling screams and ultra-loud laughing. The outfits were predictable too, the learner plate safety pinned on to a tacky piece of netting to recreate the veil with devil horns that the bride-to-be had to wear without fail and the slogan t-shirts or badges that the other hens wore stating their roles. Themed parties were interesting too, crazy eighties style fluorescent skirts with matching coloured leg warmers and sweat bands around their heads. She always thought to herself that if she ever decided or had the chance to get married, she hoped her hen night would be so much classier than any she had seen while at work.

"Excuse me waitress," came an ear splitting shrill from one of the older ladies at the table, "excuse me," she repeated just a tad bit louder with her arm aloft waving her phone.

'Oh here we go,' Kate thought, then politely answered, "yes madam," as she approached the table.

"Ah, hello there," the reply came, with another drunken cackle of laughter and slurred words, "could you take a picture of all of us please."

'At least she asked nicely', Kate thought to herself.

"Make sure we all fit in it, won't you sweetheart," the lady said as she passed the phone to Kate not waiting for her answer, "come on girlies, everyone get in," she wafted her arms around once more to usher everyone to look the same way, "and bloody smile love, you're getting married next week, think of the wedding night sex or something," she nudged the bride-to-be who was sat next to her, and, who in Kate's opinion, didn't look like she was having the time of her life right now.

Kate obliged and took a few snaps then handed the

phone back to another woman in the group. The lady who'd asked was busy already pouring some more wine from the bucket in the middle of the table.

"Has everyone finished here?" asked Kate as she began piling up the near empty plates and cutlery. No reply came but no-one was eating so she continued clearing up with another member of staff.

As they approached the swinging doors of the kitchen, Kate paused for a moment leaning on the worktop. She felt so tired tonight and was glad to see that her shift was nearly up. The birthday weekend must have taken it out of her more than she thought. She was looking forward to returning home and getting some sleep.

"Are all women as crazy as that?" asked Leo, the waiter she had been working with tonight.

She laughed as she replied, "not all of us Leo," she giggled, "hens tend to get a little carried away at these parties sometimes."

"You're not wrong there," he nodded towards one of the women who had now turned her attention to him, "she grabbed my arse earlier when I served their drinks."

"Ha-ha, that's so funny Leo. You obviously have a bum worth grabbing hey?" she jokingly said, scanning him up and down and laughing.

He blushed slightly as he nudged her arm, "stop it you big flirt you."

She really loved the banter between them and all

the staff there that she worked with. The workforce was strong, and they all rallied together as a great team. Although it was a tough job at times, especially at the weekend when they had large parties to cater for, they all helped each other and got through the shifts without much trouble.

She was particularly fond of Leo, and they'd been working the same shifts for around two months now. He was a few years older than her and had worked there for three years more so when she first started, it was him that she shadowed to learn everything in the first few weeks. They had bonded from there and their friendship blossomed. He lived just a ten-minute car journey from the restaurant too which meant that they could finish their shifts and have the occasional takeaway back at his. Many nights they had ended up at his place, just chatting into the early hours about everything foody related mainly. His dad had been a chef in one of the top hotels in London so, used to teach Leo to cook as a child. Unfortunately, as much as he loved cooking with his father, he hadn't mastered it so opted for serving food instead. Kate really enjoyed his company and cooked for him several times at hers when they got the time but most weekends, they were just too busy with work, and he had a very active social life. Much more than Kate did.

"Do you wanna grab a drink later? There's a new cocktail place about five minutes' walk from here just opened last Friday," Leo asked as he piled the last stack of plates towards the pot washers, "two for one on martinis I believe," he winked, creating a clacking sound in his cheek.

"Ooh, tempting Leo, very tempting, but no I won't tonight actually," she replied wearily, "I'm shattered to be honest. Just a solid eight hours of sleep is what I need tonight, thanks though, another time?"

"Sure, no worries, I'll check with Annabelle and Olivia, see what they're up to. Oh, how did your birthday go anyway?" he asked as they made their way into the staff room for their ten-minute break.

"Yeah nice actually, just chilled round my aunt and uncles with drinks and that," she reached for her phone out of her locker and started sifting through the photos to show him her cake and the vast number of cocktails and wine that they had got through.

"So sorry I couldn't make it in the end. Mum's funny turn was a bit much for dad this time." He replied, looking sad. His mum had been diagnosed with dementia the previous year and it was taking its' toll on them all. His father was trying to cope with it all by himself but sometimes it just got on top of him, and he would call Leo to come over and sit with her while he took a break.

Leo would sit with her and read her favourite books. He never quite knew how much she was listening and taking in, but the time was precious with her whatever communication they had.

"It's okay, family must come first. How is she doing and how's your dad coping?"

"Mum's fading too fast unfortunately, way too fast. Dad feels like he's losing her more every day, you know mentally but, bless him, he keeps so strong in front of her. I know it's killing him inside though, it's sad to watch," he tried to answer without getting emotional himself as Kate glanced up, "Anyway, enough of my drama life, how was the birthday party?" he asked, shaking the tense situation.

"Well…I err, it was interesting."

"Interesting.? As in?" he asked.

"I sort of met someone as it happens."

"Oh er, missus Ellington, there's a glimmer of hope for your romantic lifestyle hey," he whooped, "tell me more, tell me more," he joked, sitting himself down on the bench rubbing his hands together, "is he fit, what's he look like, do you have a pic for your old pal to check him over for you? He must be approved by me personally first you do realise that don't you babe."

"Leo, stop it. Erm, pictures. No, I don't think so anyway," Kate scrolled through the pictures but realised she must've been too busy to take any and then immediately felt a bit gutted, "Seems not I'm afraid. He's really nice, good looking and we only had a brief chat, but then the night was over. We shared a cab and then,"

"Then?" he exclaimed in excitement, interrupting

her.

"I went home," she replied sternly, nudging him in the shoulder with her hip, "alone."

"Booo," he hissed, giggling at her nonchalant expression, "that's not what we want to hear. We want sordid details of passion and seduction, mixed in with some naughty love and all that jazz."

"Leo, what are you like?" she joked, smiling back at him.

He could be so funny at times, and she loved having a natter with him and he nearly always ended the conversations making her giggle.

"I'm just a fun guy you know." He smirked waving his hands in front of his face and placing them under his chin.

"Right, I'm going to pop to the loo and then finish this blooming shift so I can mosey on home to catch some zeds in my bed." Standing back up and having a quick stretch of her back, she then left him still booing at her.

Just as she got to the door, she turned round and playfully stuck her tongue out at him, blowing a raspberry to finish off the gesture.

When she eventually got home and totally exhausted, she fell back onto her bed, kicking off her shoes which had now made her feet sore. Her new pumps seemed to be taking forever to break in and her big toe was tender to the touch. It had taken longer than usual to travel home after her shift tonight, because of a delayed train. The announcement came just as she got to the station *'due to a problem on the track...'* it began. Kate knew from her hundreds of tube and train journeys, that it usually meant some poor soul had thrown themselves on to it somewhere along the line. It seemed like someone did that every week now, she would read about it a few days after the event and always felt sad that an individual could be so sad and so distressed that their only option was to contemplate going down that route. Tonight, she really hoped it wasn't that scenario and that a fault on the line was indeed the reason for the delay.

As she turned onto her side, she noticed the note from Dan that she had placed carefully on the bedside that morning and inwardly smiled. Just the thought of him hiding a note made her tingle with excitement and wonder. It was nearly midnight, and she was shattered, but without acknowledging what her fingers were doing, suddenly she had pressed the send button, with a short message just saying, *'Hey, it's Kate...x'*

"Shit," she mumbled to herself, biting her lip feeling slight regret in realising it was too late to stop it going through, *"what's wrong with me."* She asked herself and threw the phone further up the bed cupping her hand on her forehead. Before she had time to think anymore, the phone lit up with the sounding 'trill' of an incoming text. Jumping forward onto her knees, she grabbed hold of the phone. He had seen her text and had replied, now what? Now what should she do? She just stared at his message for a few seconds, her heart thumping and throat feeling as though it may close with nerves, then another message popped up on the thread, *'hey gorgeous, you took your time, slow coach'.*

'Cheeky sod,' she thought, but instantly feeling a tad bit guilty, she replied, *'sorry, I don't usually keep people waiting. I've been at work all afternoon and didn't get back till late. Another rail problem, sorry again…'*

'I'm joking silly…x' was the reply within seconds and then, another ding, another message from him, *'can I come over and see you now that you're home then?'*

Her mouth widened, she couldn't believe he was being so forward, wanting to come over at midnight – and what for, as if she didn't know. Or was she just tarring him with the same old brush of past boyfriend experiences, was he going to be any different? The stunning bunch of roses certainly had never happened with other men before. Was he more of a romantic kind of guy? What was she going to reply to that message with, without seeming desperate or lonely or worse still, easy? Her sleepy mind was now wide awake all of a sudden, but she didn't want to seem too keen, so busied her fingers and replied, *'I'm going to go to bed now, sorry, maybe another night?'*

Super speedy and again, super cheeky, a text pinged back almost immediately, *'that's all good for me*

;) I can be at your bedroom door in about five mins…xx' it
said, adding another winking face emoji a few seconds
after, which made her snigger.

"Crikey," she whispered to herself, he was really
going for it. But she wanted to play it safe, keep him
hanging, so she texted back, *'it's been a long day for me,
how about meeting up in the week maybe? X'* This time she
added a kiss on the end and immediately felt silly for
doing so after pressing send. She didn't even really
know this guy and had never added the kiss symbol
to someone she barely knew before. Kisses were for
true friends and family only usually.

*'Okay gorgeous. I give up. You get your beauty sleep, not that
you need it. You've got my number so just don't leave it too long
next time hey? xx'* Within seconds and before she had
finished reading, another line of text appeared below,
'next time I see you, I'll bring you a decent vase for those roses.'

Her eyelids suddenly snapped open in surprise.
There it was, now she knew it had been him that sent
the flowers, Sally was right, as always. How did he
know she needed a vase though, she suddenly
thought, feeling a little uneasy? She looked over at
the window, the curtains were still open. As she
scoured the street outside with a strange feeling of
being watched, her phone lit up once more. Looking
down, it was him again, *'sleep tight beautiful Kate'.*

Although she felt slightly creeped out, she also felt
slightly excited. A strange twinge of something was
happening in her tummy, like nerves before a job

interview, butterflies, nervousness, and she felt silly for a second, like a teenager drooling over their favourite movie star or pop idol. She closed the curtains and laid back down on her bed smiling, holding the phone to her still thumping chest. Glancing over at the flowers which she had placed in three containers on the shelf, two of which were tall pint glasses as she only owned one small vase, she inhaled the scent. They were so strong, and it filled the air in her little room. Maybe he had seen the flowers through her window, but why would he be watching her, and should he be stalking her home? Right now, all she needed was to get some rest, she felt even more exhausted from the adrenaline that had been rushing through her veins from all the text message excitement, and it didn't take long until she was fast asleep, the phone still clasped in her hand.

Chapter Five

Dating Daniel...

It was morning way too soon for her liking and as the sunshine beamed it's hot and full set of rays in through the window.

Gently opening her eyes, she grinned sweetly at the colours and silhouettes of the amazingly gorgeous looking flowers adorning the wooden shelf opposite her bed. Their strong scent had engulfed the room during the night, and it made her feel wide awake, fresh, and more than ready for the day ahead.

Stretching her arms up over her head, and yawning, she then heard the familiar tone of her phone with a text message. She rolled over onto her side, following the sound quickly and grabbed it from under the duvet. Her tight grasp on it as she had fallen asleep must have loosened at some point in her sleep and it wasn't the first time it had been hidden and lost in the bed somewhere. Unlocking it calmly with her fingerprint, and blinking away the tiredness in her eyes, she looked down at the screen and smiled. It was Dan again.

'*Good morning gorgeous Kate.*' it read.

Her heart did another fluttering sensation, and her cheeks flushed a shade of rose as another message popped up before she had the chance to write anything back, '*how did you sleep beautiful Kate? Any nice dreams to tell me about?*'

She was indecisive whether to seem so keen to answer back too soon, she didn't want him to think she was at his beck and call, whenever; but she so wanted to answer him, it was insane how much she wanted to have this conversation. With her hands feeling clammy, and her cheeks almost hurting from smiling so much at having this type of attention, she replied, '*Good morning you. I slept well thanks, how about you? x*' There was that kiss at the end again. Typing it without realising it this time.

'*All the better for dreaming about you all night sweet cheeks,*' he returned quickly, making her blush even more. She couldn't recall the last time anyone had made her feel like a naughty schoolgirl getting cheeky messages. It was a weird feeling but then again, a feeling she quite liked from this mystery guy.

She rolled over onto her back holding the phone

with both hands above her face, just smiling at the digital writing. She was doing everything in her power to make this feeling last before she could work out what to reply. He was on the ball with it all, that was for certain but, she loved it, it made her tingle inside of her tummy looking at every word. Trying to snap herself out of the dreamy state she was in, she began to type, then another message from him appeared, *'Call me later, I'm off to work now but I'm free tonight to come over? I've bought some cava for us anyway. Saw you downing some at your party so clocked it must be a fav of yours? I can't promise I'll get the same brand though. Anyway, looking forward to seeing your beautiful face again soon...So, I'll be over around seven o'clock tonight, yeah? That cool with you gorgeous? xx'*

Kate thought to herself, *'How fast can this guy type?'* She only remembered Leo being as super-fast at typing texts like Dan was. The other girls at work would tease him for being as fast as a short-hand secretary, he was so nimble fingered. They'd even had competitions to see who could type the fastest without looking and Leo had always won. He did make her laugh with his random skills.

Dan was certainly making an impression on Kate though and he was raring to get together with her again and as soon as possible it seemed. She wasn't sure what to make of it or what to think right now so, she decided to jump in the shower and then see if Sally fancied a shopping trip to get herself a new dress for the evening. She raised her phone one last time, quickly texting back, '*Sure…see you tonight then. X*' *and* got off the bed squealing excitedly like a child who'd just been given a new toy or a large chocolate bar to chomp on. Maybe it was time to have a bit of fun and romance in her life and this guy was definitely going the right way about it with his efforts of wooing her. Maybe romance wasn't dead after all, and if the first bunch of roses were anything to go by, she was on to a winner with this one and it felt good. Really good.

She turned the water dial round a little bit more to the hotter side, the room was rapidly getting steamed up by the heat. She rubbed the shower gel across the top of her shoulders and let it run smoothly down her slender body. Washing her hair next, and with shampoo once again managing to work its way into her eyes, she shook her head. No matter how careful she tried to be, she always seemed to have this problem but, somehow, today, it hadn't fazed her. She just shrugged it off once she had put her head under the shower head to rinse it all away. Nothing would spoil how elated and excited she felt right now, and it wasn't long before she was ready for the day ahead. Grabbing her jacket, phone, and keys, she then made her way over to Sally and Robs' house with a joyful expression now seemingly glued on her face.

As she approached the house, Rob was just walking

down the pathway, his phone pinned to his ear as per usual. He leant down as he passed by her, kissed Kate on the cheek, and mouthed, "she's in the kitchen," then continued chatting away to whomever was on the other end of the line. He was a busy man most days during the week with the majority of his business being carried out remotely online. He had two phones, but his work mobile was a constant accessory stuck to his ear or on loudspeaker if his hands were busy typing away on the keyboard of his mac book.

Kate smiled as she watched her uncle bustling onto the street in his dark grey suit, thinking to herself that he hardly ever walked for work so must have a meeting nearby. He always looked so smart and professional, even while he worked from home. She remembered when she was younger that a few of friends had had a crush on him. The dark thick hair, broad shoulders, and amazingly toned legs that he loved to show off while barbecuing in the garden was all her teenage friends needed to become 'in love' with the older man scenario. She sniggered back a little laugh and then let herself in to the house, making her way to the kitchen to find her aunt.

She could smell the strong aroma of the extremely expensive coffee machine brewing their favourite dark roast cup of joe. They'd had it imported from Italy somewhere after falling in love with the brand of coffee over there one summer.

"Hey darling, you must have smelt me brewing this hey?" Sally said noticing her niece's arrival. She passed a coffee in Kate's favourite mug that she'd left there when she had moved out. It wasn't anything special, but it was 'her' coffee vessel. A large, rounded mug with cherry cupcakes and cake slices printed all over it. The handle was chipped, and Rob had got the superglue out more than a few times to try and fix it, but that one spot just kept breaking.

"Can smell your superb coffee brewing a mile off auntie," laughed Kate, taking her drink, "Jeez, I really need a new one of these don't I?" she said, rubbing her finger over the chipped area.

"Yes I thought that this morning when I got it out of the cupboard, we should look in that new shop in town, they have some gorgeous dining sets and that in there. I believe some of it is vintage. We should visit sweetie. What do you think?"

"Erm. Maybe, although I can't afford a new dinner set this month to be fair. Anyway, listen up, I have some news," Kate exclaimed, plonking her bottom onto the chrome bar stool.

"Sounds intriguing." Sally answered.

"So…Dan's coming over about seven o'clock tonight," she watched as Sally's eyebrows raised in surprise.

"He's coming to your place. Tonight?" questioned Sally as she sat down opposite at the kitchen breakfast bar, cracking open a tin of all butter shortbread biscuits.

"He is. I can't believe it really Auntie," she continued, "I don't know what's got into me but, well, I like him. I really do like this guy, so I'm running with it for a change. You said it was about time I had a bit of fun?" she said, sipping her drink.

"Yes I believe I did," Sally replied.

"Anyway, I thought I better try and get something new to wear. All my summer dresses look too boring now," she reached for one of the biscuits and dunked it into her coffee, "fancy a quick trip into town with me? You know the best places to get something a bit…I don't know, a bit, fancier, you know, a little bit more upper class than the cheap junk I have in my wardrobe."

"Well, yes of course darling. I'd love to come along, it's just…" she paused looking at her beautiful niece whose face was full of excitement. She hadn't seen her this happy about a guy in a very long time. She didn't have the heart to give her the package that she had planned for this morning,

"What is it auntie, is there a problem?"

"No, no. Well, it's just, I need to be back by four, that's all sweetie…I have a zoom meeting with my nurse, just a check up on the blooming diabetes nonsense." She lied, quickly thinking on her toes to come up with a story. She felt anxious and a little bit worried for her niece and really needed to give her this package but maybe not today after all, not while

TELLING LIES

Kate was beaming from ear to ear about her upcoming date tonight. She just couldn't tell her today. It had been so long since she had seen her like this, and Sally loved seeing her happy. Kate had clearly forgotten about why she was there too in all her excitement about her date later that evening, so they finished their drinks and biscuits, then set off to go shopping.

The town was busy as per usual, mothers fighting through the tiny aisles of the fashion boutiques with their huge pushchairs, kids crying because they were getting bored and wanting feeding or playing with. Their partners, mostly men sitting outside the shops puffing away on their vapes, or head down in their phones oblivious to the outside world waiting for their wives, girlfriends, or partner to finish up their lavish shopping habits. It was the norm for this town. But nothing seemed to get in the way of Kate's happiness today, she almost glided from shop to shop holding tightly onto Sally's arm as they laughed and chatted about all the clothing styles they had gone through over the years and what trends were always springing back. Sally knew all the best boutiques to visit but Kate still loved to venture into the smaller more independent shops and wouldn't go a shopping trip without visiting a few charity shops either. She'd always grab a bargain or three from those and loved a bit of vintage fashion. The fact that the money was for charities she loved too was always a bonus for her.

The cancer research one was her favourite, and she would always donate any change into their pots on the cashier desk. After losing her mum, she had started collecting the pin badges from that store and had them all attached to one of Fiona's old scarves in memory of her. It seemed the fitting thing to do.

"So, is there any master plan for tonight dating soiree?" Sally asked as they paused for a coffee break and sat on a bench near a large patch of grass that was called, 'the green'.

Kate placed her three bags of shopping by her side, "Well, not really. He just said he'd be round at seven with a bottle of cava. Do you think I should cook something," she asked with a puzzled look appearing on her face, "oh, I don't even know what food he likes or anything, should I text him and ask?" her voice sounding anxious, "do you think I should cancel, do you think it's too soon to have him over to mine?" She turned to face Sally.

All these questions were suddenly racing through her mind. She wanted it to be a good evening, her first date in a while and this was one she really didn't want to mess up. The last boyfriend she cooked for was a vegetarian and she had booked them into the local steakhouse where he'd promptly ordered a lovely avocado salad while she had to get through her 8oz sirloin steak and ribs main course. She had felt terrible, and she wasn't at all surprised when he didn't call her for a second date.

"Look darling, try and calm down a little bit hey," she gave Kate's arm a reassuring squeeze, "it's lovely that you are so excited. Just go with the flow tonight. Play it cool when he arrives and then see if he's hungry. If so, get him to order a takeout, you don't want to have to worry about cooking and then there's all that cleaning up nonsense. Then you'll get an idea of what food he does like, avoid any problems that way."

"You're right; you're always right. I'm over thinking it all aren't I?" Kate replied, relaxing her shoulders from being so tightly hunched up with fret.

"Yes you are my darling, just a tad little biddy bid but it's sweet to see you like this. You just need to, well…" Sally paused, "you know what I'm going to say don't you?" she reached to touch Kate's hands this time, which were fiddling nervously with the cuff of her jumper.

"Be careful?" chuckled Kate sarcastically, reciprocating holding her aunt's hand, "I will. I'll be careful, I'll be safe…I'll be fine. Thanks for always saying the right thing and being there for me."

"Always darling, always," Sally replied, smiling back, "Now are we all done with shopping, it's nearly half three already, I can't believe how fast the time has gone."

"Yes I'm all shopped out I think, and you needed to get back for something didn't you?"

"Oh...yes that's right, I did.." Sally stammered

remembering her fabricated story she'd made up, "good job you've reminded me," she laughed nervously, "can't be late for these zoom things hey."

Kate decided to walk back to hers, giving her some time to think about which outfit she would wear so they said their goodbyes. She was going over in her mind what she would say when he arrived, how she would stand, which wine glasses she would get out for the wine they would drink. What plates she should use if they did get a takeaway meal. Should she play some romantic music or maybe some smooth jazz, she also had no idea what he liked concerning that either. Tonight, she'd have to ask him more about himself, get to know a little more about him in the hope that there would be many more dates to come where she'd be prepared with food, music and more. As much as she tried to concentrate on anything else, she just couldn't get him and her important date night out of her mind, and it was the most excitement she'd had in a very long time. Tonight's date was going to be something just a little bit more special than any others before, she just felt it deep down somewhere and she couldn't work out why. And if she was honest with herself, she didn't care why right now. She was ready for some fun and this guy was certainly bringing it on.

Getting home and having a quick brew of coffee, she went upstairs to her bedroom. Asking her smart radio to play her 'pop' playlist, Kate began to get ready.

She had narrowed it down to three choices of outfits and quickly sent a photo of herself in each one to Sally, who replied, *'defo the red one, although you look gorgeous in all of them darling, I'd go with the red for tonight, it's beautifully smart and elegant but not too full on, if that makes sense. xx'* ending the message with a smiley emoji, a dress emoji and three red hearts.

Kate smiled down at the screen and messaged her back with six big kisses, then started curling her hair and applying just a tad bit of makeup. She didn't want to plaster it on for a night in, just enough blusher to brighten her cheeks up and a must-do set of killer curly, lashes full of her newest mascara to open her gorgeous blue eyes up.

Before she knew it, it was quarter to seven and she was now rushing around the lounge ensuring that everything was tidy and looking a bit more organised than it had a few hours earlier. She had thrown the shopping bags on to the table in haste, grabbing the items and running upstairs with it all to try on.

'What am I doing?' she mumbled to herself as she plumped the sofa cushions twice more and threw them back into the corners of the seats. If he didn't like her way of living, what did it matter? Was she being too fussy and why was she so worried were all the thoughts that were now running around like Mo Farrow in her brain? She shook her head at herself and laughed, then was startled as she heard the

doorbell chime.

Gasping, she felt instantly nervous, knowing he would be on the other side of the door. A final, rapid glance around the room before making her way to answer it, this was it. As she reached the end of the hallway, she took a few seconds to straighten her dress and check her hair and face in the wall mirror before calmly composing herself and opening the front door.

Chapter Six

Quite The Gentleman

There he stood, he had arrived and the handsome figure that was Dan transfixed her gaze like some sort of magnet. A silhouette of pure manly perfection standing there in front of her and in her doorway, at her home. The strong scent of his aftershave wafted in instantly, causing her nose to tingle as she couldn't help by inhale it, taking a long hard breath. He was dressed in a smart casual style, donning skinny fit, black jeans, and a sky-blue Ralph Loren polo shirt, with all three buttons done up. His brown brogue shoes were super shiny, looking brand new and she thought how different he looked from the last time she saw him at her aunts. A hoody and joggers were such a contrast to tonight's view.

In his right hand he was holding a bottle of cava, as promised, which had a big red ribbon tied neatly around its neck. As she scanned him up and down, she noticed a large rectangular shaped gift box in his other hand and her tummy fluttered to think he was buying her gifts again, after the amazing flowers yesterday.

He looked down seeing her eyes stuck towards it, "For you gorgeous," he said softly smiling as he lifted both hands up to show off his purchases.

"Oh, wow, thanks," she replied, stumbling her words awkwardly, "you really shouldn't have though. The flowers were enough yesterday but, thank you, thanks."

"My pleasure. Now are we doing this date on the doorstep?" he replied cheekily winking and giving her that smouldering stare deep into her eyes.

She giggled, "Sorry, yes, no…I mean…Oh come on in." She took hold of the items and used her elbows to usher him inside. Her tummy felt so weirdly nervous, like no other time and it was puzzling her more and more as to how this stranger was making her feel.

He closed the door behind them, and followed her up the hallway into the kitchen, "lovely little place you got here Kate," he said as he glanced around.

"Thank you, it's a bit small to be fair but it's just the perfect size for me."

"Small things come in great packages, that's the saying isn't it?" he joked, giving her another smouldering smile.

Blushing, she replied, "I'll just grab some glasses; do you want to open the wine?" as she placed the bottle on the dining table and reached for her best fancy crystal style wine glasses from the cupboard next to the fridge. They didn't get out much so she gave them a quick once over with the tea towel, hoping he wouldn't notice. They weren't real crystal, but they looked fake enough she thought after buying them from a local charity shop haul day she'd had with Leo. They'd been gathering as many kitchen bits as possible after she'd had a re-vamp and chucking out session at home, in the hope that it might inspire her to start spending more time in her own kitchen again.

"No problem, I can certainly do that," he answered as he started unwrapping the foil covering the cork, then proceeded to ask, "have you eaten?"

"Erm, not yet actually. Not since lunch anyway, and that was just a cake and a coffee in town," her hands were shaking slightly as she placed the two wine glasses on the table, chucking the tea towel into the sink, "did you want to order something in? There are loads to choose from locally."

"Sounds like a great idea, anything in particular

you enjoy eating?" he said as the cork suddenly popped in his hands, making her jump.

"Chinese, Indian, Thai maybe?" she began removing the ribbon from the gift that she'd now picked back up from the worktop side.

"Hope you like it," he nodded toward the box as he moved the glasses nearer to him in preparation for pouring the fizz.

She just smiled back as she delved into the unboxing with her hands still trembling slightly. He paused as he watched her open the box and then laughed at the gasp that came next.

"Oh, my goodness, this is so beautiful Dan," she exclaimed as she opened the box revealing a stunning, and very large crystal vase, "thank you so much, it's amazing, and very heavy," she exclaimed placing it on the table and gesturing the weight of it.

"I thought it would go beautifully with the flowers I got you," he paused, admiring her smiling at the vase, turning it around and watching the sparkle reflecting in her eyes, "let's have a drink now shall we, you can re-do your flower display into that later."

"Yes. Oh, it's perfect, and absolutely beautiful. And yes, it is exactly what I need. I am afraid to say that I had to use pint glasses as well as the tiny cheap old vase that I had. It's the only one I own but they will certainly look so much better in that, thanks again Dan," she turned on her feet, picked it back up, holding it tightly and placed it carefully by the kitchen sink. She couldn't wait to fill it up and get the stunning roses displayed in it.

He began to pour the wine into her glass first and then his. The fizzing seemed so loud; it wasn't a cheap bottle like she was used to getting on a Friday night for Fizz Friday at Leo's. No supermarket cava for her tonight. After he'd half-filled the glasses, he reached for her hand, noticing her twiddling the only ring she had, "No need to be nervous, beautiful, I don't bite. Well, not unless you're into that sort of thing," he looked into her eyes and winked again, and she felt totally immersed within them, she was mesmerised.

The atmosphere was intense, and she felt those butterflies in her stomach once again, flickering their wings hard with excitement around her insides. She hadn't been this nervous for a very long time, but she was also enjoying the weird feelings too. He leaned forward and gently kissed her on the cheek, pulled back smiling and then turned to go and sit down on the sofa in the lounge area. Kate could feel her heart thumping like a bass drum inside of her chest, and she wondered what the hell was going on with her body and how it was reacting. She'd never believed in love at first sight, those movies where instant romance was played out. Was he some sort of magician putting a spell on her? How was she falling so hard for this man that she'd only just met and more importantly, knew nothing about?

"Are you coming to join me?" he called, making himself comfortable, moving the cushions behind his back, "we need to make a decision about what food to order in, I'm starving."

She stood and stared across at him not saying anything. She felt so confused as to why she was overly nervous like this. It took her back to her teenage 'first love' memories but she was a grown woman now and needed to sort it out. She didn't want him thinking she was some weirdo, love struck, crazy girl.

'Snap out of it woman, for Christ's sake' she thought to herself. *'He's not a serial killer, and Rob wouldn't have introduced them if he was anything strange or dangerous.'*

His gentle kiss felt nice, the gifts were incredible, it was just wine and something to eat with a nice guy for a change, albeit a rather hot one at that. She couldn't help but think back to the conversation earlier with Sally. Her aunt's words ran through her brain, *'be careful.'* She promised she would so she must be careful. He was practically a stranger, only meeting him a few nights back but something was different about him, something she really liked. Something that she was going to embrace and enjoy for a few hours anyway, while she got to know more about him. All that was needed was her to relax and not seem so amateur in this dating game malarkey, so, reaching for her glass of fizz, she made her way into the lounge.

Sitting closely next to him, she sipped the wine and watched on as he scrolled through the apps on his phone looking at the various food options for delivery. She was determined to enjoy this evening with this new and mysterious guy.

*

"Morning sleeping beauty," came a soft voice as she slowly blinked and opened her eyes.

There he stood, a mug of coffee in one hand, standing next to her bed looking over her. Just his boxer shorts on, with his clothes in his other hand. His highly defined torso bronzed and muscular. It was such a beautiful view to wake up to and she couldn't help but stay silent and just take it all in for a moment as their eyes gazed at each other for a split second. Snapping out of it, she started sitting herself up from under the bed sheets. She yawned and then wiped her eyes clearer as he handed her the steaming hot coffee, "Morning," she said shyly, taking a quick sip of the rather strong-tasting liquid. She would have to explain to him about using the branded instant coffee instead of the granules.

Chucking his clothes onto the dressing table chair, he sat on the side of the bed facing her, just looking, admiring, his eyes moving over every feature of her face. "How did you sleep?" he leaned forward and picked off a strand of her hair from her face near her eyes.

"Yeah good thanks, you?" she replied awkwardly,

sipping the drink again but this time more carefully as it was hotter than she'd expected.

"Perfectly, thanks," he replied, staring at her again, tilting his head, "you have such gorgeous eyes you know."

Blushing and again, hiding behind a sip of coffee, she just looked at him.

"Have you got to work tonight?" he asked.

"Yes I do unfortunately, no rest for the wicked," she chuckled back, "eight o'clock until half eleven I think it is. There's a stag-do in as well, so it will be a bit of a crazy one I expect, and we'll probably have loads of stuff to clear up afterwards."

"Can't you get someone to cover your shift instead, then we could go to the cinema or something?" He stood up and grabbed his t-shirt, pulling it over his head. When he reappeared, he straightened his hair, leaning down to see his reflection in the dressing table mirror.

"Sorry, no. We are short staffed as it is. There are a few people off on holiday so it's just me and Leo in charge tonight and only two other girls' waitressing. Maybe Friday we could go to the cinema? I'm off that night," she watched him dressing. He was so fit, and she loved his body already, what she had seen of it anyway. The rugby training every week had probably helped build that sort of physique.

"No worries, yeah maybe Friday then hey?" he replied, sounding slightly disappointed, "Anyway, look, I've gotta get off. There's a match meeting at eleven and then I've got to go visit my mum, so I'll text you later," he pulled on his trousers and returned to her bed side, kissing her on her forehead, "let me know when you've finished work and we can have a video call, if you're not too knackered that is?" and then he swiftly left the bedroom before she could answer or say anything else, "See you later." He called finally before she heard the front door closing.

She sat for a moment, a little stunned at his rather sharp exit. She wondered if she had said something to upset him or was that just his way of leaving in the mornings? No long goodbyes, his now statement soft kiss on the cheek or at least a hug. Her thoughts were again, trailing away with her but she couldn't help it. He was a bit mysterious in some of his ways, especially last night.

When the moment had come to go to bed the previous evening, she had remembered feeling her heart racing fast as he kissed her so smoothly and full on the lip as they drank their wine, ate their takeaway, and sat close on the sofa. Her emotions were overflowing with something she'd not recognised before when she had suggested they continue the evening upstairs, but he'd shocked her with his reply, stating, "The sofa is cool for me tonight, just need a blanket and maybe an extra pillow if you have one?"

He had turned down her invitation to the bedroom,

just when she had plucked up the courage to be brave enough. Being so forward in the first place. She'd spent an hour or so trying to pluck up the courage to ask him and then felt deflated with his answer. She had no clue that he would turn around and say that he wanted to stay on the sofa while she slept upstairs. Totally confused, she'd just replied, "sure, I'll get them for you now," and had left the room puzzled. When she returned with the spare quilt and a few pillows for him, he was already undressing and starting to lay down. As she left him to it, she had slipped into bed thinking what she could have done differently. Maybe she was just looking too deeply into it, a bit deeper than she should be. Maybe he was just being the ultimate gentleman after all. Whatever the reason for his rejection, she still liked him, she liked him a lot and wanted to see him again soon.

She sat there in her lonely bed, finishing her coffee, and trying not to think about the situation too much. Her mind seemed to be wondering off every second since meeting him. Suddenly, she had an idea. Maybe it would be a nice surprise for her to message him first this time round, before he could send her his cheeky little texts. She swung her legs out of the side of the bed and grabbed her phone from the bedside cabinet, tapping away a text to him, smiling like a Cheshire cat and feeling very off the cuff for a change. She had never chased someone like this or typed such soppy messages. *'I really enjoyed last night, and the vase is stunning, thank you again. You are a sweetheart xx.'* Reading it back, she deleted the two kisses and then put them back in, shrugging her shoulders, and then pressed send before she changed her mind. Looking out the window, she smiled to herself, waiting to hear that ping of a message coming through, waiting for his usual super quick response, but nothing came.

'Maybe he's driving or has no signal.' she thought to herself after a minute or so with no reply. She couldn't help but keep refreshing the message, closing it, turning the phone off and then frantically thinking she may have missed a text from him, turning it back on again. He had really stirred up her emotions and she was so eager for a reply but after an hour, she gave up waiting. Putting it down to him just being busy with the rugby meeting or visiting his mother so she stopped looking, convincing herself that she was being too much of an eager beaver and needed to give him space to do his own things. She assured herself he would be in touch very soon.

Chapter Seven

Smitten

"So, my little minx. You had a cheeky stay at home date instead then?" Leo asked her when they had a ten-minute coffee break at work that evening. She had texted him on the train while she made her way in tonight to explain most of what her evening had entailed. The food, the gifts, the kiss. Mainly about the hot man she was now having heart palpitations about.

"Yes, it's been a while since any date, hasn't it," they laughed, "but, you know what, it was sort of nice to just chill at home instead of a noisy club actually or having to get all fancied up and go to a restaurant. I didn't have to cook either, we had an Indian delivered. That newish one on the high street.

He bought a bottle of very expensive cava too, not like our cheap supermarket rubbish," she winked as she gave him a shy grin, "and…" she continued, "he had wrapped up the most beautiful gift. Look," she grabbed her phone from her pocket and showed him a photo of the vase that she'd taken before she left for work. She had put the flowers into it as soon as she'd got out of bed that morning and Dan had been right, they looked amazing in it and fit perfectly, "It's crystal Leo, real crystal. Isn't it gorgeous, looks better in the flesh, but, how lovely of him to buy me that? I've never owned anything so stunning, Leo." she continued admiring the photos of the vase. The flowers only just fitted in it, and she knew how gutted she would be when they eventually wilted off and died. She really hoped they would last a good week.

"Wow, it looks fabulous darling, really classy and that, check you out having real crystal in your little abode," he joked, nudging her arm with his elbow, "he's certainly going all out to impress my Kate, isn't he? But, come on," he continued, "let's skip to the good part…let's get down to the nitty gritty shall we babe…" he then lowered his voice to whisper, leaning in closer to her, "how was the…you know, the bedroom antics, how was the sex?"

"Leo, stop it," she shoved him back, punching his arm, playfully, "it's not all about sex you know."

"Ouch…" he shrieked, "No need for physical abuse, I was only asking a simple question babe," he laughed. It hadn't hurt at all; Kate didn't have it in her to hurt anyone and she was only playing about like they did.

"Sorry." She apologised.

"No it's cool, didn't really hurt these tough old arms," he replied, flexing his muscles, "I'm sorry darling, it's none of my business, but come on, do tell your old pal, how was it?" he tried to lean in again and they both ended up laughing at one another as she moved, and he nearly fell off the chair.

"We better get back to work now, you crazy fool," she said, unwilling to discuss the matter any further. She didn't want him to know that she had actually been turned down for sex. The fact that Dan had slept on the sofa while she lay alone upstairs with a raging set of sexual hormones and emotions to contend with. Total confusion along with it, not something she wanted to chat about over coffee for sure.

"Oh, you are a big tease Miss Ellington, I will get the gossip at some point, "he answered as they made their way back into the restaurant, "I will you know sweetie! There's no hiding information from me." And he pushed the kitchen door open to begin serving again.

The restaurant was super busy tonight, and the stag-do table was getting louder as the evening progressed. With the beers freely flowing and not enough food being eaten to soak them up, they were all beginning to reach that stage of having just one too many and Kate wasn't enjoying it this shift. Leo had been great and had tried to deliver as many of the orders as he could but as they were low on staff as it was, Kate dealt with the situation the best she could.

It was nearing closing time and whilst Leo was serving another set of customers, she had to have a turn waiting at the stags table, so she carried another tray of alcohol shots and pints from the bar towards them. As she placed the final pint glass and began turning to clear the table next to them, she suddenly felt someone grab her behind. She spun around immediately, angrily facing one of the men nearest who had a smug expression on his face, sniggering with the guy next to him. The beer in his hand was overflowing from being too drunk to be able to hold it properly and Kate noticed it sloshing onto the floor.

"Alright darling? Fancy a drink with us later?" the guy asked in a gruff sounding voice.

Before Kate knew it, her anger took over and boiled up, turned physical. She slapped him as hard as she had ever hit anyone, right across his face. All the other men in the group just laughed and jeered loudly and obnoxiously as though it was some sort of victory slap. Immediately, Kate felt terrible but so humiliated by them. Leo came over as soon as he heard the jeering and saw the expression on Kate's face, who was now hastily leaving the situation and heading away from the table. Within five minutes, the manager had got them all to leave the premises.

"I'm so sorry Max, I didn't mean to hit him like that," Kate apologised as Max, the manager came to see if she was okay in the staff room where she'd taken some time out to compose herself again.

"Don't you apologise, it wasn't your fault the guy was an egotistical imbecile. Have a coffee and take your time," he rubbed her shoulder which was still shaking slightly, "do you want me to call the police?"

"No, no. It's fine, honestly. As you say, he was just a bit of an idiot." She had shocked herself at reacting that way. She'd never hit anyone before, not like that and her hand was still stinging from the slap.

"Are you ok Kate?" Leo asked as he walked in, wrapping his arm around her, "I made you a strong coffee, sweetheart, here you go, drink up...or do you want some brandy in it or something."

She managed a snigger of laughter, "Thanks. No coffee is fine. It just shocked me to be honest, urgh, men sometimes. No offence Leo but why do some of you think they have the right to do that? Haven't they heard about personal space and that by now?"

"Hey, look. I've never done that to a woman, unless we've been dating of course but I don't know, testosterone, beer, peer pressure, it's the mix of that most of the time I think. We're not all stupid idiots like that darling. Anyway, are you sure you're okay?"

"Yes honestly, I'm alright," she answered, rubbing the palm of her sore hand, "I didn't half whack him," they laughed.

With the shift over quicker than planned, Max told them both that they could leave a bit earlier so Leo decided she shouldn't take the train home alone tonight. He really cared for her so much and they had such a good friendship, in and out of work, so they shared a taxi to hers and then said their goodbyes.

She practically fell into the hallway, exhausted, locked the front door and kicked her shoes off under the hall side table. She wasn't bothered about any mess tonight because all she wanted to do was rest after what turned out to be a horrible and extremely busy sort of an evening. Hooking her jacket onto the banister, her mind wandered back to Dan and the fact she hadn't heard back from him yet. All day and no messages. She really wanted to at least speak to him just briefly before she went to bed. Just to check he was alright more than anything. Making her way upstairs, she scrolled to his previous message to find his number and pressed the call button, but it rang off after a few seconds.

Disappointed and confused, she threw the phone onto the bed, undressed, throwing her work clothes to the floor, and slipped into her favourite pink negligee. The soft satin felt cold at first but smooth and comforting on her, now very tired body. She massaged her thighs firmly as she sat on the bed and leaned back. Her legs had done so much walking to and from all the tables tonight, they were really aching. Just as she began to feel sleepy, her phone began to vibrate. She grabbed it quickly and was relieved to see who it was on the other end. Thank goodness it was him, it was Dan, finally.

"Dan, hi," she answered, trying not to seem too excited to hear his voice. But she was, she was so excited to hear from him at last.

"Hey gorgeous," His voice sounded a bit subdued and raspy, but Kate put it down to the time, and the fact that he must've been tired or had a long day, "are you alright?" he asked sniffing.

"Yes I'm okay. Bit of a rubbish shift tonight but I'm glad to be home now and finally talking to you. How's your day been, busy? I thought you'd forgotten about me," she rambled quickly forgetting herself not to seem too much.

"Oh Kate, no. I couldn't forget about you, who would do that to someone so beautiful," he continued, "It's not been too bad of a day if I'm honest. I had that rugby meet up thing and that, bit boring actually," he yawned, "do you want to switch to Facetime? I want to see your cute face and what you're wearing."

Her cheeks blushed and her heart skipped a beat. She looked down at herself in the pink negligee wondering if she should quickly fetch her dressing gown so at least she could cover up a little bit. She hadn't ever been asked that question over the phone and felt slightly nervous as to where it may lead.

Sensing her silence, he whispered, "I won't ask you to do anything weird Kate, I just want to see you," he said, interrupting her thoughts.

"It's not that I think it's weird, sorry. Just not been asked that before. Give me a second," taking a deep breath and lowering the phone, she pressed a few buttons and within seconds, she had switched it to a video call.

"Hello," she waved shyly towards the screen, trying to move it to the best position so she didn't look like she had a double chin.

"Ahh, there she is…simply beautiful, even at this time of night," he replied, not quite filling the screen with his face.

"I looked better earlier to be fair Dan," she replied, blushing, "I can't see all of you, why are you hiding?" but he then stayed silent for a few seconds, "Dan? Is everything alright?" His pause made her anxious and his voice still sounded strangely coarse, "Dan?" she repeated.

"I just wanted to see you, I didn't say I wanted to show my face," he moved it more towards the ceiling meaning even less of him that she could see.

"Oh, come on, play the game, let me see you. It's only fair,"

After a brief pause, she watched intently hearing

him huff a bit but then as the screen began to reveal his face, she said, "Dan!" and gasped, holding her hand to her mouth. She looked closer at the image in front of her and saw all the blood down the side of his face and across his forehead, "What the hell has happened? Dan, are you alright?"

"Hey, hey," he waved his hand in front of his face, "don't panic yourself babe. It's rugby, that's what happens sometimes, just scrum madness again that's all."

"Jesus, why is it still bleeding so much though?" she asked, "wasn't rugby this morning? Do you need to go to the hospital and get some stitches or something, it looks nasty? Did Rob see it? Dan, you must get that looked at."

"No, no. It'll stop soon enough; don't you fret your little self.

"Dan, I…" she stuttered, concerned about his face and the blood trickling down his cheek.

"Katie, sweetheart, stop worrying. Just let me see more of you. That'll help soothe the pain. I want to see that gorgeous body of yours, that's cheer me up no end."

Kate didn't answer, she was transfixed to the cuts and the fact that it was bleeding so much.

"Look," he showed her a tissue and wiped his head, "it looks so much worse than it is. Blood goes a long way you know," he said as he moved his face nearer to the screen, "come on, cheer me up, make this injured face smile." He put his finger towards his mouth, blowing a kiss back to the screen at her and winked.

Still unsure of his story, she couldn't help but fall into those beautiful eyes of his, even with the blood, he still looked hot. She glanced down at her body again wondering if she should be even contemplating agreeing to his request. But, although it felt kind of strange, it also felt kind of naughty but nice at the same time. She smiled sweetly back at him and lowered the phone slightly so that he could see just the lacy detailing of the negligee that was covering her breasts, "that's your lot," she joked, her face blushing red and moving the phone back up.

"Aww, you tease," he smiled broadly, "can't I come over? See the rest of it? I'll be good I promise, you could play nurse and mend my wounds. I'm a good patient." he said cheekily.

His deep brown eyes were staring at her through the screen, now closer. She felt enthralled by them, and she couldn't believe how they were making her feel. Something inside of her was bubbling and she thought she may burst any moment if they carried on this conversation over the phone. Without even thinking anymore and before she knew what she was saying, she replied, "Yes, come over now if you want," and in the blink of an eye, he had hung up, the screen went blank.

She threw the phone onto the bed and hurried to

the bathroom searching for her deodorant, "shit, shit, shit" she laughed to herself as she sprayed it under her arms, almost missing completely through all the frantic rushing around. Grabbing her favourite scent from the shelf above the sink, she then spritzed a few puffs of it onto the sides of her neck and wrists. "What are you doing woman?" she asked her reflection in the mirror, grabbing a dab of toothpaste and fingering it over her teeth, "make up, mascara, no, you're fine," she blew out some air as if to calm her speeding heartbeat and tousled her hair, checking one more time in the mirror how she looked. Then there was a knock at the door.

Chapter Eight

The Night of All Nights…

Spinning on her feet, and glancing towards the bathroom door, she grabbed her dressing gown and quickly slipped it on, her hands fumbling, trying to make sure the belt was tied properly and covering everything that needed to be hidden away for now. She felt clumsy and clammy with sweat from the excitement. Scrutinizing herself again in the mirror, she then made her way down the stairs, almost floating on her feet, to see his recognisable dark silhouette through the glass of the front door. He was here, and she couldn't wait to see him. Inhaling a deep and confident breath she flicked the lock down and opened the door slowly. Standing there, head down, looking much more casual than the previous evening, in tracksuit bottoms and a hoodie, he gradually lifted his head. She gasped loudly as her eyes met his battered face. The blood still looked fresh with small droplets dried on his cheeks. He had one deep gash across the side of his forehead and a cut lip.

"Oh my god Dan. You look terrible," she said innocently, pulling him inside gently and shutting the door behind them, "Why is it still bleeding, let me sort it out for you. I think I have some of those paper stitches in the kitchen, come through," she held his arm ushering him to follow her.

He groaned slightly with pain, as he reached forward to stop her, grabbing her wrist firmly, "Kate, Kate, sweet Kate," he said looking into her very worried eyes as she turned round, "please, stop fretting, it's fine. I bleed well, that's all. It'll stop soon. Now come here," and he pulled her close towards his body.

Even with the bitterly cold weather he'd just come in from, she could feel the warmth of his torso. He was hot and sweating like he'd run there but right at this moment she didn't care what he looked like. His breath calmly blowing onto her skin. Those feelings in the pit of her stomach had reappeared, giving her some weird passionate sensation that she'd not experienced before, and she loved how it was making her feel. They stood staring into each other's eyes for a minute. She was drawn into them, even with the blood surrounding his face, she couldn't take her eyes off his. He pulled her petite body closer and tightly against his. She could sense by his body language that things were about to get serious as he began kissing her neck. With his cold hands, he untied the dressing gown and gently moved his hands underneath to feel her body. She gasped softly as they touched her hot and even more clammy skin but didn't stop him. His soft lips caressing her neck like no one before and she was frozen on the spot, captivated by the sexual tension, his sexy presence, and the pure gentleness he was giving her.

As he brushed the palm of his hand past one of her breasts, she let out a tiny sigh of pleasure and he looked straight at her, "I want you Kate," he whispered, "I want you right now." Their eyes locked again as his hands caressed her sides, sending shivers down her spine. She could sense goosebumps appearing all over her body and she felt electric pulses rushing through her veins. She didn't say anything, just nodded as he beamed his beautiful eyes deep into hers, which were glazed over with excitement. Her heart was pulsating like a bass drum, and she instantly knew she wanted exactly the same. Her dressing gown was now at her feet after he slipped it gently off her shoulders without her even realising. She thought to herself how utterly sexy this moment was and how amazing he was making her feel, how special he was making this impromptu meeting. He turned around, kicked off his trainers, and led her up the stairs holding hands in silence.

*

As she lay there next to him, watching him sleeping, all she could hear in the room was his peaceful breathing and the ticking of her clock on the wall. They'd made love for over an hour, the most gentle and loving experience she could only ever have imagined. He had made her feel like the most special woman in the world. As she continued to admire him lying next to her, she couldn't help but scour the cuts on his face. The bleeding had stopped after their shower together but the injury on his forehead looked fairly deep and quite an open wound. She just wanted to get the stitches and try and close it a little but didn't want to wake him now, he needed the rest.

'Bloody stupid rugby', she thought to herself, dragging her gaze away from him, and quietly shifting her body to sit up. As she began creeping out of bed, he made a noise but then turned onto his side, reaching his arm across the bed toward her but fell silent in his slumber once more. She noticed his hand was cut over three of his knuckles. Surely rugby scrums wouldn't have caused those types of injuries but, at the end of the day, she didn't take much notice of the game to have any knowledge. Maybe

she would have to go and watch him to see exactly what they did during a match. Or maybe he'd just done it while in his day job as a labourer? Building walls is a very hands-on, manual job after all. Not thinking anymore of it, she gently covered his arm with the sheet and made her way into the bathroom, grabbing her phone from the side on the way. It was late but she wanted to text her aunt Sally. She hadn't spoken to her since the first date night with him and just felt compelled to let her know how happy she was right now in the hope that at the same time, it might help to stop her worrying so much.

'Hey Auntie,' she began typing as she sat on the toilet seat, *'Tonight was the night with Dan. It's been incredible, he's so lovely, I need to give Rob a big hug to thank him for getting him round that night. I'm so happy, please don't worry about me, chat with all the deets tomorrow, love u xx'*, signing off with a pink heart and a smiley love heart eyed emoji.

Smiling to herself as she finished typing, she switched the phone to silent, had a quick wee, and crept back into the bedroom, laying as close as she could by his side.

The following morning, she woke up before Dan so, leaving him peacefully sleeping, she decided to make him some breakfast in bed. As she sizzled two slices of bacon in the frying pan, her mind drifted off to what had actually happened last night, and she couldn't help but grin as more fluttering emotions began to soar through her body. It felt like some sort of crazy firework display going on inside her body and it was thrilling.

Just as she was cracking an egg into the frying pan, suddenly his arms appeared wrapping around her tiny waist, and he whispered softly into her ear, "Good morning beautiful," then kissed her neck gently.

Slightly startled, she replied, "Oh, good morning you," she turned round to face him, and he pulled her closer to his body, running his hands down her back gently stroking up and down, "I was going to bring you breakfast in bed."

"Mmm, you're all the breakfast I need," he replied, giving her bottom a squeeze, "Man, your body…" he said almost through gritted teeth, "it's bloody perfect," and he pulled her even further into his hips.

"Dan," she said, blushing, "come on, stop that now. Didn't you have enough last night?" she smiled up at him.

"No way near enough babe," he said kissing her forehead.

"Cheeky. Anyway, how's the injuries now, let me have a quick look?" She tilted his head so she could look at the main cut, but he pulled away from her and made his way over towards the table.

"Kate, you have got to stop worrying so much, honestly, I've had loads worse than this before, it's just a few cuts. It'll be healed in a few days, you wait and see, okay," he said, trying to reassure her, "what have you made me then? It smells delicious," he asked, stretching his neck up and taking a deep inhale of the aromas that had filled the whole of downstairs now.

"Sorry, I just wanted to see if some of those paper stitches might help close up that bad cut," she paused, still trying to look but, it was obvious he didn't want them, so she turned back to the hob, "You've got the whole caboodle," she chuckled, "I'm doing sausages, mushrooms, avocado and eggs, scrambled and fried as I wasn't sure which you'd like. Or I can do poached I guess…oh and do you like tomatoes?" she said, looking towards him with spatula in hand.

"Wow, super food breakfast hey?" he said, eyes widening at the thought of eating such a big breakfast, "Oh and no tomatoes for me, thanks, and a couple of fried eggs would be awesome, not a great fan of scrambled, cheers."

"Okay cool, it won't be long, just waiting on the sausages to finish," she turned back round to start plating it all up.

"You know how to win a man over don't you? Can I make a quick brew?" he asked as he walked back over to switch on the kettle. He was only wearing his boxer shorts meaning that she could admire his amazing body once again. She couldn't help but glance over at his backside as he stood leaning onto the counter. The bright green boxer shorts fitting tightly around his pert behind were showing off its full potential, and she was loving this morning's view no end. Shaking her head and blinking her eyes quickly, she needed to concentrate on the food now. She wanted to impress him with her culinary skills as well as him being so impressed with her body. She'd not cooked such a massive breakfast for a long time and had to get the timing perfect.

"Hey, listen. I've got the night off," she said, as she placed the sausages on the plate, "do you fancy watching something at the cinema or a meal out maybe?" Kate asked, as she set his breakfast on the table, passing him the salt and pepper shakers.

He answered, stirring the spoon in his cup of tea, "Erm, I might be able to yeah. I do have to pop and see my mum again, but I'll let you know once I'm finished round there," he then sat down, picked up his cutlery and began eating.

"Okay great," she said, sitting opposite him with the coffee she had already made earlier, "where does your mum live?" she asked.

"Oh only a few miles away," he said with a mouthful of sausage and egg, "she's in a care home across town. Do you have any ketchup?"

"Yeah sure," she stood back up, grabbing the small bottle from the cupboard.

Taking it from her and squeezing a dollop onto the plate, he continued talking, "When my dad died, she couldn't cope being alone. She was a lot older than him and had a few health issues," he slurped some tea, "I offered to take her in at mine, but she didn't want to burden me having to be her full-time nurse and all that, so she basically arranged it herself to get booked in there. It's good though. She has everything she needs, anytime day or night and she loves it."

This was the most conversation that they'd had since meeting. Kate listened intently and it felt nice to know that he could open up to her about his personal life so early into their friendship. She watched him scooping up his last bit of fried egg onto his fork. She had managed to fry them perfectly and she watched as the liquid gold yolk dropped back down onto the plate which he swiftly wiped with his finger in and then licked it clean. She chuckled at him, "Was that okay?"

"Okay? It was bloody lovely that darling, cheers, I'm full to the eyebrows."

"Good, I'm glad you liked it all. I've not cooked a big breaky like that for ages, I quite enjoyed it actually." she finished her last glug of coffee and began clearing the plate and cutlery.

"What about your folks?" he asked, sitting back, rubbing his very full belly, "I know Rob and Sally obviously, but is there anyone else?"

"Oh well, not really. My mum died when I was a teenager, so I was brought up by my aunt and Uncle until I moved out to this place. Mum had brought me up on her own, so I never knew who my dad was, and to be honest, I never really asked about him." She began filling the sink with water and squirted the washing up liquid into the bowl, "Rob sort of took over that role I guess. I didn't need anyone else by then really." She came back over to the table with the sponge and wiped the area over swiftly drying it with the tea towel in her other hand.

"Sorry about your mum darling, that must've been tough losing her at such a young age?" He sat forward and gulped his last bit of tea, stood up and placed it next to the sink, "I knew you were Rob's niece but didn't know any more than that, not my business to ask really, sorry."

"It's okay. She got cancer, my mum. It all happened so quickly too. Pancreatic, one of the worst and most rapid ones apparently. She only got a matter of weeks after being diagnosed."

He gently rubbed her back as she swirled the bubbles in the sink and started putting the plates in to soak.

"Cancer is a bloody pain in the arse, whichever type it is," he replied sternly, "anyway I don't mean to eat and run but, I really must get a move on," he said as he kissed her cheek. "Would it be ok to have a quick shower and then I'll get out your hair?"

"Yeah of course, you know where it is, I'll just clean this lot up, do you want another tea or anything?"

"I don't think I could manage another drop babe,

breakfast was amazing, thanks again for that. Set me up for the day that has," he rubbed his belly again as he smiled broadly at her and puffed out his cheeks jokingly making his face look fat.

She just stood and watched him walking off whistling some tune. Just as he reached the kitchen door, he turned and wiggled his butt playfully back at her, accompanied with a cheeky wink. He was like some buff guy from a movie. His tight, muscle packed, body bronzed and gleaming, with not an ounce of fat on it. *'Perfection'*, she thought to herself unable to stop smiling, thinking about spending even more time with him, and soon.

Chapter Nine

Games...

Later that afternoon, she had a quick meet up with Sally in town. Their bench on the green was available as usual, so they sat and ate their muffins and drank their takeaway cups of coffee.

"So, little Miss Ellington, you have some news updates for me hey?" questioned Sally, "you've done the deed with Mr Howard?" she nudged Kate's arm in jest, making her blush.

"Done the deed," Kate repeated, "I wouldn't call it a deed," and she laughed as she looked at her auntie who had her eyebrows raised primed and ready to take in all the juicy gossip and details.

"Haha, anyway, come on, I've been waiting all day to hear about it after seeing your message this morning."

"Okay, well…oh Auntie, it was, well it was incredible actually. I mean, the very few times I've slept with someone before, it's been well, it's just been sex really. But with Dan," she paused reliving some of the moments in her head, "it just felt so, oh I don't know…it just felt more special than any other time before, with anyone else."

"Ooh err, sounds intriguing?" Sally turned her body and reached her arm across the back of the bench, "tell me more, tell me more."

"I don't know auntie; I really don't know what's happening with me. Just, well, it just felt completely different, yeah, that's it. It was different and so much more," she sipped her coffee, "I think I'm falling for him already. He's put some sort of weird Harry Potter spell on me I think," she laughed as she glanced across at Sally who was almost hiding behind her cup, giving Kate a strange googly eyed expression, which made them both giggle, "stop that," she said as she playfully tapped her aunt on the knee, "what do you think of him anyway? Does Uncle Rob know much more about him other than how good he is at Rugby?"

"Erm, well, I couldn't really say my darling. He doesn't tend to discuss his players personal lives that much. Do you want any more cake?" she held out the muffin box, Kate shook her head, "He did tell me that his dad died quite tragically. I'm not too sure as to the ins and outs of it but it wasn't a 'normal' death from what we can gather. Anyway, whatever the situation, Rob thinks it hit Daniel quite hard. I think he suffered badly with depression afterwards, not sure how close he was with him."

"Yes, actually, he told me about his dad dying this morning." Kate replied, "just briefly mind."

"To be honest sweetheart, Uncle tries not to get too involved with his players, but Dan is one that he knows a little bit more about than the others. He has been through a lot apparently, maybe have a chat with Unc next time you come round?"

"Maybe. I don't want to seem like I'm prying into Dan's personal life, without asking him first, you know, so early on in our relationship. I don't want to spoil things."

"It's not prying at all darling but, well…" she paused rubbing Kate's shoulder, "just take it slowly and do as I always tell you, be careful. We do worry about you still so much; you know that don't you Kate? You're our special princess."

"I know you worry auntie and it's really sweet of you, but I am a big girl now."

"I know, I know, but old auntie Sally still has the right to worry about her little niece, no matter how blooming old you get, so you'll have to let me."

Kate just smiled back at her. She loved her auntie so much and they had been amazing bringing her up. Although sometimes she felt as though they worried too much, she couldn't fault them for what they'd done for her and the life they had provided after her mother's sudden death.

As Kate started packing her rubbish away and collecting the muffin cases, Sally held onto Kate's arm, "Darling, promise me that you will be careful, won't you? I mean, just take it slow like I said. You don't know him or enough of his past yet so…"

"Auntie please," Kate interrupted, "I thought you'd be happy for me having someone in my life. I know what I'm doing. I've not just jumped into bed with someone off the street," she snapped back and immediately saw the expression on her aunt's face which made her feel awful, "look, I'm sorry for snapping, it's just. Well, you were adamant the other night at the party that I should get together with someone. You even said someone from uncle's team, and now I am, it's like you don't want it after all," she paused, "Please, trust me on this one. I'll be fine, okay?" her voice softened, and she held her aunt's hand again, looking into her eyes. They had glazed over slightly, and Kate felt terrible for upsetting her and snapping at her like that. "Look, I've got to go. I promised Leo I'd drop by the restaurant to go through some new menu ideas with him. I'll text you tomorrow, okay?" She gave her a peck on the cheek and stood up, chucking the rubbish into the bin next to the bench, "I love you very much auntie, I'm sorry again for snapping. Do you forgive me?" she asked, pouting a sulky expression in the hope of dropping the tense atmosphere that had arisen between them.

Sally glanced up at her niece and smiled, "of course I forgive you," she said, "it's just auntie being auntie. Now go on, get off and create that menu. Say hi to little Leo for me too," she finished up, blowing a kiss with her fingers.

Kate formed the I love you sign with her hands and then hurriedly made her way to the train station to get to the restaurant.

The town seemed so much quieter than usual this afternoon which made it easier for Kate to catch up on some ideas and notes about the new menu while on the train. She couldn't help but think about the conversation with Sally earlier though, so she sent a quick text to say she loved her with three kissing emoji faces at the end. A love heart came back within seconds, and she smiled down at it, feeling a bit less tense about how their little meet up and chat had turned a little bit sour, then carried on writing her notes.

Her and Leo had been asked by the manager to create a new summer menu along with cocktails and they were so excited about it. They'd already had a few discussions about it, but time was ticking, and they had a deadline to meet now.

Before she knew it, it was her stop, so she gathered her bag and notebook and made the five-minute walk to meet with Leo. Just as she approached the doors of the restaurant, her phone began to ring in her jacket pocket. She fumbled about answering it while juggling her bag, not even noticing the number on the screen. The sultry voice on the other end melted her within a millisecond as she realised who it was.

"Hey sexy," he said seductively, "what is my gorgeous little lady up to right now?"

Stopping to catch her breath, Kate leant against the wall. It was just a sentence but hearing his voice after the evening they'd had, warmed her insides and once more, her heart started thumping hard through her chest cavity, "Hey you, missing me already?" she giggled quietly, smiling away.

"Missing you is an understatement beautiful. I'm missing you and that body of yours every second babe. It's just too much to be without you near me now," came back his reply making her blush instantly.

She could feel the redness working its way up her cheeks and her hands felt clammy. Just hearing his voice was making her insides flip over, "Dan, you're making me blush," she whispered.

"Let me make you blush some more," he whispered back.

"I'm just going for a meeting at work, should only take an hour or so. Are you alright?"

"I will be when I can see you, touch you, make love to you…see you blushing."

The silence for just a few seconds was intense and

Kate's breathing was getting faster, her heart pounded at the thought of seeing him, seeing that body of his, and more importantly, having sex with him again. She couldn't speak for a minute.

"I just needed to hear your voice and tell you that…" then the line went quiet again.

She moved her phone from her ear to check if the call had ended but it hadn't so she asked, "Dan, are you still there, are you alright?"

"Yes, I am indeed still here beautiful. I was just watching you getting all embarrassed, it's cute."

She stood up straight and looked up and down the street confused as to what he meant. As she scanned the pathways, left and right, she looked across the road and spotted a figure in a doorway just opposite. As it moved into the daylight, she could see his face looking straight at her, just smiling. He lifted one hand up to wave at her. It was Dan standing in the building doorway.

"Hey." She heard him say down the phone.

"Dan, what are you playing at?" she asked in a quiet voice, but smiling widely back, lifting her hand to wave back at him, "you're not spying on me are you?"

He chuckled, "I want you Kate. I want to touch that body of yours, hold you in my arms and kiss you all over, from head to toe," he gestured with his fingers for her to come to him, "I want you now gorgeous, right now. You know I can make you feel special again, even more than last night."

He was making her want him so badly and her emotions were overflowing in every area of her body. That voice was so hypnotic, but she had promised Leo and didn't want to let him down. Now she was torn between her new man and her work mate and didn't want to upset either of them.

"Dan, I'd love to come over there, you know I would but, I can't now. I've got to go do something at work," she shook her head gently over to him, "I won't be long if you want to wait but I've got to do this quick meeting, then I'm all yours, I promise," she blew him a kiss from her hand, "will you wait for me?" she asked, "it should only take an hour? You could even wait in here and have a coffee, I'm sure they wouldn't mind."

Suddenly the call ended. He'd hung up and stood there in the doorway, staring at her for what seemed like minutes. Just as she went to call him back, he turned and disappeared into the darkness so she couldn't see him properly anymore. Feeling even more anxious and excited at the same time, she realised he was playing some sort of game and as much as it was weird, she felt intrigued by him and his actions. Surprisingly, she wanted to play along and now needed to see him to see what he was up to, so placing her phone back into her jacket pocket, she went to the restaurant entrance. She knocked on the door and after a few minutes, Leo answered.

"Hey, I thought you'd forgotten, come on, we've got work to do missus," he said jokingly, widening the door open for her to come in.

"Leo, I'm so sorry. Something has just come up I need to sort out. I can't stay," she glanced back round across the road but couldn't see Dan anywhere, "can we reschedule for tomorrow or something, I'll come in early, or I can come to yours after work?" she said turning back to face Leo's confused expression.

"Sure, no worries mate. Is everything alright though, nothing serious is it? You looked a bit red and flustered?" he asked wafting his arms at her face as if to cool her down.

"Yeah, I'm fine, it's just a friend needs me urgently to do something," she lied.

"Okay," Leo replied still puzzled at her strange behaviour, "I've got a date in a few hours, anyway, I need to spruce myself up for that. I can text over my ideas for you so you can have a butcher and then we can chat on our break tomorrow night, is that cool?"

"Yes. Amazing. Thanks Leo, you're a superstar, oh and good luck with the date, see you tomorrow," and with that she turned to cross the road, frantically avoiding the traffic, and trying desperately to see where Dan had gone.

When she got to the doorway where he had been standing just minutes earlier, it was empty. She looked up and down the street once more but couldn't see him. Digging her phone from her pocket, she called his number, but it just kept ringing and then cut off.

'What the hell is he playing at?' she thought to herself. Tapping away on her phone, she tried sending him a text message instead to see if he would respond that way. Her fingers shaking, she eventually managed to type and send the message, *'Where have you gone? x'*. Standing alone in the doorway, staring back at the screen waiting for him to answer seemed to take forever, and then the typing back bubble appeared. She moved it closer to her face and eagerly waited. It felt like five minutes before the writing finally appeared.

'Meet me at yours, I'll be waiting, and Kate…hurry..."

She wasn't one for silly games like this and had never met anyone who played them. She'd seen this type of thing in the movies and couldn't quite believe that this was happening in her usually boring and quite simple life. Shoving her phone back into her jacket pocket with frustration, she leaned on the wall wondering what to do. In one way, she didn't want to play along and just thought to herself that she should ignore him, play him at his own game but she was feeling a slight rush of adrenaline. The excitement now brewing inside of her, she opted to go along with it this time.

As she hopped on the train, she looked at his message again, remembering the sound of his voice as he had looked at her across the road. Feelings came flooding back of their passionate night before and now, she was getting more excited. As strange as it seemed, it was exciting and made her want him even more. Hitching the nearest cab at the other end of the train station, she couldn't wait to see him even though he was acting a bit cryptic. It was just a bit of fun after all.

Hurriedly, she paid the cab driver, telling him to keep the change, and rushed towards her house. Arriving at the gate, she looked around the pathway leading up to the front door but couldn't see any sign of him. "*Where the hell are you?*" she whispered to herself.

Glancing down at her phone again to see if he'd sent any other messages, there was nothing new there. No messages, no missed calls, nothing. Throwing the phone into her bag with more frustration, she rummaged for her keys. Her hands were trembling, and she wasn't sure if she was cold, excited, or just angry. With the keys finally secured in the lock, she turned them round and it unlocked. As she started to take a step in, someone grabbed her from behind, cupping their hands firmly around her mouth. She tried to scream as she was pushed indoors but the hands were so tight on her face, she could hardly breath. The door slammed as she struggled to get free, then the hands loosened, and she jumped away from their grasp, turning immediately to try and grab something to use as a weapon. The only thing close enough was an umbrella on the sideboard so she grabbed it and opened her mouth to scream as she turned back around. Shocked, she then promptly dropped it to the floor. Looking back at her, smiling weirdly, was a familiar figure, it was Dan.

Her chest was heaving so much it felt as though her heart could smash out of her rib cage, "What the hell was that about Dan," she cried, holding her chest, trying to get her breath back, "Shit. You scared the bloody life out of me."

She felt so angry, but he just stood there watching her as she threw her bag down and tried to calm her breathing. Looking at his almost smug expression, she said sternly, "Dan. Seriously, that was not funny, not funny at all," she replied, seeing his smile gradually grow wider. His eyes were peering deep into hers and she felt a little uneasy but those eyes of his were mesmerising. They just watched each other for a minute as her breathing finally slowed back to a normal rate. "Dan, this is all freaking me out a bit, what's your game?" but he didn't answer.

Before she could say anything else or do anything, he slowly moved towards her, his eyes transfixed on hers. As he neared her body, he started kissing her passionately and fast and she quickly forgot being scared or angry with him. It was like nothing she'd ever experienced, yet it didn't feel at all horrible, it was turning her on, more than she could ever have imagined this type of thing would. This was like a movie scene that she was acting the lead role in, and it felt fantastic. They began ripping each other's clothes off, still standing against the wall in the hallway. This was one of the sexiest experiences in her life, and she was loving every second of it. She just wanted to feel his body against hers now, to make her feel special, to make her feel safe again. And that is what he did.

Chapter Ten

Doubts

"Did I really scare you that much earlier?" he whispered in her ear as they lay on the floor in the lounge where their passionate encounter had all ended. Just a woollen blanket covered their entwined bodies that she had quickly grabbed from back of the sofa afterwards. Thankfully, it wasn't a cold evening, and she hadn't even thought about putting her clothes back on just yet. She wanted to embrace this moment for as long as possible. Never had she done anything so exciting, so thrilling and yet, so immensely sexy at the same time. This was a night she wasn't going to forget in a hurry.

"Err, yes, just a tad," she replied nonchalantly.

"Aww sweet Kate." He replied, kissing her

forehead as she turned to face him.

"It wasn't funny doing that, I was really shitting it for a moment until I knew it was you," she reached one arm out of the blanket and stroked his dark hair.

"Did I make up for it though?" he asked, looking deeper into her eyes, making her tummy flutter all over again.

"I guess you've made up for it, yes." she couldn't help but smile at him. He had made her feel safe, but she wasn't sure how many more games like that she wanted to play. She wasn't sure if her heart could take those sorts of surprises or shocks. In one sense, she had been scared but it was also something very exciting at the same time.

"Well, there's a lot more of that to come I can tell you, the making it up to you stuff, not the scaring," he winked at her, turning onto his back with one arm still wrapped around her body.

His torso was now poking out from beneath the blanket, and she couldn't help but glance down at it. She gently pulled at the inside of it to expose him even more. The definition on his abs was incredible, his rugby and building work must help create that sort of structure.

"Sorry darling, it was just a bit of fun though, you know that right? You really turn me on, I can't help it that I want you like I do," he ran his fingers along the top of her arm, making her shudder with delight at his gentle touch. The goosebumps seemed to pop up fast on her skin made her gasp air.

"How did you know where I was today anyway?" she asked, "you're not some serial killer or stalker type of guy are you?" she questioned him, frowning her eyebrows together and tilting her head.

"Haha.," he chuckled back, "no, sweetheart, like I said, I can't help it. When I want you, I want you and that's it, end of." With that, he got up from the floor, the blanket sliding off his body and stood there completely naked.

His pert behind looked even more amazing than last night somehow she thought, her gaze stuck fast on his body as she pulled the blanket over her chest. His cute butt leading down to the most amazingly perfect, and very muscular toned legs, she was in awe of it and sighed to herself without realising. "You're so toned Dan."

"Oh stop it you charmer," he laughed, waving his arm in jest, "it's the strict rugby training your uncle has us doing. Anyway, fancy a coffee?"

She sighed once more, and answered, "yeah can do," in a dreamy state, leaning up onto her elbow. This really was beginning to seem too good to be true, like a dream that she hoped she wasn't going to wake up from any time soon and it felt so good, so nice. Nice to have this new man bringing excitement romance and maybe even a bit of love to her life.

Watching him leave the lounge area, Kate then gathered up her clothes and put her t-shirt and knickers back on and made her way into the kitchen where Dan was standing, still stark naked, in front of the boiling kettle. She quietly crept up behind him and wrapped her arms around his waist. He didn't seem to even flinch, not like she had earlier after him grabbing her. She kissed his back and took in his manly smell before getting on tiptoes to glance over his shoulder. He had her phone in his hand and was scrolling through the photos.

"What are you doing?" she asked, loosening her arms, and moving to his side.

"Just checking out your photos, that's all. You've nothing to hide from me, do you?" he looked at her waving the phone from side to side.

"No, of course not but…"

"But what," he interrupted, "If you're not hiding anything in here, it doesn't matter if I look, does it?" he put the phone down and slid it across the worktop, "did you want coffee or tea?" he asked her as he looked at her dazed expression.

She was confused by his tone but then instantly blamed herself for being defensive about the situation. He was only looking at photos after all. She didn't have anything to hide. Why did she even question it, she thought to herself as she sat at the table, "coffee please?" she answered back.

The next few minutes remained silent between them, just the clinking of the mugs as he stirred his tea and chucked the spoon into the sink. After he'd finished making the drinks, he gave a mug to her and went off upstairs to shower leaving her a little bewildered by the awkward silence that had ensued. Sometimes he acted strange, his reactions or tone of voice was a little weird but maybe that was just how he was, and she was looking too much into it. Her newfound love was making her feel amazing most of the time, especially the random and spontaneous sex they were having. It had only been a few days, but she felt as though she'd known him so much longer. She was looking forward to what the next few weeks, months, even years she hoped were going to bring and what other mad experiences they may have together. She wanted to get to know him even more, more than any boyfriend before. He was so intriguing, so she wasn't going to jinx it or complain.

'*Just enjoy this guy,*' she told herself as she grabbed her phone and scrolled through her notifications, sipping on her coffee waiting for him to come down. As she checked, she put a slice of bread in the toaster, fetching the butter and marmite out of the food cupboard. She was hungry for some carbs, something to perk her energy back up.

About fifteen minutes later, Dan appeared in the kitchen again, wet hair slicked back, and now fully dressed, "I'm going to shoot off now babe, I'll be round later about five ish with a meal and a bottle or two. Give us a kiss," he said, leaning down towards her and placing his hand on her shoulder.

Kissing him back, full on the lips, she felt the warmth of his skin against her face.

"Mmm, marmite lover hey…" he said, licking his lips and smiling at her, "you will be here later won't you darlin'?"

She replied, "Sure. I'm going to get a bit of housework done and then I was thinking I might do some baking for a change, any cakes, or biscuits that you fancy me making for you?"

"Anything sweet is good for me babe but as long as I can have a slice of you, I'll be a happy man. See you at five," and then in a flash, he had left, leaving behind a trail of his scent which now filled the room.

For a few minutes, she just stared into her mug of black coffee, thinking about what had happened last night. It made her tingle and she felt completely loved and sexy along with it. No one had ever made her feel this desirable before and it was all because of Dan. This fit, young, gorgeous guy that had stepped into her life at just the right moment. Smiling to herself, she got up and began getting the rest of her clothes together from off the floor in the lounge and hall where their passionate session had taken place. The lounge cushions were all over the floor, she had some clearing up to do before another night of passion tonight. At least that's what she was hoping for.

As she straightened up the sofa and folded the blanket, her phone text tone dinged. It was Leo with all the new menu ideas that he had promised to send over for her. She fetched her notebook and pen from the coffee table and started jotting all the suggestions down. She still felt bad cancelling on him like she had and sent him a reply saying she would reschedule the meeting as soon as she could and that she was sorry. She knew by the returning message of a blowing kiss emoji that he forgave her. He was such a good friend and work colleague and always made work that little bit more interesting. After toing and froing texts to each other regarding his disastrous date that he'd had the previous evening and more menu ideas, Kate had a few pages full, and they were excited to get started on them in the next few days.

*

Before she knew it, the time had flown by and all she had managed to get done was the washing up and a light hoovering of the downstairs rooms. It was nearly half four already and Dan would be back soon. She wanted to make a bit more effort and get into something a little bit sexier than her current scruffy t-shirt and joggers so quickly ran upstairs to rummage through her wardrobe and drawers. She pulled out the new dress that she had brought when she had her shopping trip with Sally thinking that would certainly do the trick. All she needed to do now was a light freshen up, so she hung the dress on the back of her closet door and jumped in the shower.

She sat at her dressing table, drying her hair that seemed to be taking ages, in just her bra and knickers. Just as she flipped her head to one side, she gasped, noticing Dan standing there, leaning in the bedroom doorway, "Jesus Dan," she cried, as she switched the dryer off, "you have to stop making me jump like this," she turned round on her stool, "You're gonna cause my heart to stop one of these days," she held her chest, "I didn't hear you knocking or ringing the bell, did I leave the backdoor open?"

He slowly started stepping towards her with his hands behind his back. For a second, she thought he was playing another game and the feelings of anxiety, but excitement began reeling through her body once again.

"No need to knock. I took your door key earlier," he replied honestly, "now who are these for I wonder?" his hidden hands came from behind him, producing another wildly amazing, large bunch of red roses.

"Wow," she gasped as her eyes widened, "Dan, they are stunning," she said, taking hold of them as he got closer to her, "you really shouldn't have though, I still have the other ones there, look. I'm not sure they will all fit in together."

"Don't matter, I'll buy you another vase. You deserve flowers every day," he stroked her still damp hair and flicked it back over her shoulders, "Man, you look so sexy with your hair like that. And this underwear...I'm liking this little set a lot." His eyes were full on swooping up and down her body and again, the moment became intense, silent and the air was filled with passion. She began to feel her heart beating faster as he ran his hands up and down her body.

"It's not dry yet?" she innocently corrected him, shaking her head and ruffling through her tresses, "I don't know if my hairdryer is on its way out, may have to get a new one."

"Let's go out tonight hey?" he suddenly interrupted, "I've got an idea you might like. Oh, and I've brought a few bits of my clothes to keep here," he pointed back towards a holdall that was in the doorway, "is that alright with you or am I being too presumptuous in thinking you would like me here a bit more?" He moved back slightly, looking into her eyes, smiling.

"Erm, no. No, that's fine, I love having you here and a night out would be great, what's the idea?" She ruffled her hair again and moved back to the dressing table to continue drying it.

"It's a surprise. Just get dressed. I'm nipping for a quick shower; it's been a long day." and he left the room to go into the bathroom leaving Kate with her new bunch of flowers. She placed them on the side to sort out once she had finished drying her hair with no idea where and what she would actually place them in. She'd have to get the old pint glasses out again until the other ones started dying off.

She continued drying her hair and decided to put it up in a messy bun for quickness. Her hair had been a nightmare just recently, drying out quicker than normal although it was still thick and manageable to some extent. She hated the way she had to use products and heat on it each day. It was always tied up for work for hygiene purposes, maybe all that tightness was stressing it out. Maybe she needed to invest in a hair mask or some sort of treatment which would give it a boost? Securing it with a few bobby pins, she then began applying her makeup, when her phone pinged. It was a message from Sally.

It was a message from Sally, *'Hey lovely. How are you? What are you up to? X'*

Texting back, Kate wrote, *'I'm great thanks, how are you? Just getting ready to go out for the evening with Dan, he has a surprise for me. ???? x'*

Sally: *'OK darling, sounds like you're having fun. It's just that I've still not given you that thing I was supposed to give to you on your birthday, keep bloody forgetting when I do see you. Have a nice evening, hope to see you soon. Love you. Miss you lots. X'*

Kate: *'Aww, thanks, Miss you too. I'll try and sort something for tomorrow or the next day, just been so busy lately, love you lots too. Say Hi to Uncle Rob for me. Xxx'*

Sally: *'Will do darling, take care, and keep us in the loop. Lots of love. Xx'*

Kate just replied with a single kiss and finished

applying the last bit of her makeup which looked flawless as usual. She then stepped into her dress, grabbed some heals from the bottom of her wardrobe and checked herself over in the full-length wardrobe mirror. She was ready and happy with how she looked tonight. Taking a quick selfie, she smiled back at her reflection. It was nice to get a bit glammed up for a change and this would be the first date night out with Dan which she was excited about.

Whilst he finished up showering and got himself dressed, she made her way downstairs to try and find a container to put the new flowers in. All she could muster up were the pint glasses, so she cut and arranged them and put them in the middle of the table. Tying the ribbon from the packaging around one of the vessels to try and make it look a little bit prettier in some way. She chuckled to herself standing back and admiring her handywork.

Chapter Eleven

Just A Night Out...

"So, where exactly are we going?" Kate asked as they got comfortable in the back of the taxi about half an hour later.

Dan looked gorgeous and smelt amazing as usual too, he'd obviously packed his aftershave along with his clothes too and she loved the scent. She hugged his arm and moved closer to him secretly hoping it would be a romantic restaurant somewhere. Somewhere in town where maybe she would see someone she knew and could introduce her new man to them. She wondered if Leo might be out tonight, he usually was out most nights in town, and she would love them to meet. Just so they could gossip about it at the next work shift.

"You'll see soon enough babe, you just have to be a bit patient and wait a little longer," and he turned to kiss her head, rubbing her knee gently and seductively. Just brushing over her skin causing the hairs on the back of her neck to stand up and increasing her breathing.

She looked down as he began to move his hand further up her leg towards her inner thighs. His hands were soft, but she could still see the cuts on his knuckles. She put her hand over his to stop him going any higher and he chuckled quietly. She was sure the moment could have got a lot hotter if she had let him have his way. She was excited for the evening ahead and just kept hold of his hand, rubbing his pained knuckles as if to try and fix them.

They arrived about twenty minutes later in the middle of the town and got out of the taxi where there was a bustling crowd of people outside a pub. Loud chatter and the sounds of clinking glasses filled the street, the normal drunk who had been at it all day and now didn't have steady legs to stand up and get home unaided. It reminded her of the stag do that they'd had in the restaurant a few days back, and she really hoped this wasn't the place they were going to.

"Don't worry babe, I wouldn't take you into that shit hole," he said, noticing the concerned look on her face, "it's around the corner here. We just need to walk about five minutes, come on," he grabbed her hand and directed her, hastily walking on past the groups of pub goers. She tottered behind on her heals, trying her best to keep up with him but he didn't let go of her hand. He had that firmly in place with his and she felt safe in his hold.

Within a few minutes, the long-awaited venue appeared.

"A strip club!" she exclaimed as they stopped outside the building. She looked up at the large swinging metal sign showing a girl in a giant martini glass. The two sturdy bouncers at the door looked sternly down at them both from the top steps.

"Yeah," he said, "I thought it might, well, you know, spice things up a bit," he nudged her in the arm playfully, "I mean, with your tight body, you could get a job here instead of that stinking place you work at," he smiled and winked at her, turning his nose up in disgust.

"Dan, I like my job, it's not a stinking place at all," she replied a little offended that he would even say that "and there's no way I'd work here, Jesus. What do you take me for?" she asked him.

"Why not babe. You're bloody gorgeous and I've seen that body in action. You could teach some of these girls a thing or two, I'm sure," he smiled again pointing to the pictures on the posters outside.

She shook her head at him, "Dan, I'm not really into this type of place, I'd rather not go in here, can we just go somewhere else?"

"I've booked us a private booth," he said, rubbing his hands together, "just us two."

"Is this a joke?" she asked, suddenly hoping, and praying that it was, "are you playing another weird sort of game on me?" she nudged his arm, hoping he would turn round and lead her somewhere else. Anywhere but here.

"No. Why would I play a game like that, come on, it'll be a laugh if nothing else," he grabbed hold of her hand, pulling her towards the steps, "I could order you a lap dance if you like, most girls are into that at some point, aren't they? You know, girl on girl action and that."

"No!" she exclaimed again, "Dan, no. I'm not going in, please. Can we do something else," she pulled back at his arm, pleading with him to not move further towards the doorway.

"Kate, sweetheart. Come on now," he turned round, stroking her face, "you've not gone all shy on me now have you?"

"I just don't want to go to a bloody strip club Dan, it's just not my thing." she pleaded again.

"Look, I've paid for the tickets, I'm not wasting all my money. They're VIP tickets as well. You can wait outside if you like with these boys," he pointed to the bouncers, "but I'm going in, so I'll see you later."

"Dan," she called out as she watched him pass the doorman his ticket and momentarily glance back down to her.

"You coming in or what?" he asked, shrugging his shoulders.

She looked up and down the side street that she was now standing in and decided she didn't feel at all safe to wait out here, "okay, okay," she answered reluctantly, and within seconds, she had joined him at the top of the stairs having her hand stamped with some horrendous looking women's body logo. A few steps more and they were in the club, being shown to their private booth by two topless girls wearing only silver sparkly hotpants, that clearly didn't fit their plumped-up butts. Their bodies were amazingly toned and tanned with no sign of any tan lines. Their hair and makeup absolutely perfected with the longest eyelashes Kate had ever seen.

Sitting down on the purple velour curved sofa, Kate felt more than uncomfortable. She had seen these places in movies and watched some documentary about the girls who worked there but in the flesh, it seemed worse. The darkness of it all felt seedy and she wasn't enjoying the attention the girls seemed to have on her man. She fidgeted in the seat and then was shocked as the blonde girl leaned over and kissed Dan on the cheek, after he had sat down.

"Hey Danny boy, it's been ages, where have you been? Me and the girls have missed you."

Kate watched as the girls' pert breasts almost touched his face, she got so close. Her excitement for tonight had turned into a nightmare situation which she was not enjoying one bit and she didn't like this feeling at all, especially as he seemed to be fine with everything.

Dan replied to the girl with, "Busy my darling, you know me," and proceeded to slap her pert little hot pant covered butt as she walked off. Noticing Kate glaring at him in disbelief, he then innocently questioned, "what?"

"Why did you do that?"

"What, smack her arse? It's okay babe, we've been friends for years, she's cool with it." He shrugged.

"Well maybe I'm not?" she said back, but he didn't reply, "I take it you've been here before then?" she folded her arms looking sternly at him.

"Of course I have, what man hasn't? It's the best one in town, you know. Now, what do you want to drink? Wine? Cocktails? Gin…?"

Staring back at his oblivious face, Kate felt horrible, and she thought she was going to cry any minute. This was slowly turning out to be a terrible evening that had been so full of promise from the outset. After the passion and the romantic flowers, she couldn't believe what an extremely tense atmosphere that had now grown in such a short space of time. Feeling humiliated and saddened hadn't been on her agenda and she didn't want to be part of what might happen next.

"I don't want anything to drink Dan, I want to go home," she said emotionally as a lump appeared in her throat making it feel like it was closing up on her. She swallowed hard watching him just ignore her pleading. He didn't seem to even notice how upset she was.

"Here you go sweetheart, thought you might like your usual to get started," said another busty blonde as she placed a drink in front of him, "did your lady friend want anything extra from us?" she commented, flicking her hair back and looking suggestively at Kate with a smirky smile on her face.

"No, I bloody don't, thank you very much," Kate butted in before he could answer and then stood up, knocking into the table making his drink wobble, "Dan, I'm leaving," she spoke raising her voice over the music that had now begun as two brunettes climbed on the stage in the middle of the room, "this is not my idea of a fun night out," she paused in the hope that he'd get up, apologise for even suggesting it and take her home. Take her back to bed and make her feel better, special again like before but he didn't move. She felt infuriated, "Dan!" she cried at him, but no reaction came. He was too busy sipping his drink and now watching the stage girls behind Kate dancing and throwing their perfect bodies up and down their poles like gymnasts but with much less clothing on. She shook her head and held back the tears feeling completely crushed by the whole thing. She swiftly grabbed her handbag, left the table, and rushed out of the club.

On the street again, alone in the doorway, just one of the huge doormen watching on, she began to weep. What was going on in his head right now to do this to her, she had no idea what had changed to make him behave like he had. She waited for five minutes in the hope that he would come rushing out to see where she was, to see if she was okay, but he didn't, and she was so annoyed.

"Do you need anything Miss?" asked the bouncer as she wiped more tears away, trying her hardest to compose herself.

"No, thank you," she sobbed, "I'll be fine," she sniffed back the tears, then got her phone out of her purse and dialled for an uber which arrived within four minutes to take her home. She slumped herself in the back seat and rested her head back. As they turned out of the street, she took one last glimpse back to see if Dan may have come out of the club after all, but he wasn't there. He'd stayed inside that hell hole and let her leave.

"Actually, is it ok to take me somewhere else please?" Kate then asked the driver.

She didn't want to go home tonight; she didn't want to be there if and when he arrived back. Now that he'd helped himself to a key, she didn't want to be alone with him being too angry, too hurt, and so upset. She needed to go to her aunt's house and sleep in her old bedroom, gather her thoughts together before facing him whenever he decided to check back up on her. She began texting Sally quickly, *'Please can I come over? Issues!! :('* and within seconds, a reply came back telling her to come straight round. Kate gave the driver the new address and felt relieved to not be on her own tonight.

"Hey what's up darling?" Sally asked, ushering Kate in when she arrived twenty minutes later.

Her eyes were now stinging and red from tears that she had sobbed out uncontrollably after getting out of the taxi and breathing in the night air. She felt humiliated and worried about how she was going to explain this to her aunt without Sally turning round and hating Dan for treating her that way. Kate now found herself trying to convince her mind that it wasn't so bad because she didn't want her family to think bad of him. At the end of the day, he was a young man who wanted to have a bit of fun and he'd just got her wrong, thinking she may enjoy the strip club. Maybe he was just having a bad day and wanted some time to himself. Maybe he did come out after her, but she left the club too soon. Her brain rambled on with scenarios as to why this had gone so wrong. Then she realised she was making too many excuses for his behaviour, and she would sort it out with him when she felt a little bit better tomorrow. Talk it over first before bad mouthing him and the evening to her aunt and uncle. She didn't want them to worry unnecessarily.

"I'm okay really, I just didn't want to be at home

on my own tonight, we had a bit of an argument," Kate lied, "I'd rather not go into it though auntie, can I just sleep here tonight and maybe we can chat about it in the morning?" She begged, hugging her aunt tightly.

"Of course, sweetie, of course. Come on in the warm, you look frozen," She replied as she rubbed her nieces' shivering arms, "here," and passed her a tissue from the sideboard where there was always a supply elegantly displayed in a silver tissue box. An ornate but modern box that covered the cardboard décor of any shop bought tissues, "you clean that beautiful face of yours up sweetheart and get some sleep. Everything always seems better in the mornings when you've had some shut eye. Do you need a hot chocolate or anything else, something stronger?" she stroked Kate's back lovingly. She hated seeing her upset and hoped it wasn't anything serious, but she knew deep down, Kate would talk when she was ready, she needed to rest for now. Convincing herself that if it was too bad, they would be talking about it now. She trusted her niece and didn't want to push her or upset her any further.

"No, I'm fine honestly, thanks auntie," Kate said wearily, and then climbed the stairs to her old bedroom which was immaculately kept just how she'd left it when she moved out. Closing the door behind her, she glanced round the room. All the happy memories of living with Sally and Rob returned as she walked forward and lay silently and tearfully on the bed. They had been the best stand-in parents she could ever have wished for, and her mum would've been so happy and proud of her sister. She glanced over at the photo of her mum which was hanging on the wall by the dressing table. She missed her so much and wished she had spent more time with her before she died. Fiona's ever-calming voice and playful games they used to play together, the messy baking episodes, the silly biscuit shapes they used to try and create and then test out on the neighbours. She often wondered why life was so cruel taking special people like her mother away and so suddenly too. She was too young to die, and they could have had so many more fun times and years to enjoy each other. She turned onto her side and lifted her knees up close to her chest and wept quietly wishing her mum was there to just give her a cuddle this evening. How had things turned upside down like they had tonight? And what had made him behave like such a pig that way with her. Those girls being around him had made her feel so inadequate and inferior to them. She knew her body wasn't perfect and for him to be ogling at them like that, hurt. Her brain was in turmoil thinking it all over, trying to comprehend and understand it, but before long, she drifted off to sleep, exhausted.

Chapter Twelve

Forgiveness...

The sun beamed brightly through the bedroom window, causing Kate to stir. It was morning already and she hadn't closed the curtains last night so as soon as the sun had risen, it had woken her. She hadn't moved an inch all night, waking up in the same position as she'd fallen asleep with a crumpled-up tissue still held firmly in her fist. She must've been more tired than she had thought.

As she squinted her eyes and blinked hard, she turned away from the rays shining onto her face and began thinking once more about the previous evening and what she would do or say next. She wondered about the best thing to say to her family after turning up there in such a sad state and untalkative mood last night. How was she going to explain it to Sally and Rob, and what would her excuse be? They had to be her priority. She had spent the night in their house and so they'd definitely want to know why that was in the first instance. They'd be concerned as to why she had been upset enough to not want to go home, to not want to talk about it when she'd arrived. She honestly didn't want to explain the whole sordid truth about the club and how he'd not left with her, how he had ignored her pleading for them to leave together and worse, leaving her on her own outside the dive of a club.

She didn't want them to think bad of Dan, she just couldn't face that so early on in their relationship. She was falling totally head over heels in love with this guy and that realisation was clear as day this morning as she thought about him. All she wanted to do now was see him, talk to him. The chance to explain that she just wasn't into that sort of thing and then they would be okay, surely he would say sorry, he would understand her rash choice to leave like she did, and they could get back to their hot steamy passionate moments together. Surely, everything would be okay once they'd had the chance to talk it all over. She just had to get back to hers and see him.

Quickly, she sat up knowing she had to get home sooner rather than later. Gathering her coat and purse, she hurriedly straightened the slightly ruffled bed covers, made her way to the door of the bedroom, creeping on her tiptoes, carrying her heels so she didn't make any noise.

It was just before six o'clock and Sally and Rob must have been still in bed fast asleep. The house was silent apart from the birds singing in the back garden, so she crept downstairs and made her way out the front door, closing it slowly and carefully behind her. She felt a pang of guilt for sneaking out this way but convinced herself that her aunt and uncle would understand, they'd forgive her once she'd explained her strong feelings towards Dan.

Ordering an Uber, she slipped on her shoes and waited at the corner of the road for her car to arrive. The short journey home to where she hoped Dan would be waiting for her, ready to say sorry for his behaviour and then they could put it behind them. Start again where they'd left off the previous afternoon.

As she closed the front door, she noticed his shoes in the hallway and his jacket was hung on the banister. He was there and in some way, she felt relieved that he'd actually come back at all.

"Dan," she called out, putting her keys on the sideboard, "Dan," she repeated, looking into the lounge. But he wasn't downstairs, so she began walking upstairs.

She could hear water flowing, he was in the shower, so, chucking her coat into the bedroom on the way, she tried turning the bathroom door handle, but it was locked.

For a second, her mind raced once more with images playing of him on the other side of the door. She had an awful feeling that he could have had someone else in there and that's why he had locked the door. That image made her feel sick but all she could do was wait and hope her mind was just playing tricks on her. The times she had been cheated on before meant almost always expecting the worst to happen but maybe, just maybe, she thought to herself, she was wrong about Dan, maybe she'd gotten last night all wrong and it was just an early relationship hic-cup. She had to give him the benefit of the doubt, so she sat back on her bed and anxiously waited to hear the shower stop.

He appeared five minutes later with just a small grey towel around his waist, his torso dripping wet as he stood in front of her rubbing his hair. Breathing a sigh of relief, trying to stay calm, she couldn't help but feel thankful that he was in fact alone.

"Decided to come home then?" he said as his deep brown eyes stared intensely into hers, "where have you been, aunties and uncles? Or round that bloody Leonard's place?"

She didn't like his attitude and his sarcastic tone was sharp, unnecessary. He sounded angry at her for not being there last night, knowing she hadn't come home. He was behaving horribly again, and she didn't like it. She didn't like the fact that he'd brought Leo into the equation either.

"Yes, I stayed at Sally and Rob's. And it's Leo, not Leonard." she replied, correcting him.

"Thought so." He shrugged back coughing.

"Dan, what's the matter?" she calmly asked, not wanting to sound too pushy but at the same time, wanting answers as to why he was being off with her.

He shook his head and continued rubbing his hair dry.

"Look, I'm sorry about leaving that place last night but I just didn't want to be part of that. I'm not into strip clubs, never have been, never will be." she explained, hoping he would now take his turn to apologise.

He gave a sly laugh back, "well, Miss goody two shoes, maybe you should live a little and get into them," he replied with sarcasm again, "it's more fun than you think. You never know, you might enjoy yourself hey?"

"Really?" she returned sternly this time, "you really think I would like that sort of trashy shit?" she stood up, now trembling inside with his uncaring reaction. She had to try and stand up for herself now as he didn't seem to be listening to her honest answers, it was almost as if he didn't want to listen or understand.

Suddenly, he came stomping toward her and cupped her face with his strong, clammy hands, "yes. I do actually," he replied, "it can be good for some relationships to spice things up. You should try letting your hair down a bit more, be a bit more adventurous." With that, he leaned down and kissed her hard on her lips, pulling his towel off and chucking it behind her on the bed. His now naked and still slightly damp body was rammed against hers; she could feel the heat coming off him.

She didn't know if she felt scared or excited. He made these moments feel like movie scenes somehow and she wasn't sure how she was supposed to react to it this time. Surely he knew she wasn't happy, surely he knew how unreasonable he was being towards her and how rude his words seemed? She couldn't work it all out and her mouth seemed glued shut, the words just wouldn't come out for some strange reason.

He pulled back from the kiss and looked down at her worried face, his mesmerising eyes drumming deeply into hers as usual. Just as she was about to try and murmur something, he let go, turned around and grabbed his clothes off the floor. She took a deep breath with her heart thumping hard in her chest, but still, she just stood there watching him unable to speak or move.

"Look sweetheart, it's cool alright," his voice now softened as he stepped into his boxer shorts, "if you're not into it, you're not into it…I won't suggest we go there again okay?" he turned to look at her and she nodded silently still motionless, "The thing is

Kate, it's just, well…" he stuttered, "guys need that sort of stuff at times so if you're alright with me going every now and again, we will be all cool, alright?" his face now changed from angry and stern to casual and carefree, wanting her forgiveness but she just stood frozen with shock as he continued, "Anyway, let's just forget last night hey babe, there's something else much more important that I wanted to talk to you about," he said as he pulled on his jeans and tightened the belt.

He was now so calm and collected yet she still felt too shocked and bewildered to even reply or try and interrupt him. What was he going to come up with now, she wondered?

He reached for a small gold gift bag which was sitting on the side next to her bed. Tugging his t-shirt over his head on the way back, he held it by the little black string handles and swung it in front of her, smiling that all-encompassing and infectious grin, "here, I wanted to give this to you last night when we got back," he pouted a sad mouth, "but you didn't come home so...anyway, you forgive me yeah? You know you love me really, don't you darling?" he passed her the bag and kissed her on her cheek.

Her body still seemed paralysed with total confusion, her heart beating fast, but he was slowly working his magic on her like some magician. She was being drawn into him like all the other times and she couldn't help herself as she looked down at the gift bag now in her hand.

"Kate, please," he whispered, moving even closer to her, and gently lifting her head back up to face him, "I'm sorry," he finally apologised, "I just hope this makes up for it. I didn't mean to be so horrible last night. Please, open it and tell me you forgive little old me hey?"

She wanted to say something, but her mouth wouldn't work. Taking the bag, she slowly pulled it apart, and looked down inside. She could see a small red box, so she reached in and took hold of it.

He grabbed the gift bag from her other hand, throwing it onto the bed, "I can't wait to see your face babe," he said excitedly, "go on, open it, open it, have a look."

She glanced back up at him, he was smiling so widely, like the cat that had got the cream, and suddenly, she felt her heart gradually melting and her anger subsiding. He really was the most beautiful looking guy she'd ever dated, and she couldn't help but want him even more. Peering down at the box again, she lifted the lid and gasped. A huge diamond ring was staring back at her which sparkled as she moved the box nearer to her face to get a closer look at it, "Dan," she finally managed to utter after gasping, "what is this for?"

"What does it look like babe. A gorgeous ring for my gorgeous girl," he looked at her excitedly, "Kate, it's an engagement ring you silly sausage," he gently pushed her shoulders to get her sat on the edge of the bed, "I want you to marry me," he softly said as he knelt down on one knee in front of her, "So I guess this is the part where I ask you," he cleared his throat and gazed into her eyes which were now widened, "Will you marry me Kate Ellington…please? Be my wife. Kate Howard, it flows lovely that name doesn't it?" he asked wading his excitement into her glistened over eyes.

Her mouth gaped open in shock, she looked down at his face, "I... I don't know what to say Dan, I mean…after last night, we need…"

Before she could say anything else, he took hold of the ring box from her hands and took the ring out. Chucking the box to the floor he then clasped at her hands, "Look, this is the truth babe. I've totally fallen in love with you over the past few days, it's crazy but I have. You do something to me inside," he held his hand to his chest, "and I don't want to lose you," his eyes were now tearing up and Kate thought her heart was going to burst out of her chest any minute as the following words hit her ears one more time, "will you marry me Kate?" he paused, "go on, please say you will, you'd make me the happiest man on the planet if you would say yes to me. Be my wife, I love you."

All the previous evening stress and this morning's anger, doubt and weirdness seemed to disappear in that moment. His gorgeous eyes, his beautiful face, even with the cuts and bruises that were still raw, she couldn't believe how handsome he looked staring up at her asking her to marry him.

After a few seconds, she let the tears escape from her still puffy red eyes, took a deep breath, and answered, "Yes. Yes of course I'll marry you."

"Woohoo!" he shouted as he placed the ring on her left finger and secured it with a kiss.

She giggled back admiring this now shiny new addition to her hand, "it's so beautiful Dan, so, so incredibly beautiful…and so big." She exclaimed giggling again.

"And so are you babe, the beautiful part not the big," he chuffed, "you are the most beautiful girl I've ever known. It suits you too. A diamond for a diamond. Now come here, give your future husband a cuddle." He stood up and lifted her up in his arms swinging her round in a circle. They laughed loudly as they landed on the bed, and she couldn't help but continue to stare at the huge diamond ring now having pride of place on her hand.

"Look, Kate. I know it's only been a matter of days," he said as he gently lifted her chin up to look at her, "but I've never felt this way about anyone, you've made me feel things, I mean. You just do something to me inside here," he patted his chest, "you are all I want from now on. Just me and you baby girl. It's just us now."

As she looked at him, she could clearly see that he had tears welling up in his eyes, and her heart was totally engulfed in the moment. She had fallen head over heels for him all over again, not really understanding how it had happened so quickly either, but she didn't care. He had messed up last night, but he'd said sorry, and she knew she had to forgive him for that one silly mistake. She loved him so much too. No-one had ever made her feel this way either, so it seemed like they were the perfect match, and she adored the way her tummy turned somersaults every time he was close to her. Even the strange, tense moments that she couldn't work out felt right in some weird way. He was intriguing, exciting, enthralling, and the spontaneous moments that they'd experienced so far made it all the more fun. He was right, it had to be them together now, they were engaged, they were an official couple, and she wouldn't be letting him go anytime soon. She was ready to live life to the full, just a bit more and with him beside her, she knew her future would now be more exciting than she could have imagined.

Standing there together at this very moment, with his smouldering eyes warming into her body, she felt complete. Her heart was beating so fast, and she couldn't wait to tell everyone her news and celebrate with them as soon as possible.

Chapter Thirteen

The Party...

A small engagement party was arranged within a month, with just a few close friends and family coming along to celebrate the occasion. It was only mid-October, and surprisingly, the weather was milder than normal. Today, the sky was a vivid hue of blue, and the sun was hot, shining its warm rays down on them without a single cloud to be seen, it was perfect weather for entertaining outside. They'd decided to have the small gathering at Kate's place in the garden. Some buffet food and the bonus food option of a barbecue. Then they would have the obligatory cocktails and drinks as a late afternoon/evening mingle session.

Dan had moved more of his clothes and belongings into her house over the past few weeks, and he rarely missed a night staying over. He had claimed his drawer space and one rail in the wardrobe with toothbrush, shaving kit and even purchased a set of new towels for the ensuite. He'd told her how his towels got ruined quickly because of how dirty he would get at work, so he liked to have new ones regularly. She didn't question it; she just liked the fact that he was becoming part of her home. It was almost like it was their place now. It had become theirs more each day and Kate liked the feeling of having him to come home to after work. She also loved it when he would get home from rugby practice or work and they'd slip into the bathtub together, shower together and spend the evening as a couple, like real couples did when they started out.

Sally had arrived nice and early to help Kate with the buffet food, although she ended up doing what she did best and prepared the ingredients for the after food, evening cocktails. When Kate announced to them that her and Dan were engaged, they had insisted on paying for the party. They'd wanted to bring in caterers, but Kate had insisted she was able to do the food prep herself with Dan taking charge of the barbecue food. Sally had taken her to the supermarket the day before, insisting that she paid the bill, swiping Rob's credit card to get whatever Kate needed.

Rob helped erect a small gazebo in the tiny garden with Dan, just in case the weather changed at a moment's notice. It was also now serving as some shelter with the unpredictable sun that had now shown its face.

"Thanks for all your help with this auntie, it's looking great isn't it?" Kate hugged her aunts' shoulders as they continued creating fancy shaped sandwiches and laying out the salad on various silver platters that Sally had hired in especially just '*to jazz it up*', she had told Kate.

"Oh, anything for you sweetie, you know I love a good party gathering," Sally answered, slicing some lemons, "and yes, it looks fabulous as I knew it would with your creative skills."

"It's mad though isn't it, I'm engaged auntie!" she exclaimed lifting her shoulders in disbelief.

"Yes…" Sally hesitated, "It's all been a bit…well, a bit of a whirlwind romance hasn't it?" she said, glancing up at Kate who was now carefully getting the chicken drumsticks out of the oven, ready to go out for a final roast on the barbecue.

"I know," Kate answered, throwing the oven gloves onto the kitchen side, "it's exciting though."

"Exciting is definitely the word. We are pleased for you darling; you know that right?"

Kate nodded and smiled back.

"But, you are okay, yes? It's not too rushed?"

"Yes auntie, we are awesome, I really can't believe

how good it feels to have someone who's so," she paused and held her head towards the ceiling thinking of just a word that could describe him in the best way possible, "captivating," she finally said as she smiled across at her aunt.

"Aww. He has certainly made an impression on you my darling," came the reply with a wink and smile back, "Oh, I meant to ask actually," she continued, "you never told me what happened the other week, you remember, when you came over late and slept at ours after your evening out. Did you have an argument or something? I take it everything was sorted out?"

"Oh, err," Kate stuttered, "yes. It was nothing really," she fibbed, feeling herself growing internally hot from lying, "well…we went out and, err," she turned her back on her aunt for a moment to gather her thoughts together, fiddling with the bread sticks that needed to be brought into the middle of the table, "we bumped into an old flame of his and I just got a bit, you know, well, a bit jealous I guess. I over-reacted, stupidly to be honest. I mean, look at him, he's just bloody gorgeous," she glanced out to watch him and Rob still struggling and fighting with the gazebo fabric and poles, it made them chuckle, "he was bound to have some past girlfriends, wasn't he?"

"Oh yes sweetie, we all have those past lovers who we would rather not bump into with the new beau on our arm," she raised her eyebrows, "as long as he didn't upset you, we have been worried about you, it's all happened just a bit, well quick."

"I know. Like you said, it has been a crazy whirlwind affair I suppose, and I understand that you're both concerned and it's lovely to know you are there for me, but," she took a deep breath, "I'm in love auntie, I really am, I've never felt this way about anyone before, and look at this blooming thing," she held out her left hand with the enormous diamond ring adorning her engagement finger, "he treats me like a princess auntie, and I love how he makes me feel so special. I'm so happy right now auntie, please be happy for us?" her face beamed with joy and for the past week or so leading up to the party, he had been by her side continuously without any weird or shocking happenings. He had apologised more than a few times about the dreaded 'strip club' incident but Kate had thought about it over and over and had decided it was just a tiny blip in their early relationship. New couples always had a few ups and downs when they first start dating, it was inevitable so, they had agreed to not mention it again and just enjoy getting to know each other as much as they could over the coming weeks.

Sally smiled back at her niece, seeing how her face was still beaming, she didn't need to say anything, she just touched Kate's hand with a gentle and reassuring squeeze.

Finally, having got the gazebo structure to stay up,

the men came into the kitchen to get a cold beer each from the fridge, both lingering around the snacks trying to pinch a sausage roll or three while the ladies weren't watching.

"The grill is flaming up nicely now, so it won't be long, and we can get all the meat out there for a nice roasting. Get this feast of a barbecue going hey mate?" Rob said as he swigged on a bottle of beer, not before clinking it with Dan's bottle to praise themselves for a job well done.

"Can't wait Rob, I've heard all about your barbecue skills." Dan said as he walked round the kitchen island and put one arm around Kate's waist, leaning in and kissing her cheek softly.

He smelt amazing as usual, and Kate looked toward her aunt and uncle standing together. She loved how their relationship was so strong, something she now aimed for herself.

"My hubby takes his barbecuing very seriously don't you darling?" Sally said, rubbing her husband's arm, "And well done on the gazebo thingy, both of you, everything looks great out there," she continued, "make sure you don't burn the king prawns this time though hey?" she joked nudging him and rolling her eyes in jest.

"No-one likes burnt prawns Uncle," Kate added smiling at them both, "Oh, auntie, I've just remembered, weren't you supposed to give me something weeks ago, you said that you forgot on my birthday?" Kate passed Sally a glass of prosecco, chinking their glasses together.

"Erm, yes, I did, erm," Sally replied, a little anxious sounding, "but it doesn't matter now though my darling, not today. This is your special day to concentrate on, it's not urgent. We can meet up during the week or something, and…" but before Sally could finish her sentence, the doorbell chimed.

"Ooh our guests have arrived," Kate shrieked excitedly, quickly untying her apron and hanging it on the door hook as she scuttled off out of the kitchen and into the hallway.

Sally chuckled and sipped on her wine, secretly relieved to not have to go into the subject any further, "will your mother be coming over to see us today Dan?" she asked, turning to see him trying to sneak another sausage roll into his mouth.

They were still a bit hot, only leaving the oven five minutes earlier, so he tried his best to answer between, puffing, and wafting his hand in front of his mouth, "no, she's not able to make it this time, unfortunately," he mumbled, "she's not been feeling so good of late, so we thought it best she didn't come. You know how the older folk can pick germs up so quickly, so no, she won't be coming."

"That's a shame, it would've been nice to finally meet her, maybe we should arrange something else in the next few weeks, we all need to meet her before the day of the wedding hey?"

"Yeah, maybe?" he answered, taking a swig of his beer before placing it back on the table. He then swiftly left the kitchen area to find Kate and see who the first guests were to arrive. It was Leo and Jessica, another one of the waitresses from work.

"Wow, Kate, that's bloody stunning," Jessica said, admiring the sparkling ring that Kate was proudly holding up towards all their faces. They'd not had a shift together since the big engagement announcement and she'd only sent a text message picture of the ring so far, "looks way better than the picture you sent me, jeez…it's massive too!"

"I know, it's incredible isn't it. I love it Jess and it fit me perfectly, just look at the way it glistens when it catches the light?" Kate replied turning her hand to catch the sunlight coming in from outside.

"Oh, it's simply gorgeous K, you're a very lucky lady. I'll have to get Dan to tell my future husband where to go for mine?" she laughed, noticing Dan moving closer to Kate's side.

"Hi, you must be the famous Leo I keep hearing about?" Dan said as he stopped next to Kate, firmly wrapping his arm around her waist, and holding his other hand out towards Leo's.

"That's me, don't know about the famous part though?" Leo replied, chuckling, "and you must be Daniel?" he asked back, reciprocating the handshake gesture.

"Dan," he replied, "just Dan is fine mate."

Kate clapped her hands together in excitement, "Oh, it's lovely for my two of my favourite men to finally meet," she continued smiling widely at the two of them shaking hands, "come on in, let's get you both something to drink. Ooh, and there's oodles of food to eat," she hooked her arm into Leo's and held Jessica's hand to usher them through the hallway, leaving Dan behind as two of his teammates had also just arrived walking up the pathway.

"Dan looks familiar," said Leo, as they approached the kitchen table full of food, "I swear I've seen him before Kate. Are you sure he's not eaten at the restaurant or come into the bar area at some point?" he asked picking at the mini sausages as Kate poured him a glass of wine.

"No, I don't think so anyway. Maybe he looks like someone else you know. Tall, dark, and handsome, you know the sort Leo, bit like you," she nudged him playfully as she glanced over to see Dan who had made his way back into the lounge area. He was now watching her intently as he chatted to his friends.

"Oh stop that you flirty minx." Leo replied nudging her back.

"He's gorgeous though, isn't he?" she winked at Dan, and he blew a kiss back to her with his fingers, "can you believe I'm getting married to that gorgeous hunk of a guy, Leo?" she whispered, passing him his drink, "I mean…just look at that man…and he's all mine."

Leo put his other hand around her shoulder, "I'm really happy for you Kate, and I can't wait for the wedding madness to start. Please, please, let me help with the dress finding malarkey that every woman loves to stress out about. I'm sure I'm the best person for the job."

"Ha-ha," she giggled. "That's actually not a bad idea. It's only going to be a really small affair though. Dan didn't want anything massive and that's ok with me, you know I don't like to be the centre of attention," prodding him in the ribs, making him spill a bit out of the glass, "oops, sorry," she apologised.

"Does he have any of his family coming along today?" Leo asked, wiping the spilt wine from his hand onto a napkin from the table.

"No unfortunately not. He only has his mum and she's poorly so I'm going to have to meet her another time. Anyway, I best go see if he's alright, he doesn't know many people here apart from those two, see you in a bit. Oh, and make sure you eat loads will you, we still have the barbecue food to be cooked outside yet," she pointed out towards the garden, and almost skipped off over to Dan. She was genuinely thrilled to have all her close friends and family with her today and had been waiting to introduce her new fiancé to her good friend for what seemed like forever.

Leo watched on taking note of their body language as Kate approached Dan with a kiss and hugged him tightly around his waist. Trying not to stare, he thought to himself that Dan had acted a bit distant from her. He didn't seem to be hugging her back as an excited fiancé should do at their engagement party. He sipped another mouthful of his wine and thought to himself that maybe Dan was a bit shy only knowing the few people who had just arrived, like Kate had mentioned. When they'd met in the hallway, he'd seemed to make sure that everyone saw that he had his arm around Kate, tightly and the handshake between them had been firmer than normal. As he grabbed himself a tuna sandwich, he racked his brain again wondering where or if, he had seen him before. Leo knew all the local bars and clubs, so it could've been one of those nights or maybe he'd been to the restaurant before Kate had started dating him, when she wasn't working a shift or something. He concluded that, wherever it was, if at all he knew of him, it would come to him eventually, if he was correct in thinking he knew him from somewhere anyway. Today was about his good friend, Kate, and celebrating her engagement to someone she was obviously smitten with. As much as he was bursting to share his own exciting updates with her, they would have to wait for now. It wouldn't be long until they were back working together. Once he had her sat down and ready for his big news, he would reveal it all to her and cross his fingers in hope she would be as excited as he was.

Chapter Fourteen

New Beginnings...

The next few days were full on. Halloween bookings were already coming in thick and fast at the restaurant, so Kate and Leo had been busy decorating and creating a few crazy spooky meal options. Dan had been spending more time than usual visiting his mum. He'd told Kate that he planned to take her to meet her very soon, but she had been too poorly to have any other visitors but him. A little disappointed but understanding and accepting his reasons, it gave Kate a chance to spend quality work time with Leo at the restaurant now that their new menu was in place.

As they sat having a coffee just after closing time, Leo finally decided tonight was the night he needed to tell her his long-awaited news.

"So, yeah, he's now asked me to go and work for him privately, but full time," he said, stirring another sugar cube into his drink.

"Leo, that's amazing. Well done mate, you deserve this break," Kate replied excitedly, "but I will miss my work buddy here," she pouted a sulky face.

"Well Miss Ellington, that's the thing you see, I have some other news," he paused as she looked on curiously, "he wants me to find one other person who would be professional enough to work alongside me on a regular basis. As his catering team if you like."

"Right," she replied, slightly puzzled.

"Oh Kate, sometimes…you really do need to get your brain into gear a bit quicker," he laughed, nudging her shoulder against his, "I told him about you and that you would be my only choice of person to work with there."

"What?" she cried, "seriously?"

"Of course, you doughnut, of course I have suggested you. What do you think of the idea?" he sat forward, "no more horrible stag-dos, tacky hen parties and certainly no more weak wages. Look at it here," he then unlocked his phone and showed her photos of the house of the person he was talking about. "It's all in-house, private jobs, we would be the guy's personal chefs and the wages are almost three times what we are earning at the minute mate. He's a top footballer with a ten-acre piece of land, indoor swimming pool, sauna, gym; which he's said we can use, and…check this out…" he scrolled along to the images of a kitchen, "this would be our new place of work, what do you think?"

As he continued to swipe through the pictures on his phone, Kate realised, this could be the ultimate chance of a lifetime and she knew she needed to join her friend on this adventure. The place looked simply incredible, and she wouldn't be tied to all the commuting anymore.

"Oh my god Leo, look at that gorgeous worktop, that oven? We could create so much trouble in there," she chuckled, "and that sort of money will certainly help with the wedding," she sat back as the pictures ended, "can I speak to Dan first and let you know? It's not that I need his permission or anything like that, but, well, we are a couple now, so I need to see if he's okay with it don't I?" she asked.

"Sure, yes of course. I've said I'll let the guy know by the weekend so if you could get back to me by then, otherwise I'll have to try and think of someone else," he made a pouty face at her, "to be honest though mate, I'd much rather it be you," he held his coffee cup up to cheers hers, "we're such a good team and he loves all my ideas for the copulas amounts of dinner parties and events that he holds in that place," he unlocked his phone once more to show her the kitchen in the hope that she would just say yes there and then, "just one more look at it

Kate, you know you wanna." he joked, waving the image around.

Her eyes gleamed at the phone and at Leo. She was so elated to have been asked to be his right-hand woman and this was a chance she had always dreamt of, "I'm going to text Dan now to say I have some news and then we can talk about it tonight," she took her phone out and began typing a message, "I'm sure he'll love the idea and be as excited as me, especially when I tell him how much money I'll be getting."

Her and Dan were getting married in a few months' time so they would become a pair, they would be a partnership so she felt it only right that they should make this decision together, like married couples do. She decided to add in another line quickly, telling him to bring home a bottle of something sparkly to celebrate with a champagne emoji at the end. She couldn't help but smile as she typed the message frantically.

Leo watched her tapping away excitedly on her phone. He hoped so much that they could do this job together. They worked so well together, and she was his number one choice.

Within minutes, a text message pinged back to her, "Yay, he's just left work," she said reading it quickly, "right, I best get off home and discuss it with him. I'll let you know asap okay, woohoo," she shrieked, and with that, she gave him a peck on the cheek, grabbed her bag and made her way home feeling even more excited for the future working days with Leo in that fabulous kitchen that was now imprinted into her brain images.

On entering the hallway, she noticed his work boots, covered in mud, and yet again in the middle of the floor. He didn't seem to remember the discussion they'd had regarding just popping them over to the side instead. She sighed with a smile and carefully pushed them with her foot to try and avoid any of the mud crumbling off. She decided there and then that she would clean them later for him, they needed a good banging off first once they'd dried completely. But for now, all she wanted to do was tell him the news about the new job. Hearing him singing in the distance, she guessed he was in the shower or bath, so she ran upstairs, chucking her bag and coat over the banister.

"Hey there, fiancé," she joked, "you ok in all that?" she asked as she opened the door and leaned against the wall, folding her arms. Grinning from car to car at him seeing all the bath bubbles surrounding his body. He never usually had a bath and obviously didn't understand how to control the dosage of bubbles to the water.

He turned suddenly hearing her voice, "oh, hi babe, yeah all good," he replied, sloshing some water onto the floor as his arms came out the tub, "just a bit sore. Rough day at work and then rugby practice for two hours. Thought I'd have a bath and soak these bad boys," he held his arms up and flexed his biceps smiling at her.

As she admired his structure, something strange came over her, something she had never done before and only seen in movies. Slowly and seductively, she slipped down her dress, letting it fall to the floor at her feet, "they look perfect to me," she said quietly and in a cheeky tone of voice.

He froze and watched on as she then unclipped her bra, pulled down her knickers and began walking towards the bath, stepping in facing him. Instantly aroused, he shuffled his body towards her, kissing her gently, touching her soft, now wet, covered in bubbles, body, which she didn't refuse one bit. There was that adventurous side coming out again and she loved it, taking control of the situation this time, his wild ways seemed to be rubbing off on her.

After ten minutes of pure sensual passion in the bath, they dried themselves off and moved into the bedroom, climbing beneath the freshly washed covers, and made love.

As they lay together, her head on his warm chest, she felt content. With their wedding fast approaching, and a new job about to give their finances a big influx of money, she really was feeling better than ever before. Her future was framing a beautiful picture and it was more than fun.

Smiling up at him, as he scrolled through his phone at some rugby match information email, she decided to fill him in on the job prospect. She didn't want to keep Leo waiting too long, she wanted to secure her place with him. But just as she sat up, her stomach turned over and she felt nauseous. She must have looked terrible as Dan looked at her and immediately reacted with, "Babe, you alright? You've gone green like."

But she wasn't alright at all. She cupped her hand over her mouth thinking she was going to throw up everywhere any second if she didn't move fast. Jumping out of bed, she ran back into the bathroom, fell to her knees, and met the depths of the toilet. For a minute or so, she stayed in that position throwing up heavily, then heaving as nothing was left inside her. Her eyes were watering, and her mouth tasted awful.

Dan grabbed himself some shorts and had followed her in. Seeing her on the floor, he came and sat beside her, rubbing her back, "Babe, what's going on? Have you eaten something weird again?" he asked. He knew she liked experimenting with various weird types of food. All the new menu ideas had to be tasted before they could offer them out at work.

"Maybe," she spluttered back, wiping her mouth, "Urgh, how embarrassing, sorry," she apologised, she'd always hated being sick, suffering with it a lot after her mum had died. Shock sickness, the doctors had said. A natural reaction for some people, a coping mechanism they told her. Everyone deals with grief differently apparently; she remembered them all saying.

"Here, use this," he passed her a long piece of toilet paper to wipe her mouth properly, "I'll get you some water," and left to go downstairs.

She thought to herself as she wiped the remains of vomit from her mouth, what was it that she could have eaten that would make her throw up like this, but as she racked her brain, she couldn't even remember eating anything at all today. With all the excitement of the wedding plans and the job offer that she still had to talk to him about, she realised she'd not had anything, let alone something that would make her feel this way. So, what could possibly have caused this?

'*Why am I throwing up like this?*' she thought. Whatever it was, she didn't like this sicky feeling and doing it in front of Dan too had been so embarrassing.

As Dan returned with a glass of water, she had remained in the bathroom, sitting up but, leaning against the bath next to the toilet, just in case she threw up again. This outburst of nausea had made her feel terrible and as she hadn't eaten, she felt weak along with it. The spare of the moment, bath, then bed passion had taken the last of her energy and she truly felt exhausted.

"Here you go sweetheart," he said as he passed the glass, "drink that up and rinse your mouth, then we can get you back into bed for some rest."

"Thank you," she replied wearily sipping some liquid. "I must have picked up a bug or something," she said after swigging some more water and swiftly spitting it out down the toilet, "I've not eaten anything all day so it can't be down to food," she wiped her mouth with the last of the tissue, threw it down the toilet where Dan then flushed it and put the seat down.

"That's weird then? You don't think, you know, you're not…" he paused, "you know," he repeated, pointing to her stomach, rounding a shape with his hands.

"What?" she questioned before realising what he meant, "pregnant?" she replied, shocked he would even think about that sort of thing, "no, no, of course not," she paused again to give her mouth a final swill of liquid. She was beginning to feel a little fresher now, "well, I don't think so anyway…Oh god Dan, what if I am?" she said, racking her brain, trying hard to remember where she was in her menstrual cycle.

The whirlwind romance, crazy dating adventures, engagement party and everything else had taken over her mind lately and suddenly now, she couldn't even think straight to when she'd had her last monthly. *'When was I last on my period,'* she thought to herself as she glanced up watching Dan brushing his teeth. She used to be so hot on recording the dates in her phone so she would have to check in on that before any panic ensued. It couldn't be that, not so soon surely.

"Well, I'm not going to know about that girly stuff am I darling, don't you have an app or something?" he spat out the paste and rinsed his mouth, "I don't know if we are ready for baby Dans' just yet though hey?" he joked holding his hand out to help her up.

"No," she replied, "certainly not yet," she carefully stood up and he linked his arm into hers as they made their way to the bedroom where she laid on the bed, grabbing her dressing gown on the way to cover herself.

"Stop there for a bit, I'll do you some toast in a minute if you want," he pulled a blanket over her legs, "maybe you need something to eat, that's why you've been sick," he paused, "sorry, I'm not so good at this sickness thing."

She smiled back at him, "It's okay thanks," she wiped her clammy brow, resting her head back, "maybe just one slice of toast might be a good idea, just with butter for now." She watched him sorting some of his clothes out that had been thrown by the side of the bed, "I have some news I wanted to run past you actually Dan. I've been offered a new job. It's a private chef position. Some footballer that Leo got chatting with after he tried our new menu in the restaurant wants some in-house cooks."

"Oh right," he replied as he threw some socks

across the room trying to land them in the washing basket, "what do you mean by private? Not anything dodgy is it?" he remarked, fist pumping himself for getting the socks straight in.

"No, no, of course it's not dodgy. Leo wouldn't be into anything like that," she insisted, "so, the guy is minted, he has this massive mansion and needs two permanent chefs for when he has parties, events, and things like that. Anyway, Leo has the job and has asked me to be his partner, to work alongside him there. What do you think? The money is crazy, and it will help with the wedding fund, we could have so much more on the big day and even have that honeymoon in Mexico that you wanted?" she shifted her bottom and sat up again, smiling now but his expression was more concerned than excited.

"You don't have to live there do you, I mean...we've only just hooked up together in this place. I don't wanna live on my own again babe."

"No, we would go there each morning to prepare his meals for the day and then when he has any larger parties or events, that would be extra money," she began to feel wheezy again so laid her head back against the bed.

"Oh right, well, whatever you think Kate. It's your life I guess."

She looked on as he finished folding his clothes up and pulled on his hoodie, "well, no, it's our life now Dan. We're going to be a married couple, so we need to make these choices together. Shall I tell him yes then because he needs to find someone else if I can't do it, or if you don't want me to do it, I won't. I just need to let him know one way or another."

"Yeah fine babe, go for it…look, I've gotta go, mum needs to see me urgently," he continued, grabbing a pair of his jeans from the dressing table stool, "I missed her call, so she left a message for me. I listened to it when I went downstairs earlier, so I'm going to have to shoot off and see what's happened."

"What, now? But it's so late, is she okay?"

"Yeah, I expect so, just wanna check on her you know. Sorry babe. When she needs me, she needs me, I can put a slice of bread in the toaster, but you'll have to go down and finish it, sorry," with his jeans now on, he bent down and kissed her forehead.

"Oh. Okay," she answered confused by his sudden urge and needing to leave so abruptly, "when am I going to meet her Dan? The wedding isn't long away now, would be nice to get to know her before then, I could come with you now if you like?" Again, she tried to sit up but gagged as the sick feeling returned. She held onto her tummy, hoping there was nothing left to bring up, "just give me a minute and I can get dressed."

He shuffled on his feet uncomfortably and just replied, "probably best not hey. You need to get a bit more rest. Don't want you throwing up all over my mother, do we? That would not be a good first meeting hey?" he said with a weird snigger, "I'll see you tomorrow. I think it's best if I stay over with her for tonight, as it's getting a bit late and all that," he grabbed his jacket from the back of the bedroom door and reached for his trainers which had been thrown as per usual at the end of the bed.

Kate sat back up against the bed watching him. She hoped so much that his mother was alright but also wondered why he had to leave like this. She just nodded with a disappointed look on her face.

"You know I love you' Kate."

Again, she nodded and tried her best to smile at him.

"See you soon yeah?" he said as he hurried out of the room, ran down the staircase and slammed the front door behind him, leaving her sat alone and a little bit bewildered.

He was certainly building more of a mysterious side to him, and it seemed on a daily basis now. Did he have secrets from her and if so, when would she find out what they all were? Why hadn't she met his mother yet, why was he so secretive about her at times? She tried her best to get comfortable and rubbed her tummy. Deciding to wait up for a while, she grabbed a book from her bedside drawer, then after a minute, threw it towards the end of the bed. She just couldn't concentrate, and it was driving her mad.

Chapter Fifteen

Surprise…

It was nearing midnight and Kate felt awful knowing that she would be alone for the night now feeling the way she did. She stared for a moment at the bedroom door thinking, maybe this was another joke he was playing. Imagining he would poke his head around the doorway and come back to bed with her, hug her and make her feel better, but he didn't return so she tried to get comfortable by lying down and pulling the covers snuggly up over her body.

She laid there staring at the ceiling, willing her eyes to close and sleep, get some rest, like Dan had said to her. But it was no good, her mind was racing, and she still felt sick. Sick with something going on in her tummy and sick with worry now about where he was and how his mother was too. Her brain wouldn't stop whirling round about the new job offer either; she needed to make the decision herself.

"Sod it" she said to herself and grabbed her phone from the side, quickly texting Leo to give him his answer.

'Yes, yes, yes. Let's do this!' she typed and sent.

'WOOHOOO….!!! ☺' Came the text back within a minute.

Smiling down at the reply and laying there imagining working in such a beautiful house made her grin even more. If only Dan hadn't left so abruptly so they could celebrate together, if only she didn't feel so bloody sick. She held her hand to her mouth and took some deep breaths to stop it happening again. Thankfully, she managed it and began massaging her tummy and before long, she had fallen asleep, dreaming of all thing's food and the fantastic new job she was about to embark on.

Morning arrived way too quickly, she still felt worn out from last night's events. Yawning and stretching her arms up, she looked around the bedroom where there was no sign of Dan having returned during the night. She really had hoped that when she opened her eyes, he would be there lying beside her with his loving and mesmerising eyes peering into hers. But alas, it was not happening. His side of the bed had not been touched; he'd stayed out as he said he might do. She looked over at the flowers that he'd brought her just a few days ago. Ever since the first huge bunch that she had got from him, there hadn't been a week where no flowers adorned her stunning vase. Without fail, every Friday evening, he would return from rugby and present her with a new, fresh bouquet and although she had never been into flowers previously, she loved this routine and the romance it brought along with it. This had, so far, been the most romantic person she had ever been with, and the floral gifts made her feel even more special.

Reaching for her phone by the bedside, she decided she needed a girly chat and to catch up with her aunt.

'Hey Auntie. Could you pop over for a chat this morning?' she texted.

The reply was instant as per usual, *'Of course, I'd love to. Do you need me to bring anything? Cakes, Chocolate, Wine. lol.'*

Kate laughed, *'Erm...'* she started typing. She had an idea of what she needed but was unsure of whether she should ask that of her aunt. Last night's sickness was still playing on her mind. Did she really think it necessary to worry that she could be pregnant and then go and worry the hell out of her aunt at the same time? But, this morning, she didn't feel like going out herself right now, so she replied, *'probably best lay off the cakes with your diabetes hey but, yes please, I do need something..."* she paused, finger poised to continue typing, unsure if she really did need this thing, "*could you bring a pregnancy test. Eek.'* she quickly typed back confidently and added a confused face emoji.

Sally's reply this time was delayed, and Kate stared at the screen for a minute, hoping she hadn't made a mistake in asking but then she saw that Sally had started typing, *'ok…see you soon. xxx'* the message appeared saying finally.

Within half an hour, Sally was standing at the front door holding up a chemist paper carrier bag, eyebrows raised in shock.

"Auntie, please don't look at me like that?" she joked as she closed the door behind them.

"Like what darling?" Sally shrugged her shoulders, "I thought you wanted to get married first before a family ensued?" she asked, laughing softly.

"It's just a precaution. I was quite sick last night and," she paused, "well I've not been keeping track of my periods so…I just wanna make sure I'm not, you know, just to be on the safe side."

"Oh, okay then," Sally's eyebrows raised again.

"I can't imagine it will be positive. I think it's more over excitement and everything going on right now," she started unwrapping the box as they made their way upstairs to the bathroom.

"What else is happening then, have I missed something?" Sally asked, following Kate.

"Oh yes. I must fill you in on the new job info I've been offered, let's get this out of the way and I can tell you all about it."

"Okay sweetheart, I'll wait in your room, you go pee on the stick thing," she fluttered her arms to usher Kate into the bathroom.

Within a few minutes, Kate returned with the said stick in her hand, looking ashen pale and shocked.

As they sat on the edge of the bed in silence, all that could be heard was the leaky, dripping tap from the sink and a bird outside singing at the top of its voice, like it knew it would be heard during this awkward moment of silence.

"Shit, shit, shit," Kate suddenly said through gritted teeth, breaking the tense atmosphere, "what the hell am I going to do, this wasn't the plan," she turned to see Sally equally expressing a stunned look on her face, "I've got the wedding coming up in a few months. I can't get married being pregnant, and my new job, oh god, my new job," she sighed heavily, "a baby was not in the equation for a very long time. Auntie, what the hell am I going to do?"

"Well…" Sally started to answer.

"Oh Christ," Kate interrupted, "I never even thought about, well, you know, contraception. Dan was so out of the blue and it's been so amazing, I didn't think to ask him either. I hadn't bothered getting any because I'd not been dating for ages. Shit, shit," she repeated standing up and pacing the floor in a confused state.

Sally watched her beautiful niece, fraught with

worry. She thought the absolute world of Kate and wanted her to be happy like she had been since meeting Dan. Yes, they'd all agreed that it had moved ridiculously fast after their initial meeting, then to get engaged so soon, but she had not seen her niece this happy with someone and she deserved happiness and love in her life.

"Come here, sit down my darling," she reached for her hand and sat Kate back on the bed beside her, "now listen to me. Sometimes, things happen for a reason and many of them are sent to test our souls but," she paused stroking Kate's hands which were now cold and trembling, "why don't you see it as a blessing instead. You could have the baby sweetie, you know I'll be there to support you with everything, don't you?"

Kate just nodded, staring down at the stick that clearly stated her predicament of being pregnant.

Sally continued, "you can reschedule the wedding so no need to fret about that. I know the owner of the venue, she'll be fine with a move of the date, I can arrange that so that's no problem, okay?"

Kate just sat silent listening, her eyes stinging from wanting to let all the tears out that were brewing in there. She felt like exploding with sadness and just wanted to sob into a pillow.

"Nothing is set in stone regarding the wedding yet is it? That is the benefit of having a smaller wedding, hey?" Sally held Kate's hands again, giving them a gentle squeeze of reassurance, "come on sweetie, take some deep breaths now."

"Thank you," Kate finally spoke, "but, I'm just not sure it's something Dan wants. Not right now anyway, he's been so looking forward to the wedding. I've not even met his mother and now he's going to have to tell her she's going to be a grandmother, with a girl she's not even met, she might not even like me auntie…" with the thought and realisation that she could lose Dan, her tears escaped rolling down her now, flushed cheeks and she was heartbroken.

"Hey, hey. Come on now, you, stop this, stop those tears," Sally said as she wiped the wetness from Kate's cheeks, "you might be surprised, it may be just what he needs. A family of his own to love, I mean, it's been him and his mum for a while now. I'm sure as a grandmother, she'd be more than over the moon."

"I've not even met her yet though," replied Kate sadly.

"Well, that can be sorted I'm sure, and look at it this way, the baby can then be part of your wedding when you do it in the future." She rubbed Kate's arm again, trying her best to reassure her, "a little flower girl or page boy to add to the special day."

Kate just sat silent once more, contemplating the future and how a baby could add something to their lives. Bring them even closer, maybe help with his sudden mood swings. Although, the only thing that was now racing in her brain was remembering his words last night, *'I dunno if we are ready for babies just yet though hey?'* and he was right, they both weren't ready for that sort of commitment so early on in their relationship. She had always imagined adulthood to be so different, landing her dream job, meeting, and settling down with someone special, getting married, buying a house together and then having a family much later. That had been her mindset anyway but now fate was about to take some control of her life, and she felt so confused but also angry with herself for letting this happen. Her emotions were wading in and out like the tide.

Sally moved closer to her, wiping the tears away as they silently fell into her lap, "Kate, darling Kate. There's something I need to tell you which might help you decide what to do," looking straight into her nieces' eyes, her hands cupping hold of Kate's again, she shuffled her bottom to position herself to face her, "I've been meaning to tell you for a few weeks now, since your birthday party actually. But then it all happened, the Dan thing and you were always so busy with work etc, etc," she moved her head toing and froing, "anyway, you know the package I had for you?" she paused to take a deep inhale of breath and Kate was now staring at her, puzzled by the serious atmosphere that had now changed, "your mum, my darling sister, Fiona. Well, she made me promise to give it to you on your thirtieth, but I thought your twenty-first birthday would be better, anyway, as you know, I forgot and then, I kept forgetting and then you met Dan and then the engagement," Sally was rattling on about random facts and her words became slightly flustered, more with frustration at just not being able to blurt out what she really wanted to.

"Auntie, please you're starting to freak me out, what is it?" Kate interrupted, "please just tell me already."

"Sorry. Okay here goes…" Sally took another deep breath, puffing her chest out in preparation.

Kate looked on and she couldn't work out if she felt worried, excited, or just plain sick again, but their moment was stopped suddenly when there was a loud knocking at the front door.

"Oh, bloody hell, who could that be? I had better get it," Kate carefully stood up, but her head felt woozy, and her body swayed slightly, "whoa," she slurred, blinking her eyes rapidly to try and stay up straight.

"Easy now," said Sally, holding her tightly, "I'll get it darling; you lay back down, we can talk about this later," relieved, Sally sat Kate back down and gently laid her flat covering her legs with the blanket, then quickly made her way downstairs. On opening the front door, she was faced with two policemen, "can I help you?" she asked, confused.

"Good morning madam, yes. We are looking for

Daniel Howard," the taller officer checked his notebook as he asked, "we have this noted as his current address. Is he home right now?"

"Erm. No, he isn't, he's visiting someone. What's this all about? Is he ok?" she asked, trying to stretch her neck to see the notes that the other officer was now looking at in his pad.

"We just need to talk to him about an incident, do you know when he will be back? Are you his partner, relative?"

"Incident," she repeated, "what sort of incident? And no, my niece, his fiancé, this is her place. She's upstairs, but she's not feeling well at the minute, can I help with anything?"

"Do you have a contact number for him so we can get in touch, the one we have for him on the system doesn't seem to be in service anymore," he showed her the phone number on his pad, "is your niece okay, not hurt in any way?" he glanced behind Sally as if to try and see inside.

"No, she isn't hurt, she's just not feeling well that's all," she answered defensively, "I'll just fetch his number from her, please wait here," then she scuttled back upstairs as fast as she could. She opened the bedroom door and was about to speak when she noticed Kate was already fast asleep. Not wanting to disturb her, she crept back out, returning to the front door.

"I'm sorry but Kate's asleep, she's got some

sickness bug we think," she fibbed, "and was up most of the night throwing up, she's exhausted. I don't think it wise to wake her unless it's urgent."

"Okay, thank you, madam. If we have your word that she is okay?" he insisted to which Sally nodded, "if he comes home before we've made contact with him, please ask him to give us a quick call will you?" he passed her a card with his name and number on, and they both turned to walk off.

"Is Daniel in some sort of trouble?" she asked before they took another step.

"If you could just get him to call us as soon as possible, that would be great. We will continue to try and contact him in the meantime, thank you for your time." And then they were gone, leaving Sally bewildered and worried.

She shut the door and went to make herself a coffee, hoping Kate would get a good sleep before they continued their conversation that she had been dreading for many years now. In another way, as much as she was not looking forward to carrying on the conversation, maybe with the current pregnancy doubts that Kate had, it could help her decide what to do for her future with Dan and a baby in tow. Whatever happened, Kate was her priority as ever and sorting out why the police had just turned up was more important. Maybe Rob could help?

Chapter Sixteen

A Letter from Who…?

"Yes Rob, the police just turned up looking for Dan about some incident. They wouldn't tell me much else," Sally whispered. She had gone into the garden to ring her husband, more concerned by what the police officers had implied about Kate being hurt. It was playing on her mind more than the so-called, incident itself that they had mentioned Dan had been involved in, "what do you think they were getting at Rob, asking if she was hurt, I mean why would they ask that if something wasn't untoward?" she continued pacing up and down the lawn.

"Darling, try and calm down, it's just routine enquiries probably, a mistaken identity or something," he said reassuringly, "you know what it's like when police are clutching at straws trying to solve crimes. Dan wouldn't hurt her, we know that."

"This isn't some bloody seedy crime drama on Netflix Robert," she snapped back, "this is our niece, not bloody Silent Witness."

He couldn't help but laugh slightly at her references, "I know it isn't but listen, Dan isn't dangerous is he, we know that of him at least. He has never come across as violent or aggressive at the club and he certainly doesn't strike me as the sort of person that would hurt a woman, especially Kate or anyone else to be fair on the guy, I'm certain of that darling."

"So why were they here then and why would they have asked not once, but twice if she was alright?" she asked again, pressing him, "it's weird Robert. I've got a bad feeling about this; I really don't like the sound of it, and I certainly do not like the fact that Kate has police at her door. Can you try and find out a bit more about him, you know a bit more regarding his upbringing, background, current family situation," she pleaded, still trying to keep her voice down in case Kate woke and heard her, "this is our Kate, our niece darling, we can't have her involved in any incidents or have her hurt," sipping her now cold coffee and wincing as she swallowed, she continued, "I promised Fiona I would take care of Kate. I can't let her down, Rob. I promised her darling, I promised Fiona," she was now close to tears herself, distressed with worry that something bad was happening and she wasn't doing her job of protecting Kate as she'd promised her sister. The last thing she wanted was more sadness or grief for Kate. Losing Fiona so suddenly as they all had was enough for anyone to cope with let alone a teenager as Kate was at the time.

"Alright, alright, I'll try and have a look into it all," he said, trying to calm her, "try not to get so upset, I'll look in his folder at the club and ask a few of his buddies. Just don't say anything about the police to Kate at the minute, about any of it, we can sort this out ok?"

"Okay if you're sure that's the best thing to do. I don't like hiding this from her Rob, I'm not happy with that but…"

"Sally, sweetheart…we will sort it okay?" he interrupted.

"Thank you," she paused as she took a deep breath, "I'm sorry for snapping at you like that."

"Don't fret. It will all be fine."

After they said their goodbyes, she hung up the phone, placed it in her trouser pocket and glanced up towards Kate's bedroom window. She thought about the new baby situation that they'd just found out together, "Oh damn it," she whispered to herself.

Now there was that issue to take into consideration, making the whole thing a little bit worse. Sally knew she would protect and look after both of them no matter what was going on with Dan. The other news that she nearly revealed earlier would have to wait a little bit longer while she sorted this situation out. In the meantime, she would try her best to keep her own mind busy. There was a bit of washing up and tidying up to do while she waited for her niece to wake so she went back inside.

Two hours later, as she sat reading the newspaper in the lounge, Kate appeared, still looking tired and pale in the face, "Hi," she said wearily.

"Hey there, did you have a nice sleep sweetheart?" Sally said sitting forward in her seat.

"Yes, thank you," she yawned back, "I must've needed it, look at the time?" she glanced up at the clock on the fireplace mantel, "is Dan back yet?" she glimpsed into the kitchen hoping to see him making himself a drink or something, but he wasn't anywhere to be seen.

"No darling, no sign yet, maybe his mum's taken a turn for the worse?" Sally tried to sound convincing.

"Oh, don't say that auntie," she sat beside her on the sofa.

"Sorry, anyway, let me make you a nice hot chocolate and get some food into that little tummy of yours, you must be hungry," she said rubbing Kate's knees, "we need to keep your strength up now don't we?" she pointed towards Kate's tummy and then walked across into the kitchen to boil the kettle.

Slowly and steadily, Kate followed her a few minutes after and sat at the table, resting her head in her hand, ""God, I do hope everything is alright with his mum, he left in such a hurry."

Sally glanced across and smiled, not knowing what to reply.

"What a mess I must look."

"You look a little fresher faced than you did a few hours back, I must admit. Are you feeling any better?" Sally asked as she scooped a heaped spoonful of cocoa into a mug.

"Yes I am. A lot better now thanks. I've not felt so knocked out like that in ages. Is that what pregnancy is going to be like for the next few months?" she smiled sweetly up at her aunt who grinned back, nodding, "I have no idea but have heard that's it's pretty awful for the first semester."

"Oh fab," Kate joked, "Jesus, I'm pregnant, auntie. I'm going to have a baby for goodness' sake."

Sally slapped her forehead jokingly and rolled her eyes which made Kate giggle, "do you want some marmite on toast, your favourite, yucky stuff?" she asked making a grimacing face, "I will need to get off shortly but can make it before I leave."

"I'd love a slice or two, thanks," replied Kate.

As Sally popped a slice of bread in the toaster, she sat for a moment on the next chair to Kate, "so, do you think you've made your decision then, you're going to keep the baby?"

"Yes, I think so. Like you said, it could be just what we need," she looked down at her engagement ring sparkling in the afternoon sunlight beaming through the window, "I've just got to break it to Dan that the wedding will have to wait a year or so, I suppose. Let's hope he's up for it," straightening her ring, she couldn't help but, secretly have doubts that he would be overjoyed at this news. They had literally only been together for months and sometimes, his unpredictable moods shook her. More than a few times she had been worried he may just leave and not return. How would he react to this unexpected predicament, what with him having to be with his mum so much? All these thoughts were running through her mind at a rate of a hundred miles an hour and as the toast popped up, wafting its usually lovely aroma, it done the opposite and made her feel sick again, "Oh god," she cried, holding her hand to her mouth. Pushing the chair back, almost toppling it over, she ran to the downstairs toilet to throw up once again.

"Do you want me to try and call Daniel from your phone, tell him you need him to come home?" asked Sally, rubbing her back and passing her a wad of tissue to wipe her mouth.

"No, no," Kate mumbled in between the wipes, "it's ok. I'll just wait until he gets back. I don't want to disturb his time together with his mum or have him see me in this state either, it was bad enough yesterday," she clambered up, holding onto the radiator for support, "I'll be ok if you need to get off, honestly. I'll have that toast if it's not burnt, or maybe some soup, that should help settle my tummy a bit."

"Well only if you're sure my darling. I hate to leave you like this, but I have a doctor's appointment in half an hour. I tell you what, let me ring them," she said, lifting her wrist to check the time, "I can cancel it, it's nothing urgent, just a menopause tablet check-up thing and monitoring of my diabetes…"

"No, honestly, you go. I'm not working today so I'm just gonna watch a bit of TV and rest until Dan gets back."

"Alright sweetie. I'll give you a call later to see how it's going and let me know what he says won't you?" she kissed Kate on the head as they made their way back to the lounge where Kate plonked her aching body on the sofa. She rubbed her ribs; the heaving was beginning to make them ache.

"Oh auntie, before you go, who was at the door earlier anyway?" Kate asked as she tried to get herself comfortable, plumping a cushion behind her back and grabbing the blanket to put over her legs.

"Erm. It was a parcel for the little lady next-door, they couldn't get an answer, so I signed for it, then took it round when I saw coming home," Sally lied quickly, surprising herself at how easily the story flowed out of her mouth. She hated lying, but she didn't want to upset her and tell her about the police until Rob had found out some more, if any, information. Maybe it was just a mistake, and they were looking for the wrong person, just as Rob had suggested. Surely Dan wouldn't have hurt anyone? She really hoped not anyway but she wasn't going to worry Kate with it all yet when there was no need to. She needed to rest for the time being, not fret about what might be going on with him.

"Oh and," Kate called again as Sally got to the doorway just about to leave the room, "what were you going to tell me? You know before I dozed off."

Sally just couldn't tell her now, she had too much else to deal with, "it's nothing that can't wait darling. Another day hey," she called back hastily, "don't you worry your little head about anything now, honestly. You just rest and take care of my great niece or nephew in there," she pointed down in the direction of Kate's stomach, giving her a cheeky wink before quickly leaving avoiding any further questions.

Closing the front door behind her, she stood there for a moment leaning back onto the side wall. Taking a gasp of breath and facing the sky, she whispered, "I'm sorry sis, I will tell her I promise, soon, I will," with tears welling up and her throat feeling tight with worry, she began to think if she didn't hurry up and do this, she would've let her sister down? She hoped for forgiveness and for everything to turn out alright. The right time would come but it just wasn't now. For the next few days, she had to find out more about Dan, his past and try to figure out why the police had come looking for him in the first place. She hurried down the pathway, got into her car and drove home.

Kate couldn't get comfortable on the sofa after munching her newly made slice of toast and marmite, so she decided to have a quick shower. All the being sick episodes had made her feel disgusting but after that, she wasn't going to do anything until Dan got home except rest and maybe do a bit of baby research. She'd not expected to even think about having children until her late twenties at least, she didn't have a clue about any stage of pregnancy, how she was supposed to feel, what was normal for the sickness part, nothing, not a clue. She decided she needed to get herself some knowledge on the subject so that she was prepared to reel it all off to Dan when they had that all important chat soon, so after her refreshing shower, she got into her favourite velour tracksuit and opened her laptop.

As she became mesmerised by the thousands of baby stage images on Google, she found herself becoming more excited and less worried as she had felt a few hours back. Maybe this was a good thing after all, maybe it was the start of her fabulous life with the most gorgeous, and intriguing man she had ever met. It was early days and an unexpected event but maybe, just maybe, it would be okay, and they could continue to be happy, as a family now.

'Yes, tonight,' she thought to herself, she would tell him tonight, make it special for both of them. Make it another special moment in their crazy and exciting relationship.

As she got up to make a glass of water and make another slice of toast, she heard the postman deliver so she walked into the hallway to collect the pile that had hit the doormat with a thud. Shuffling through them quickly, sighing at the brown envelopes that she knew were bills facing back at her, she noticed one which was a handwritten envelope addressed to her but just with her first name written. She placed all the other letters on the side and went back to sit down in the lounge gently opening the mysterious looking envelope, after switching the television on.

'Dearest Kate,' it read, *'You don't know who I am. Well, you may know who I am, but we've not met yet. I'm Daniel's mother, Anna, and he has told me so much about you.*

I must say, you sound like a truly beautiful and wonderful person. Someone my son is very lucky to have in his life. Someone I feel lucky to have taking care of my boy.

I'm also really hoping that we can maybe meet soon.'

Kate couldn't believe what she was reading and scanned the document closer, grabbing the remote control, switching the TV off so she could concentrate more. She glanced up towards the kitchen as she heard the toaster pop but couldn't move, needing to read on, she continued.

'The wedding plans sound lovely, and I am so upset that I can't be with you both to witness your special day.

To see my son marry has always been a dream of mine as it will be for you when you have your own children. That would make them my grandchildren I suppose!

I guess this is a surprise for you and I'm sorry we're not talking face to face.

Daniel cannot bring himself to tell you more about me and that's fine, I know he finds it very difficult to talk to anyone about me and where I am, but especially about what happened.'

Kate's eyes were frantically but carefully moving over every sentence trying her hardest not to miss a single word of it at the same time.

'I needed to contact you in this way because I feel like it is best for you to know a little bit more about my son and me for that matter.

As much as I would love to meet you, see you and chat to you about it all, I thought it might be too much first off, I hope you don't mind'.

As she took a breath and sipped some of her water, her body sank down further into the comfort of the sofa. Dan and his past were becoming even more intriguing now with this letter from his mother who also sounded mysterious. She pulled the blanket over her legs and continued reading.

'Okay, here goes…

Five years ago, Daniel lost his father, and I lost my husband, but it hit Daniel extremely hard, harder than I could have imagined if I'm totally honest with myself.

I tried my best to get him the help he needed, not easy in my predicament, but I did try.

I think the main problem was that he was at a difficult age, and I don't think he has ever had the time to get over the ordeal or even to grieve properly.

When he was eventually seen, the doctors finally diagnosed him after two years of forms, tests, and interviews, it wasn't an easy process I can tell you. But we got there in the end, and he's been on the medication since then.

So, why am I reaching out to you in this way you may ask? Well, it's because recently, during his brief visits to me, I've seen a change in him, in his behaviour, his attitude. He's become a little bit erratic at times and it makes me think he's not told you about the illness or worse still, that he's not taking his medication now. I wanted to make sure you knew the truth and by doing so, you could begin to take charge of it, ensuring that he continue taking his tablets every day.

The problem is that if he doesn't take them, his mood swings will get worse, and he won't be able to work either. At times when I know he's off them, he has become unbalanced, sometimes he gets very angry and upset at the slightest trivial things that you or I would generally shrug off. During these down periods; as we call them; he can just disappear, and you won't see him for days/weeks at a time. It is so worrying Kate, and I would hate for you to be going through it.

One time he went away for nearly two months without any

contact with me. I just had no idea where he had gone and if he was even alive, it is that serious.

Anyway, I'm not sure how much you know about us, and I hate contacting you this way, but I just had to, for your sake and your family too. He's told me about how you lost your own mother; I'm so sorry for you but he said you are one of the strongest persons he has ever known, apart from me, bless him. So please, please, I am asking you to not only protect yourself, but to help him, help my son…could you speak to him about it, please???

Taking a deep breath, Kate had to stop for a moment, thinking what the hell she had got herself into and what the hell was going on with this letter. The first time she gets to know anything more about her future mother-in-law is in a letter stating that her husband to be is ill in some way, on medication and that he could just disappear any day. As confused as she was, she needed to read on.

'He probably wouldn't want to know about this letter either so do feel free to throw it away or maybe hide it from him in case you need to re-read. I don't want to upset him; he might stop coming to visit me and I couldn't deal with that. Not to lose him as well. He's all I have left in this world; he's my son and I love him so very much.

Kate, I don't want to cause any trouble but after seeing him the other week and listening to him talking about you in such a loving but frantic manner, I felt it my duty that I should write to you. I hope you don't mind.'

Kate suddenly stopped and looked up as she heard

the key turning in the front door. She quickly stuffed the letter and its envelope down the side of the sofa, she would have to finish it later. Someone was coming through the front door.

Chapter Seventeen

Stay or leave...?

"Kate…Kate," she heard Dan's voice yelling as the front door slammed shut, "Kate, where are you? Kate!" he repeated loudly.

"Dan," she called back, sitting bolt upright, "I'm in the lounge."

He appeared within a second, sweating and out of breath holding his chest, unable to speak for a second. He looked terrible.

"Dan, what the hell? Are you ok," she asked, noticing how fraught and pale he looked?

"Erm, well, yes I guess so," he stuttered, pacing back and forth in front of her, "I need to explain something to you Kate," he then sat down next to her, his knee juddering up and down, "I, err," he stammered again, "I have to go down to the police station. They called me, I was on my way to see mum again but…" his face didn't look right, he was physically shaking, and his words were so slurred and frantic, "it's probably nothing," he went on, "but I just need to go. Will you wait here for me? Will you promise to be here when I get back?" he begged.

"Dan, try and calm down, you're scaring me, tell me what's happened, why do the police want to see you? Where are you going?" Kate sat forward holding his hands which were stone cold and trembling. Her head felt dizzy again and she thought to herself that if she tried to stand up, she would definitely be off to the toilet, throwing up again. She tried to take some deep breaths with him.

"Kate, listen," he said, "you know I love you right, you know that I would do anything for you, to protect you, keep you safe," he began nodding to her to agree, "I won't let anyone hurt you, babe, I must be the one to look after you now that you're gonna marry me. I, I just have to be the one to sort stuff out, make sure you are okay and that."

Kate nodded back as she tried once more to stop his hands from shaking so much, "try and breathe slower Dan, please, just slow down," she pleaded with him and wiped the sweat dripping from his forehead.

He tried a few deep breaths and then blurted it out, "I've hurt someone Kate. I saw them touch you and I just…I couldn't help myself, I just kind of lost it. Oh shit, you're going to think I'm some sort of nut job now," he ripped his hands from hers and stood up, "it's no good, No. I can't do this to you, I've got to go," he began running upstairs and Kate rushed as fast as she could after him, nearly tripping on the blanket that had fallen to the floor in all the commotion.

As she finally got to the bedroom door, out of breath, she saw him chucking a load of his clothes into a holdall from under the bed, the same one she had seen him with at her party, "Dan, stop, stop. What are you doing?" she cried, "you're scaring me Dan, please stop and talk to me." she cried.

"I've got to go Kate. I need to just get out of here, it's not fair on you. I can't be evil like my father, no, you're too special, too beautiful to be with someone like me," he swung round and grabbed another hoodie from the floor, "I can't face hurting you. I'll let you know where I am as soon as I can…I love you Kate," and he darted across the room passing her with just his bag in hand.

"Daniel," she yelled after him. She was so shocked at what was happening and so worried about how he was behaving. He looked as though he was taking everything and leaving her. But what was so bad, he felt he had to go this way. With the last bit of energy she could muster up, she shouted, "I'm pregnant Dan!"

He immediately stopped by the top of the stairs and turned around, looking back at her standing there now crying. With his eyes, glazing over with tears, he just shook his head and then continued to run down the stairs, slamming the front door behind him.

Nothing but silence now filled the air as she heard his thudding steps running up the gravel pathway outside. She stood there for a minute listening to the deafening silence he'd left behind and then it came again, the sickness. She ran to the toilet, throwing herself onto the floor crying, feeling completely helpless and stressed out. What the hell was going on? This was supposed to be the moment that the two of them became three, the precious time when she revealed her news to him and he spun her round in pure excitement that they were to be parents but no, it was not like that in the slightest. He'd come home in a frantic state and now run off without any explanation. She didn't know what had happened and more importantly if he'd be back anytime soon. His crazy behaviour was making her more anxious than anything and why did he say he had hurt someone?

Standing alone and desperate for answers, she thought about the letter that she had been reading just moments before he'd arrived. Maybe that would explain a bit more for her, give her a clue to this 'medication' that he was on and if that might explain this situation? She was so confused and upset. Life had just been tipped completely on its head and she needed to find out why?

She carefully stood up, feeling weak and dizzy but made her way to the top of the stairs. Grabbing her phone from her pocket, she began dialling Sally's number. Her hands were clammy and trembling, she was struggling to see through the tears now welled up in her eyes. By mistake, she clicked on the wrong name and began calling someone else. Frustrated, she let out a loud groan, hung up and tried again. It was all getting too much and as she stepped onto the first step down, she missed her footing, thudding down the entire flight of stairs, landing in a heap at the bottom. The phone was just out of her reach as she groaned in agony. She could hear Sally shouting on the other end of the line but then everything went black before she could utter a cry for help.

Her forehead cut, hands stinging, her body aching with pain and bruising; Kate awoke in confusion, blinking hard to try and work out where she was and why she felt so sore. Looking around, she realised she was certainly not in her bed, not in her room, not in her house in fact. The smell was different, the pale white walls and the blue curtains surrounding her bed did not seem familiar at all. The only familiar site she could see was her auntie.

"Where am I?" she asked quietly, trying to sit up but grimacing with pain as she did so.

"Hey sweetie, you're in hospital," Sally said, who

was sat beside her, holding her hand, "take it easy now, lay back down, you need to rest," she gently applied some pressure on Kate's shoulders to lay her back.

"What…what happened?" Kate asked as Sally adjusted the pillows and straightened the sheets covering Kate's frail body.

"You had a bad fall darling, at home, you fell down the stairs," she rubbed Kate's cold hands, "I'm just thankful that you were calling me as you did it otherwise," she paused to take a breath, "well, I dread to think how long you may have been there on the floor. Oh, Kate my darling," she began crying, and kissed Kate's hand, "I'm so, so, sorry I left you now, I'll never forgive myself."

Kate was bewildered, and glancing around the room, her eyes darted from side to side as she suddenly thought about the fall and the fact that she was pregnant. Seeing her auntie so upset she feared the worst, "my baby, the baby auntie, is she ok?"

Sally replied, sniffing back her tears, "yes darling, the little one is just fine. They've done a quick scan while you were still asleep. I told them on the way in that you had just found out," she paused, "I hope I did the right thing. I hope you didn't mind but I thought it best to check as soon as possible."

A wave of relief washed over Kate as she lay her head back down on the pillow. The thought that she may have lost the baby before she'd even got used to the idea of having it turned her tummy over in knots, "no, no, that's fine, thanks. God my side hurts," she said, rubbing it.

"Yes, I imagine it would darling. You had quite the tumble. Those stairs of yours are pretty darn hard you know. But it's only bruising, thank goodness, they will soon heal," she stood up and poured a glass of water for her, "you are going to come and stay with us for a few weeks, I insist. Dan is welcome to stay too but, you are the number one priority and I want to look after you, make sure you recover from this first, no arguing," she said giving Kate her 'knowing what's best' expression, "we won't take no for an answer darling. I've called your uncle and he's gone shopping for all your favourite food," she smiled sweetly at her niece who just nodded in agreement. She knew it was the best idea and felt safer knowing they would be there to help her through this recovery.

Kate then remembered why she was here in the first place, the cause for falling down the stairs, being in such a fret. She recalled Dan storming out of their bedroom with his bag of clothes. His face turning to briefly glance at her after she announced the pregnancy. That's why she had been in such a state to not concentrate on the phone call to her aunt, that's why she missed her step and fell. Her face now changed to ashen white again with the realisation that she was here because of how he had left in such a hurry taking as much as he could fit in that small holdall, and not even staying to tell her why.

"Kate, are you okay?" Sally noticed how pale she had become and could see the worried look in her glistening eyes.

"Dan's gone…he's left me auntie," tears began to escape from her saddened eyes, and she continued to explain, "he came back about an hour or so after you left. He was in a right state auntie, I couldn't get any sense out of him and then he grabbed his things and just left…he just walked out on me," she carefully shifted herself to a sitting position, "I tried to get him to explain to me what was going on, I tried to get him to stay by telling him I was pregnant, but…well, he just said nothing, he just stared at me and then, he went, he left and that's when I called you and…"

"Try and keep calm darling," said Sally watching on as Kate got even more stressed out, frantically trying to get her words out.

"Sorry," she apologised after a few seconds, taking a few deep breaths. After settling herself back in the bed, she then explained what Dan had said to her so very briefly when he had come back to her house and what had led to Kate falling down the stairs. She tried to relay back everything that he had spoken about, but it all seemed so muddled in her mind, she was confused, angry and so upset and as well as that, she really hurt from the fall itself.

"We will sort this out, try not to worry yourself. I

know it's a bit of a mess, but Rob is looking into things for us," she paused holding Kate's now shaking hand, "it will be alright, I'm sure."

"But why did he just run off then, why has he left me Auntie. Knowing I'm pregnant too and he still didn't want to stay," she wiped her tears from her face, "he's done something to someone and doesn't know what to do, he'll be alone, and I can't even help him." Kate was now sobbing uncontrollably again. There was nothing Sally could say to make the situation clearer for her so all she could do was hold her and let her get all her thoughts and emotions out. She felt so angry with Dan too for leaving Kate that way, he didn't even know she was in hospital. She wanted to get hold of him nearly as much as Kate did but for other reasons. She wanted to shout and scream at him for doing this to her niece, for walking out on her, her and the baby which was even worse. She wondered if the police would find him soon before she did. One way or another, he needed to be found and give them all some explanations.

*

"Kate," Sally said as they made their way home from the hospital the following evening, "I need to tell you something," she paused feeling nervous about how Kate would react to knowing she had lied to her, "you know when I was round yours and you were in bed, after the test and sickness, then there was a knock at the door?"

Kate nodded.

"Well…I told a bit of a fib, it wasn't a parcel for the neighbour at all,"

"Okay?" answered Kate in a confused tone of voice, looking across at her aunt.

"It was actually two policemen. They were looking for Dan and asking some questions."

"Really, what sort of questions? And why did you not tell me when I woke up?"

"I didn't want to worry you sweetie. Rob said he would investigate it and that they'd probably made a mistake, you know, wrong person, wrong house sort of thing."

"Auntie, you should've told me, why didn't you tell me?" she asked again.

"I'm so sorry my darling, it was wrong of me. You were sleeping and after the shock of finding out about the baby, well…oh I don't know," she shook her head ashamed of herself, knowing now that she shouldn't have hidden it from Kate. Maybe this accident could have been avoided if she had revealed it all to her.

Kate looked away, watching the world pass by outside the car.

"All I can do is apologise profusely. Rob assured me that it would just be a routine wrong person sort of thing, so I figured you didn't need to be worried about it until we knew a bit more."

The tense atmosphere remained silent for a few moments, then Kate said, "this must be related to what he said about hurting someone. Do you think I should phone the police and tell them what he said, tell them what I know…or more what I don't know?"

"I'm not entirely sure what's best to do right now Kate. All I do know is that we need to get you home for some rest and we can chat to uncle some more, see if he's got any news on the matter. He's usually good with dilemmas like this. I'm sorry again, please do forgive me darling."

Kate held her aunt's hand in the back of the taxi. She could see how upset and guilty Sally felt but it didn't matter anymore. All she wanted was for this stressful mystery to be over. She knew she had the right people around to help her through this so there was nothing to forgive. Sally was doing her best to protect her, that was all. Even if she did tell a little white lie. They were her family and she loved them unconditionally, no matter what Dan was playing at or the trouble he was causing.

Chapter Eighteen

The Truth will Come

. . .

A whole week passed by and there had still been no sign of Dan being found or of him returning to Kate's house. He hadn't been answering her countless attempts at calling him, dialling without even looking at the keyboard in the end. He'd made no calls to her, no text messages, no answer phone message, just blankness, just nothing. Eventually, his phone didn't even ring anymore so she could at least hear the funny answer message that he had recorded.

'Bonjour, it's Dan, you know I don't do these message thingymebobs, so coolio, just leave something funny for me and

I'll try and call you back when I work it all out, ciao for now peeps'

Just to hear that silly message, his French, English and Italian mix of a message. Just to hear his voice was all she wanted. It would be something for her to cling on to, but she didn't even have that anymore now, it was silent. And the silence was numbingly horrible.

It was as though he had just vanished, disappeared off the face of the earth, like he never existed. Like he had been a big dream, something only in Kate's imagination. The relationship that had started so well but so quickly had now almost frozen in time. Kate was growing increasingly worried about him each and every day he didn't turn up and each day he wasn't there. Her mind trawled back to the letter from Anna, echoing what she had said about him disappearing because of not being on his medication, it had to be that she tried to reassure herself of it. Surely he wouldn't have just left her like this for no reason.

Rob had been round and checked Kate's house twice a day to see if he'd turned up or at least come back to collect any more of his belongings but no luck there either. There was no sign of him having returned, he'd gone and forgotten everyone and everything. About their romance that she so thought was on the road to something a lot bigger and better than she'd known before.

Every day that passed had got more tense for Kate, and finally feeling fit enough to return home, she felt some sort of relief to be in her own bed. After spending the week at Sally's, she figured it was best for her to be at her place in case he turned up there and needed to be alone with her, or more importantly, needed to explain himself and this whole sordid situation that he'd left her in limbo about.

Sally wasn't so sure of Kate being alone so had convinced her that it would be best to stay there for a few days at least. She wanted to try to make sure that she ate and got as much rest as possible, but Kate couldn't help but grow more anxious and stressed not knowing where he was and why he had left like he did and why he was not even getting in touch with her, the silent treatment was deafening, and she hated everything about it.

Her sickness was worsening too. She would throw up five or six times a day and it was tiring her out so much that when she didn't have her head stuck down the toilet, she was sleeping, trying to build her strength back up for the next day of worry. Trying so hard to rest and relax through this nightmare.

The police had visited the house again to talk to her about anything she might have known or forgotten to tell them, and the fact that they were still looking for him made her feel even worse. The not knowing was torture. She had taken a few weeks leave from her work after the accident, and although she knew rest was key to getting back to normal somehow, she really missed her job, her work colleagues and especially missed one person: her best friend, Leo. She decided she had to see him and more than that, she wanted to apologise for letting him down about the new job they had just recently agreed to. She'd never felt so down as she did right now and needed to chat with her friend as soon as possible. She grabbed her phone and messaged him to come and visit as soon as he could.

'I need to see you Leo, I need one of your hugs' she typed in.

'Hey beaut, no problem at all' he'd replied, *'got a few errands to run and then I'm all yours sweetie, see you soon. Xx'*

And sure enough, later that afternoon, he arrived full of beans in his usual upbeat manner, "hey gorgeous," he said in a voice almost melodic, "how's my favourite work buddy?" He asked as he walked into her bedroom, smiling broadly, waving one arm in the air and with a small bunch of bright yellow and dark pink gerberas in the other. They were wrapped in yellow tissue paper which he knew was her favourite colour.

She felt more than overjoyed to see his friendly face finally and her smile beamed back at him with pure glee. They'd been text messaging each other but to actually see him, hear him and hug him tightly, was just the tonic she needed right now. It had seemed like ages since they'd had a good natter too, they had some catching up to do.

Once the initial excitement and enthrallment had calmed, he lounged himself on the end of her bed, "so, sister…" he joked, "what's the low down on everything, come on, tell me all the juicy gossip?"

She couldn't help but giggle back at him as his eyebrows raised and his all-encompassing smile warmed her heart, "well apart from throwing myself down the bloody stairs and passing out, finding out I'm going to have a child and then…" she paused as her smile wavered to the more sadder news part of the gossip, "well, Dan vanishing off the face of the earth…not much else happening here if I'm honest mate. It's all pretty…well, rubbish."

"Mmmm, nothing short of news hey?" he said, touching her leg reassuringly.

"I'm so sorry about the job Leo, I feel terrible about letting you down," Kate apologised as he leaned over the bed to grab a biscuit from the tray that Sally had brought up shortly after he'd arrived.

"Don't be silly gorgeous," he said, dunking it in his hot coffee and taking a clumsy bite of the digestive before it disintegrated, "actually," he continued, his mouth full and mumbling, "I explained to the boss what happened, you know the throwing down the stairs bit," he chuckled, smiling up at her face, "he was really nice about it," he finally swallowed, and wiped the corners of his mouth, "said the job is yours still when you are up to it and feeling better. Apparently, he visited the restaurant after he offered me the job, and took a liking to you," he winked at her, "so, no need to worry about that stuff. Anyway, enough about work, come on, give me the lowdown on the new little Kate bubba, how's the bun in the oven cooking?" he shuffled himself more into the middle of the bed and crossed his legs nodding his head in the direction of her tummy.

"It's all okay, thank goodness," she rubbed her belly lovingly, glancing down for a second, "I was so worried when I had the fall, you know, that something might've happened, that I could have miscarried, but no, it's cool," she said glancing up to him. "I'm so sick with it though Leo, it's ridiculous. I'm either in bed sleeping with zero amounts of energy or I have my head stuck down the toilet, throwing up the little bit of food that I manage to keep down there. I'm sure it's not meant to be like this, not this bad anyway."

"Not a clue babe," he chuckled, shaking his head, and shrugging his shoulders, "have you spoken to your doctor about it though? Can't they give you some anti-sickness pill, like people have for travel sickness maybe, or at least recommend something to help stop it happening so much?"

"No, I haven't. What with all that's been going on, I've not had a chance to make an appointment. I might have to ask for something though. To be honest, it's wearing me out and I'm not even getting the chance to enjoy the whole pregnancy thing yet. It's early days I suppose though?"

Just then, Sally came into the bedroom with a new tray of hot drinks and another small plate of sweet treats. Ginger biscuits this time, to add to the rapidly disappearing digestives that Leo was munching his way through, "here you go, I just had a google and read that ginger is supposed to help relieve morning sickness, may be worth a try darling," she said, rubbing Kate's shoulder, as she approached the bed, "help yourself Leo but do make sure this little one gets some hey?" she asked, "I'll just be downstairs, got some business calls to make for Rob." she gave them both a wink and left, shutting the door behind her.

"Aww, she's a gem, your aunt, isn't she?" Leo passed Kate the plate, but she shook her head.

"Yes, she's been amazing. She's never been anything else Leo, well, both have, I'm lucky to have them taking care of me." she smiled.

"You are darling, you are." He replied, wiping his hands clear of any crumbs from the new biscuit he was now devouring.

Kate watched him with fondness, he did love his biscuits.

"Look Kate," he said gently as he moved to sit beside her, "I know you may not want to hear this but, well I'm your best friend aren't I?" he asked.

"Of course you are Leo, but what are you going to tell me? You do worry me when you say things like that."

"Sorry," he shrugged, grimacing, "well, do you remember at your engagement party, when I said to you that Dan looked familiar?"

She nodded, looking puzzled and sipped on her glass of water.

"It took me a while to figure it out, but I did in the end. I know where I recognised him from."

"Okay…?" she answered, wondering what he was about to say about Dan, hoping it wouldn't be anything like seeing him in a strip club or somewhere she wouldn't like.

"Right, well, you know that evening at work when we had the rowdy stag do party meal thing?"

She nodded again.

"And the jerk of an idiot who thought it funny to slap your arse?" he paused looking at her, rolling his eyes, "well, when me and Max chucked the guys out, I noticed someone outside, across the street, he was just standing watching, almost…looking a bit shifty..." he paused again and turned his body towards hers, "It was Daniel. Kate it was Dan standing outside the restaurant."

"Seriously? But why?" Kate replied, "Leo, are you sure it was him?" she shuffled her body round.

"Yep, positive. I checked our camera footage too after you told me he'd gone AWOL. You can see that he followed the stag do guys afterwards. When we heard about the fight a few days after, that's when I put two and two together. I knew I'd seen him somewhere. I mean, don't get me wrong, I'm not accusing him of being in the fight but now…with all you've told me about what's going on…"

"Leo, are you definitely one hundred percent sure, do you really think it was Dan? Do you think he could be involved in it?"

"I'm ninety-nine-point nine percent positive Kate," he nodded, "I'm good with faces and he wasn't really hiding as such. I've not said anything to the police about the CCTV yet though. I didn't want to get him into trouble but it's only a matter of time before they ask for it. Do you want me to wipe it?"

"No, no way." She refused bluntly, "I don't want you getting into trouble because of me, because of Dan and what he might have done. You must tell them, show them it. If it wasn't him, it might get him off the hook, then he might come back?"

"Maybe, but if he was involved in the fight?" he paused, "well, this is your man, your fiancé for Christ's sake and now…well there's even more at stake isn't there, he's this little ones' daddy," he continued, "he could get locked up. I mean, I know the guy was a prick and deserved a slap for thinking he could grab your arse, but his face was properly smashed up. I saw it in the local paper last week, they were asking about any witnesses who may know anything. It looked pretty bad mate."

"Oh my god Leo," Kate said, "that must have been what he meant when he said he hurt someone," her tummy churned over, "Jesus, this is awful. I just wish I knew where he was. I could talk to him, get him to speak to the police and…" but before she could say anything else, her stomach began feeling bad and she swiftly placed her hand to her mouth, "Urgh…hang on," she swung her legs off the bed and ran as fast as her tired legs could go, to the nearest toilet, head down and another round of scaring yuckiness ensued.

"I'll get your aunt," Leo called out and he went down to fetch Sally who returned promptly to the bathroom.

"My goodness, this little one is not agreeing with ginger biscuits is it?" she jokingly said, trying to make light of the situation.

Kate felt horrendous this time and didn't have any energy left to even smile back.

"Is it safe to come in?" asked Leo, knocking softly on the door.

"Yes Leo darling, come on in," answered Sally, rubbing Kate's back.

"I'm so tired of feeling this way, it can't be right can it?" Kate asked, head in hands, her face a nice ashen shade of white.

Leo sat himself on the edge of the bath, "is this normal Sally, to be so sick with pregnancy?"

"I'm not sure Leo, as we never had our own

children, but it does seem a little extreme. I made a call to my doctor earlier, Kate. He can fit you in tomorrow afternoon. I really think you could do with getting some advice regarding this sickness."

"I was just saying about something to help with it, maybe anti-sickness pills or something herbal. You know like some have to take pills for flying or travelling?" Leo replied.

"Yes I agree, you can't continue like this, you're wasting away," Sally passed a fresh tissue to wipe her mouth with, "the little food that you do manage to get down, comes out pretty much half an hour or so later. Anyway, he's also arranged to give you an ultrasound scan to check on the baby while we are there, is that okay? I'm not taking over too much. You know, being a nosy, annoying aunt?"

"No, auntie, that's fine." Kate replied, her voice now slightly raspy from this episode of throwing up. Her throat was growing more sore, and all she needed now was a large drink of water to replenish her, some much needed rest and more sleep.

No matter what was happening right at this second, all the while, she couldn't stop her brain from working overtime, thinking of Dan and what sort of stupid game he was playing or what sort of trouble he had got himself into. If only he was here to help her through all this, get this nightmare assault worry out of the way and more importantly, be with her and their new baby bump.

As much as she loved having Sally, Rob, and Leo there to support her, it was her new man she wanted next to her more than anyone right now. Just some closure and support from the man she had fallen head over heels in love with so rapidly. If he could just show up and tell her the truth, help her believe in him that he hadn't been involved in anything untoward. That he wasn't the person that the police were looking for. The terrifying thing was, deep down, she knew something wasn't quite right by what he'd said so frantically that day, and then with the news that Leo had just revealed.

It was breaking her heart each minute Dan was gone from her life, the longer he stayed away, the more broken and hurt she became. All she wanted was some answers. All she wanted was for her normal life to return. The happy, fun, and exciting life that her and Dan had been building over the past few weeks. Even with the spontaneous moments that were off-the-wall, she wanted that back. She just wanted him back so they could work it all out, sort things out and get on with their plans for their future together. Now there would be three of them, it was even more important.

As she finally gathered her strength up again, made her way to the bedroom and climbed back into her bed, she sighed and wiped her forehead. She felt so totally shattered, physically and mentally.

"I just want this nightmare to be over Leo," she

whispered.

Leo got comfortable as well sitting next to her. "I know babe. I'm sure things will get better soon; things will work out somehow." He put his arm around her as she lay her head onto his chest.

Sally had been back downstairs preparing a fresh jug of water with lemons floating in it and a slice of toast to try and help settle Kate's tummy this time.

"Try and get some sleep darling." She said as she left them to it.

Leo switched on the TV, and they lay together, watching a movie until Kate had finally fallen asleep.

Chapter Nineteen

The Worst
Goodbye…

The following afternoon, Kate and Sally made the short car journey to the private clinic just across town. She had already been sick four times today and felt sure it wouldn't be the last time.

After the consultation with the doctor, they were then taken to the waiting area for the scan. As Kate sat waiting, all she could think of was Dan and that he would miss this important moment. She checked her phone for what seemed like the fiftieth time just in case he had by any chance of a miracle, messaged her, or tried to call. Nothing came up so she tucked it back into her handbag, angry but disappointed. She looked round at the posters on the wall of what the baby may look like on the scan she was about to have, and she began to sense a glimpse of excitement to be here at all and to be having a first visual meeting of her little one. *'If only your daddy were here too'*, she thought to herself, glancing down towards her tummy. Having a baby had not been on the cards yet but the idea and the realisation of being here was helping to make it sink in. If only she was here with her fiancé, and they could experience it together like normal couples should with their first child's scan.

"Have another cup of water sweetheart. It helps to see baby more clearly apparently, I just read it up there." Sally said passing her a clear plastic cup and pointing to a sign on the wall.

"I think I'll pee all over the floor if I have any more auntie." She laughed gently, "I just wish Daniel was here you know?"

"Yes I know darling. I'm sure he'll be at the next one darling." Sally tried to reassure her.

Kate sighed and bowed her head. Maybe her aunt was right, maybe once he'd sorted whatever he needed sorting out, he would be back, and they could enjoy this exciting time. She just couldn't help but feel sad for him not even knowing yet that he was going to be a father and the fact that this whole predicament could've been so very different if he had been here.

Two minutes later, the nurse called her name, and they made their way in.

The room was dark with just a narrow hospital bed, two chairs either side of the bed and a complicated looking machine with dials and buttons galore. As the remaining few spotlights were turned off, the sonographer then stood beside the bed, asked Kate to lift her top up and began to squeeze some gel onto her exposed tummy.

"Sorry, it's a bit cold and slimy but we will wipe it off afterwards for you," the lady said and then went on explaining the whole procedure as she went along.

Sally watched anxiously in the other chair, waiting patiently to see her niece's baby appear on the screen any second.

"As it's quite early, it may take a little bit of time to find the little one at first, so please bear with me. They are known to be a bit shy sometimes. Are you ready to get started?" the sonographer smiled across to both ladies in turn.

"Yes, I think so," replied Kate turning to look at Sally who winked back. They held hands, tightly and the lady began pushing down onto Kate's tummy.

The silence filling the room was deafening, and the nurse's eyes seemed to be transfixed to the screen studying the images with concentration, "how far along do you think you are?" she asked, still moving the transducer around searching for something to become clear. She was pressing down quite firmly now, and it was uncomfortable on Kate's very full bladder which she had to fill up before the appointment.

"Around eight or nine weeks I think, is everything alright?" Kate looked at the sonographers' expression who was still busily studying the black and white screen very closely, her eyes fixed and not turning to look at her or Sally as she spoke and asked questions.

"I may need you to go back out in the waiting area and drink a bit more water, then we can try again. Sometimes it can be difficult to see them this early on especially if they are a little small for the stage or the dates may be inaccurate," she said, as she stopped scanning, "would you mind drinking a bit more for me and we can try again in about half an hour?" she asked, lifting the scanner gadget from Kate's tummy and holding out some tissue for her to wipe the gel off with.

"Erm, sure, okay," replied Kate, nervously taking the wad of tissue.

As they sat outside the room again, Kate drank four cups of water and began worrying, "I think there's something wrong Auntie," she stared at the information posters on the wall again with the various stages of scans wondering which stage hers would be.

"No, it'll be fine, maybe it's just a bit small as she said, hiding away in there, it's early days sweetheart,"

Sally tried to reassure her.

"Maybe," but Kate wasn't so sure, something was telling her that there was a reason the correct images weren't appearing on that screen, there must be a reason as to why she has been feeling so unwell and throwing up so much, "I can't help it, it's just, well. All the throwing up, it's not normal to be sick this much, I looked it up auntie. Do you think… do you think she's ok?" she asked, pulling her gaze away from the posters.

"You keep saying 'she'," Sally replied, changing the subject in hope they would be called in soon, "how do you know it's going to be a girl?"

"I don't know, it's just a feeling. I just hope she's ok, I've sort of got used to the idea now of her being there, being a family, you know; even if it's just the two of us."

Sally smiled at her lovingly, "you have me and uncle sweetheart…" but before she could say anything else to try and reassure her niece any further, they were called back into the room.

This time, as her tummy was prepared with gel once more, the screen was turned around away from them, and the atmosphere had changed to a more tense and awkward din. The doctor was also now in the room and he and the lady sonographer were looking at the images appearing on screen, intently and almost whispering between themselves as buttons and dials on the machine were clicked and switched.

It seemed like it would never end, and Kate had an awful feeling building up inside of her. Why couldn't they just tell her what was going on, why all the whispering and deep intense faces. This wasn't how it was in the movies when everybody was smiling and happy. When that all important image of a new life would appear and everyone cried with happiness, why wasn't it the same as that, what was wrong?

Kate glanced up at Sally, Sally looked across at the doctor, then the doctor turned to Kate. In slow motion, the lady moved the equipment back away from Kate's body and slid her chair back so the doctor could get beside the bed.

"Kate," the softness and sadness in his voice said it all, "it's not the news we were hoping for. We have managed to find the foetus, but I'm afraid there's no heartbeat, I'm so sorry," he touched her leg in comfort, but she just stared back at him in a dream-like state as he continued, "there is a baby, but its heart isn't beating. We've taken some images if you'd like to see but I'm afraid the baby isn't alive anymore, this probably happened a few weeks ago."

Sally held onto Kate's hand tightly and turned to the doctor with tears in her eyes, "but she had a scan a few weeks back after her accident and everything came back normal? I'm sorry doctor, I'm confused, are you saying the baby is in there, but it has died?"

"Yes. I'm very sorry," he apologised again, "it looks like it stopped around seven weeks gestation, from the size we can measure today, probably after the previous scan in that case. If you'd like to come through to my office, we can talk it through. I can explain what happens next."

Kate sat up slowly in silence as the nurse gave her another wad of tissue to wipe her tummy clean once again. She didn't know what to say or how to react, so she had to remain quiet, in a stunned silence until her brain could comprehend what was happening.

"Sweetheart," Sally whispered, "do you understand? Shall we go and talk it through with the doctor?"

Kate moved her legs to hang over the bed still not uttering a word, not expressing any emotion. She felt empty, blank, totally dead in herself and she was ashen white with shock. She straightened her trousers, pulled down her top over them and began moving slowly, reaching her feet onto the floor, and then silently walked out of the room.

"Kate…" Sally called after her, but knew she wasn't coming back, so she just followed and waited until she finally stopped and sat down on a bench outside of the clinic.

"She's dead auntie, my little baby is dead inside me."

Sally didn't have a clue what to say back, she just held her niece's cold shaking hand and sat beside her to listen to the heartache that was now ensuing for them both.

"I knew something wasn't right. I just knew it; I told you something was wrong." Hard tears now slowly cascaded from her eyes down her cheeks and dropped onto her lap, "my baby has died inside of me Auntie. I couldn't even look after her, I couldn't keep her safe, what sort of person am I?"

"It's not your fault darling, please don't think that way. Sometimes, these things just happen, I've had loads of friends have the same, it's, well it's nature's way sometimes. Come here," she pulled her in towards her embrace, "please don't think it's anything you've done because it's not," she hugged her tighter and tears streamed down Kate's face. She began sobbing uncontrollably and Sally's heart broke into tiny pieces for her. Why did this have to happen to her incredible Kate when she had been through so much already with Dan disappearing. All she could do was hold her and let her grieve for the baby.

*

An appointment was made the following day for Kate to go into hospital to have the baby taken out. They had discussed it with the doctor after finally being strong enough to face the situation, going back into the hospital. She had to either let nature run its course or have the baby taken out by surgery. Neither choice was one Kate thought she would have to make but it was for the best as she didn't want to see it all happen with a miscarriage at home.

When she woke up from the operation, the hard

realisation set in and she broke down in tears once again when the nurse came to check on her and asked her if she needed anything, "I want my baby back, that's all I want, my little girl," she sobbed.

The young nurse had comforted her the best she could, and sat on the bed while Kate cried, her heart was torn into what seemed like a million pieces and she suddenly realised how much she had loved that little baby in the short time she'd known about her. What made this situation even worse was that Dan didn't even know what was going on in her life right now. He couldn't even be bothered to let her know where he was, what he'd done and now she was coping with this without him. She felt angry and wanted to get back to some normality as quickly as possible. Back to her normal boring life instead of all this craziness that had been the last few months.

As the nurse passed her the last of the tissues, Kate thanked her and tried hard to compose herself and calm down. Taking a deep breath she told her, "I'd like to go home, can I get dressed? Are my things in here?" She turned to reach the bedside locker.

"I'll go and check with the doctor first, Miss Ellington, I think he may just want to come and do a final check. Do you want any help getting dressed? You may be a little sore for a few hours, I can help you if you like?"

"No thank you, but I'll be fine. And thank you for sitting with me. Sorry I was a mess." she investigated the locker grabbing her bag to find her phone.

The nurse left the bedside.

Kate started typing a text to Sally, *'please come and get me auntie, I want to go home .x'*

A response came back a minute after, *'I've just got here, I'll be up when I've sorted car park. x'*

And she was. She was there just as Kate had finished getting dressed and gathering her belongings. The doctor had reluctantly discharged her, but with Sally convincing him that she would ensure the patient would be in her safe hands, he felt positive to let them go home. Kate was feeling a tiny bit stronger and ready to face the future, whatever it may bring in the next few days and weeks. All she could do was hope that it would be good news.

*

"Are you sure you are alright Kate, do you want some coffee, something to eat? I can rustle you up with a sandwich, or a salad if you have food in the fridge?" Sally asked as they arrived back at Kate's house.

"I think I'd just like a strong coffee for now actually, that would be great thanks," Kate sat down on the sofa gently. She was a bit sore from her procedure, "and maybe a few painkillers that the doctor gave me too please? They're in the front pocket of my bag," she asked, scooting her bottom to get comfortable.

As she laid her head back to try and relax, she

remembered the letter that she had stuffed down the side of the sofa from Dan's mother. It had completely gone out of her mind since the fall down the stairs, then Dan still missing and then this awful twenty-four hours. She felt compelled to read more and see if it would give her any clues as to what was going on with him and, maybe some insights into his mysterious mother too. Something needed to give her some clarity after what she had been going through. She leaned forward and reached down, grabbing hold of the slightly crumpled letter.

Chapter Twenty

The Truth Revealed…

"What's that you got there, sweetheart?" asked Sally as she carried in a tray consisting of steaming hot coffee, the prescribed painkillers, and a small plate of bourbon biscuits.

"It's a letter from Dan's mum. She sent it to me in the post and I only read some of it just before I had the fall," she paused, trying to flatten the paper out a little bit, "I hid it from Dan when he rushed in all in a state because I wanted to tell him about the baby first. Then he went and bloody left," she said rolling her eyes and sighing, "to be honest, I'd forgot about it with the accident and everything. But I just thought about it now. Maybe she knows something about where he could be? He didn't speak about her too much. He was always so, well sort of private about her, but maybe he's gone to stay with her? Maybe that's why she wanted to write to me in the first place."

"Oh, how interesting. Does it say where she lives, we could go and visit her? He could be hiding out with her or at least staying nearby to her." Sally sat down beside Kate on the sofa, putting the tray onto the coffee table in front of them.

"Well, he told me she lived in a care home so I'm not sure if he could stay with her there," swigging back a glug of water and downing the painkillers, "I don't know how it works with care homes and that, do they have space for relatives to stay over, do they allow that?"

Sally shrugged her shoulders.

Kate started at the beginning again reading the letter out loud this time to Sally who sat listening intently, intrigued at the first few pages.

"And this is where I got up to before Dan came in that day," Kate said as she continued reading, "I don't want to cause any trouble but after seeing him the other week, and listening to him talking about you, I felt I should write. I really hope you don't mind me butting in. I just want to help you understand him a bit more. Daniel doesn't think you need to know about his mental health issues, he thinks he has it under control but when he came to visit the other day, he told me he had come off his medication and he didn't want to go back on it anymore. He feels as though you have cured him somehow," Kate then paused, glancing to her side at Sally's puzzled face, "what does she mean, mental health issues? Do you know if Uncle Rob knew anything about that?" she asked.

"Well, when Rob first met him, he did tell him that he had suffered from depression quite a lot, but it was down to the fact that he lost his dad so suddenly. They'd chatted about the fact that he'd had trouble coping with the death but kept the details pretty much to himself. Rob didn't know the full story of how his father died."

"Why haven't you told me about all this before now?" Kate quizzed a little sternly.

"Because, well, because Daniel seemed fine. He was obviously on this medication stuff when he was with you. Rob said he hadn't seen him so excited and so upbeat since that evening where he met you, at your party," she shrugged her shoulders and looked into Kate's concerned eyes, "you were both so happy darling. A fresh new relationship for the two of you, we didn't want to interfere or look like we were fussing over you too much, you know, being too overprotective, or too nosy."

"Auntie, this could be really important as to why

he's behaved like this, why he's gone off like he has, so suddenly and out of the blue."

"I know that now don't I? I'm sorry darling, I really am. Rob told me I should have told you the minute we knew he'd gone. I just didn't want to spoil things for you, make you worry even more than you were already." She tried to change the subject, feeling horrible inside for keeping this information to herself, "what else does it say?" she asked, nodding down toward the letter.

Kate put her slight bit of anger and frustration aside, turned over the page and continued reading, "erm, where was I... ah, here. He feels as though you have cured him somehow, so he wants to be normal again. He's stopped seeing his therapist too and this worries me terribly. His bipolar disorder is not something that can just be fixed, and he needs to keep taking the medication." Kate paused, "He's got bipolar. Did you know that too?" she laid the pages on her lap turning to Sally once again. Her poor mind was completely mashed with all this new information coming to light and she felt so betrayed. By Dan more than anyone, for the simple fact that he'd hidden so much more from her about his past and this serious illness. If he had, things would add up in her mind, his sudden weird outbursts, his spontancity.

"No, we didn't know it was that bad, like I said, he just told us that he got depressed because of losing his father, we didn't know about any medication that he should or would have been on at any time."

Kate shook her head. These past few months had turned into nothing but a nightmare, she just wanted to know the truth and get her life back to normal. More than anything, she wanted him to come back, just walk in through the front door and explain everything to her instead of finding out from everyone else, from some random letter from a woman she'd never met. From his mother of all people, this is not how she had imagined this year to pan out.

As she began reading the next page, another shock revelation appeared. "I'm begging you to get him to start them again, please. And he must get in touch with the therapist as soon as possible so they can monitor his current state of mind. With me being locked up in this place, it makes it very difficult to be able to help him. Prison is not a great meeting place at the best of times," Kate stopped immediately, gasping, and putting her hand to her mouth in shock, she exclaimed, "what the hell," and read the sentence out again, "With me being locked up in this place, it makes it very difficult to be able to help him."

As the words hit their ears again, at this point, Sally nearly spat her coffee across the room in disbelief at hearing Kate repeat the words aloud once more. "Jesus, Christ, the woman is in prison?" she spluttered, carefully putting her coffee mug down before she spilt it, "his mum is in prison!"

They just looked at each other in utter shock for a moment and then Kate carried on reading with her eyes wider than ever, "I only see him about once a month as it is, and they are very restricted with time allowed for visitors to come in."

Kate had to stop for a second, placing the letter back down onto her lap, "she's in prison, Auntie, his mum is locked up. For goodness' sake, what the hell is this? How many secrets can one family have?"

Sally gently shook her head.

There were just one more page left to read.

"This is insane," Kate said as she perused the final notes and read them to Sally, "please Kate, I'm begging you. Please get him to take his medication again, he can get a bit of a temper and become violent without them, and I worry for you or anyone he may encounter. I can clearly see that he has fallen head over heels in love this time, you must be a very special person. But at the same time, this worries me greatly. I wouldn't want anything to happen to you or anyone else. I couldn't forgive myself, not again. Without the drugs, he can get very protective of those closest to him, those who he loves, and he will get jealous very easily. It's the illness you see, but without the control of the tablets in his system, he will do anything to keep you close. And I mean anything Kate. Whatever the cost, he can be extremely unpredictable. I'm being honest, dearest Kate and I don't mean to scare you but it's vital that you know more about my son, you had to know the truth, so I had to write this letter." Kate took a breath for a second, silenced by the words in front of them two of them. If she hadn't been sat there with her aunt, she could've thought she was in a movie or dreaming and hoping that dream would not be real. She continued scanning the writing and then read the final paragraphs, "If you would like to write back to me, and I would be glad to hear from you, then, I've added the address at the bottom of the page. If you feel like you would like to visit me and chat a little bit more about it all, I would be extremely happy to see you and to finally meet you. I'm sure it could be arranged soon as I don't get any other visitors other than my son. But, Kate, just one more thing…" Kate looked up nervously at Sally who swiftly nodded back in anticipation of what she was about to say, "I wouldn't let Daniel know if you do decide to come and visit me, not unless he's back on the medication anyway and then maybe you could come together, and we can all be open about everything finally. Anyway, I think I've probably said enough for you to get your head around, I'm sorry if it's been a shock or too much. I just don't know what he's told you and wanted to be honest. I hope he's okay…I hope you are too. All the best for now anyway. Anna."

They both just sat in shock for a few moments trying to comprehend the information that they had just read. How could this be possible that Dan's mother was in prison, was this some sort of trick, some joke that somebody was playing on them? And if it wasn't a joke, why on earth was she in there in the first instant.

"Wow," was all Sally could say, breaking the silence as she reached for her coffee mug, "I think we may need something stronger than this Katie darling." And stood up.

Kate glanced up, unable to express any emotions or expressions, "I don't get it. He told me his mother was in a care home, he said he went to see her every day, he couldn't have been. He was lying to me all this time," she said, sitting back in the chair, the letter still tightly grasped in her hands. "Where was he going everyday if he wasn't visiting her in the so-called care home? Auntie, what the hell have I got myself into? And what the hell is she in prison for?" Kate asked, dumbfounded.

Sally looked down at her niece, whose face was pale and looking more anxious than ever. She didn't have the answers to any of the questions that Kate was throwing at her, and she felt as shocked as her right now. There didn't seem to be an easy answer or a logical one for them to conclude. For a few minutes, they couldn't help but freeze on the spot, wondering, thinking, and getting more confused by the second.

Suddenly, the deathly silence was broken as they heard a loud knock on the front door.

"Oh god, get rid of them, whoever it is auntie, I can't deal with people right now." Kate pleaded.

Sally rubbed Kate's shoulder, then went to answer the door, leaving Kate still shocked, staring, and shuffling the papers of the letter in sitting in her lap. "What the hell are you playing at Dan?" she whispered to herself.

After a few minutes, Sally returned to the doorway of the lounge looking ashen white and stunned, "Kate," she said quietly, "it's the police, they've found Dan."

The short drive to the police station was tense, silent, and seemed much longer than the ten-minute journey. Kate sat in the back of the police car holding tightly onto Sally's hand. The traffic was unusually heavy and every light they approached seemed to change to red, giving Kate even more time to ponder over her thoughts and fears as to what this outing may bring.

After reading the letter from Dan's mother, she had so many questions running around in her mind. She had a huge list to ask him about his illness, his mother, the lying, his disappearing. She was trying to work out how to bring the subject up about his family, without causing any trouble for his mother. At the end of the day, Anna had taken the time to contact Kate concerned for her safety more than anything it sounded like. Maybe she would have to wait to see what his explanation was as to why he left so suddenly first. Her insides were churning around, and she still felt weak from the surgery and all the emotions that had spilled out for her during the past day. All this new information she now had on him was mind-bending, but she was beginning to kind of understand the weird mood swings that he'd been having. The sudden leaving in the middle of the night, the very impromptu sex sessions that sometimes started off a bit out of the ordinary, albeit a bit scary for a few times. He was mysterious, intriguing, but it was starting to make more sense because of the illness. If only he had been honest from the start about it, she could've helped him, made sure he was on his medication. Suddenly, she found herself taking some blame again about the whole situation that was gradually unfolding. It seemed so unfair that she was going through this at all let alone after just miscarrying their baby, a baby he didn't even get to know much about either.

Nearing the police station, the car began to slow down, then seconds later, pulled in and parked next to other patrol cars. Kate's tummy flipped over and over, doing somersaults of fear and worry. She had never seen the inside of a police station before, but she was more nervous about seeing Dan after so long than caring about where she was. She felt as if she were playing a lead part in some movie, a dream, a nightmare that maybe she would wake up soon from and all this craziness would be over. How she wished that so much right now, all she wanted was for life to return to some sort of normality again, as boring as it could get sometimes, that's all she wanted now. Thinking back a few months, she wished she could turn back the hands of time and it would just be her in her little house, living her daily routine, working hard, and enjoying life. As much as she had been excited for the baby and how amazing it had been to meet Dan, she hated dealing with all this trouble, she needed her life back without this pain and stress.

"Do you think I should tell him about losing the baby?" Kate said to Sally as they made their way into the building, following the police officers.

"I don't know darling, maybe?" she rubbed Kate's arm as she linked it into hers, holding her close.

"I know he heard me that day...I know he heard me say I was pregnant but now," she paused to swallow a lump in her throat. It was all still so raw and painful to think their tiny start of a baby had gone almost as quickly as it had appeared, and sort of wasn't relevant, "well, now I'm not pregnant." She added, the tightness growing stronger on her aching heart.

Sally didn't know what to say, she just tried to smile back reassuringly, and hoped everything would be alright for her niece. Before they could talk anymore about it, another officer approached them.

Chapter Twenty-One

Love Hurts…

"Miss Ellington," said the female officer, glancing down to see them look up at her and nod, "this way please," she added, pointing in the direction of the door she had just come through herself.

They were both directed down the narrow corridor, passing several very heavy and thick looking closed doors on each side of the walls. Interview rooms with large glass windows to see in. There were notice boards containing police information, then some wanted posters like in the movies. Kate thought to herself that they must have them in there so that police officers could identify the criminals if they were off duty. Keep them on their toes with recognising the culprits or something. She also glimpsed at the various helpline and advice leaflets that were neatly displayed in clear plastic holders. Support groups for anyone that needed it and one random Salsa dance class with a full line of paper strips of phone numbers attached to it for people to call up and book lessons. Kate assumed from the amount of number strips left, that it was either a new poster just been put up, or no-one wanted to learn to salsa.

"When can I see Daniel?" she asked as they finally walked into the interview room at the very end of the corridor.

"Not too long now. We just have a few questions to go through first and then you can see him, madam." The officer answered, showing Kate and Sally to the black, not very comfortable looking chairs.

Nodding in agreement slowly, Kate sat down. The room was tiny and very boring looking. Grey concrete walls and a small window with bars on the inside. There was only enough room for a chipped and scratched rectangular table with four hard plastic chairs around it. She almost felt like the criminal awaiting a grilling.

"Can we get you both a cup of tea, coffee, water?" the female officer asked. She had her hair tied back neatly in a bun and wore thick rimmed glasses which she kept pushing up her nose. Her uniform was neat and tidy just like in the TV programmes Kate had watched tirelessly over the years. She loved a good crime drama, but this wasn't fun at all. Being part of her own life dramatics.

"No, I'm okay thank you," replied Kate. She just wanted to get on with it and finally get to see Dan.

"I'm fine too," Sally said, so the officer left the room as two male policemen came in sitting opposite.

"Thank you for coming in today, Kate. And this is your aunt?" he asked.

Kate nodded; Sally smiled at him.

"Okay. Nice to meet you both. My name is Bruce Jones, I'm the officer in charge of the case against Daniel."

Kate turned to Sally, frowning her eyebrows perplexed at his words.

"So, like my colleague told you," Officer Jones continued, "we just have a few questions, is that alright?" he asked as he began shuffling the small folder in front of him.

Kate responded again with just a nod of her head.

"Now," he began, "on the evening of September twenty forth this year, you were working as a waitress at the…" he paused as he grabbed his glasses from the table and opened the folder, "The Olive Branch Bistro and Restaurant on the High Street, is that correct?"

"Yes," Kate agreed, watching him reading more of his paperwork.

"And that night, I believe that you were serving a stag party of around fifteen males, yes?" he asked.

One nod back again from Kate, agreeing to the information he was stating.

"What time approximately did they leave the restaurant, do you remember?"

"Erm…" Kate thought for a few seconds, the stag party night, this was the night one of the guys had slapped her behind, and they had all been thrown out by Leo and Max, the manager, "I think it was around eleven, maybe half ten ish. They got asked to leave early by my manager Max and my colleague Leo."

"Why was that?" he probed.

"They were getting too rowdy and," she paused, "one of them, well, one of them got a bit carried away," she replied shyly. She really didn't want to go over that incident again.

"Carried away?" the officer questioned, "As in…?" he wasn't giving up.

"Well…he thought it would be okay to slap my arse as I served the table," she bravely answered.

"Oh, I see, thank you for clarifying that. Was anything reported, noted down at your place of work, like in an incident book?"

"No, I don't think so. Max and Leo just asked them to leave, and they did so that was the end of it. Stag parties can get a bit, you know, out of hand sometimes but we sort of get used to it, unfortunately, it's part of the job. They asked them to leave for being inappropriate and rude and that was it really."

"Thank you Miss Ellington, and yes, they did the right thing, your friend and manager," he rummaged in the card folder, shuffling papers around, "do you remember seeing anyone outside as they left the restaurant? On the street maybe?"

"No, I didn't go outside. Like I said, Leo and Max dealt with it while I went to the staff room to catch my breath. I…err, well I slapped the guy so needed a minute out back. I never saw anything or anyone outside."

"Okay, no problem," he said as he slid a grainy image across the table and pointed to someone standing with a hoodie and jeans on, "do you recognise the person in this photo?" he asked, staring straight into her eyes as if cross examining her.

She looked down away from his glare at the photo on the table. It was Dan, she could tell straight away, and then she remembered what Leo had said to her at their engagement party about knowing him from somewhere then revealing on his visit to her house, realising where he had seen him before. As her mind raced, she remembered also that he'd turned up at her place, with his cut hand and bloodied face and in the same clothes as the photo she now had in front of her. That very evening when he said it had been during Rugby.

"Miss Ellington?" the officer pressed, interrupting her thoughts.

"Sorry," she replied, shaking her head of her

memories, "erm, yes. I think it's Dan... sorry, yes, it's Daniel."

"Thank you," he took the photo and slid it back into the folder, "so, just to clarify for the interview notes, you are identifying Daniel Howard as the person in the image I have just shown you?" They looked at her intently waiting for her confirmation.

"Yes, I am, it's Daniel but, what's happened? What has he done?" Sally grasped Kate's hand, noticing her nervously twiddling her fingers together and picking at her nails.

"Miss Ellington," the officer sat back in his chair looking serious, "Mr Howard has admitted to an assault on that evening."

"Assault?" Kate exclaimed, "what do you mean assault and on who?"

"On the customer who assaulted you that evening in the restaurant," he replied, "we just needed some clarification of the events that evening to match with his story and the victim's account. Thanks for your time today, I understand how difficult it must be for you. Would you like to see Mr Howard now? You can have ten minutes if you'd like to still see him."

She couldn't help but think to herself that she had made things worse for Dan now by speaking to the police, confirming that it was him in the picture. Leo had told her he thought Dan was outside that evening and now it turns out he was. The bloody face wasn't a rugby injury, he'd been in a fight but why?

How had he known that the guy had slapped her that night and why would he feel it necessary to get into a fight with him because of that? Her mind was again racing around, and she felt overwhelmed with the whole situation of the past few days. Did she even want to face him right now? Her brain ached, she felt hot and clammy with the fear of seeing him, wondering if she might just want to slap him now for putting her through all of this.

"Miss Ellington, would you like to see him?" the officer repeated, holding his arms out, directing Kate towards the corridor.

"Just see him Kate," Sally said, holding onto her arm gently and reassuring her niece, "see what he has to say for himself, give him a chance to explain at least? Think about the letter we just read too."

"I just don't know auntie. I feel like all I will do is cry or scream at him right now, or worse."

"Look," Sally held Kate's chin up to look into her eyes which were glazed over with sorrow, "he's been an idiot, but he's had the guts to hand himself in. Just listen to him for now and then we can kick his butt later when this is all sorted out," she whispered, trying to somehow make light of it all and help Kate make the decision.

Kate nodded back slowly in a daze, "you're right, as always…okay" she replied, and then followed the officer not knowing what the hell she was going to say to him, how she was going to feel and whether to tell him about the baby, about their baby that she had just lost.

As they reached the door, Kate felt her heart racing, "I just need a minute," she said as she leant on the wall for a moment looking up to the ceiling. Surely he wasn't such a bad person. How could she have fallen in love with him so quickly if he was a bad egg. Much of the time, it had been exciting, fun, and so different to previous boyfriends. She had agreed to marry him now, they were engaged just a month ago. She felt sure that she was a better judge of character than to get involved with some aggressive thug who went around beating people up for something so trivial as a slapped bottom. Taking a deep breath, she stood up straight again and nodded to the officer that she was ready to go in.

The door shut noisily behind her. As she stepped forward to see the image of Dan sitting at the table with his face down in his hands. For what seemed like minutes, she stood there as his head moved seemingly in slow motion to look straight towards her with their eyes meeting instantly. Her anger subsided and her heart now felt warm for seeing him. He looked so sad and tired and all she wanted to do was grab hold of him, hug him tightly and never let go. She knew she had to be brave and strong so as much as she wanted to embrace him and tell him everything was going to be okay, she kept her composure and walked slowly toward the table, sitting down opposite him. They just looked into each other's eyes for a few seconds with a deafening silence surrounding the morbid room.

"I'm so sorry Kate," he whispered finally, "I didn't mean to do this, I just…" Dan glanced across at the officer standing by the door watching them intently with his arms linked behind his back. The atmosphere was horrid, and the room was even darker and dingier than the one she had just been interviewed in, "I was just trying to protect you," he went on.

Kate didn't reply. All she could do was sit and listen for now. Her heart was beating rapidly, and she felt as though any moment, it would crash through her ribs and explode.

"I can explain everything, I swear, I'm not some sort of crazy person," he moved his hands across the table reaching for her.

"No touching," interrupted the officer in a deep voice, startling Kate.

Dan returned his hands into his lap and bowed his head in disgrace. As he lifted his head once more, she stared into his brown eyes which looked sadder than she'd ever seen.

"I'm so sorry Kate, honestly I'm not crazy, I'm not, believe me, please," he pleaded.

"I know you're not crazy," she replied, "it's alright, I believe you Dan. We will get through this together," she smiled at him, tilting her head to try and make him feel a little bit better. She needed him to feel her love through her eyes as they weren't allowed to touch each other. Her anger was dwindling away after seeing how hurt and pained he looked right now.

He managed a tiny smile back at her and for the remainder of the ten minutes she was allowed with him, they talked about what had happened. Kate purposely kept off the subject of the baby and what she had just been through in the past twenty-four hours. He was the priority now and she was determined to get him through this and work things out as soon as this problem was fixed, and she could get him back home. Before they knew it, the ten minutes had ticked by, they had to say goodbye and Kate had to leave him alone in the room.

"When will he be allowed to come home?" she asked arriving back to the main reception area with the interviewing officer.

"We have a few more questions and procedures to go through, the victim is coming in for another interview to see if he wants to press any charges, but he will be here until tomorrow afternoon as a precautionary measure. We will call you when he is ready to be collected, is this the best number to reach you on Miss Ellington?" he said as he showed her his notes on the clipboard.

"Yes. Okay, thank you," Kate replied, wishing he would have said Dan could leave now and all this be over.

"No problem at all and thank you for coming in to help us with our questions."

All she could wish for now was that the person, the victim, would not press charges on Dan and they could start to re-build their relationship again. She wanted to help him with his medication and the illness she had now found out about, she had to, she was in love with him, and this was just a big, stupid, mistake he'd made, an act of his love. An act of protection for her. Nothing made her feel any better thinking about violence and it was no excuse to hit someone the way he had but she was smitten with him, and her heart had forgiven him already.

Chapter Twenty-Two

Explanations…

"Are you okay my darling?" Sally said meeting her in the doorway.

Kate just nodded back, "I think so," and made their way outside. The fresh air hit her face and she took a deep sigh, "what a bloody mess hey?" she added.

They embraced each other with a big hug after exiting the building and walking slowly down the entrance steps to call a taxi.

"They said five minutes," Sally told Kate as she finished on the phone, "you sure you are alright sweetie?"

"Yes. Well, sort of. I don't know what to make of it all auntie," Kate replied, wearily, "I really don't know how I feel right now. I'm not sure if I'm angry or upset with him, with the whole situation or what. It's just all too much to take in. I mean, why?" she added raising her hand to her head and wiping her brow, "why would he do that to someone? And then lie to me about it."

"Maybe it's his condition honey? You remember what his mother said in the letter about coming off his medication and getting angry and protective? It could be down to that I suppose?"

"Yeah, maybe you're right, it must have something to do with that, I guess."

"Did you tell him about his mother writing to you? About her letter and what she told you?"

"No," Kate shook her head, "I just wanted to see what he said first about all of this rubbish, I just wanted to know what happened," she paused to take a breath of air as she saw the taxi arriving, "I will tell him though, at some point; I need him to know about it and then, we need make sure that we get him all the help he needs."

"You going to stay with him?" Sally asked.

"He's my fiancé now, not just a casual fling. I must help him; I must stay with him auntie. I still love him." she insisted, as they climbed into the back of the cab.

"I know you do sweetie," Sally leaned across, softly calming Kate's fumbling hands as she tried to fasten her seatbelt. "And the baby, did you tell him about what happened?"

"I didn't. I couldn't. Auntie, he looked so sad already. To do that to him in there, I think it may have broken him even further," she glanced back towards the station that was now becoming distant as the taxi drove out of the car park towards the centre of town, "I'll tell him when he's home and settled. A prison is not the place to give him that sort of news."

"Okay darling. Let's get you back home, you need to get some rest after what you've been through over the past few days. I'll stay with you unless you want to come and stay at ours? You know Uncle Rob won't mind, he's got a few days away in Switzerland for work so it would be just the two of us anyway, what do you think?"

"Thanks auntie but I think I'd like to be in my own bed and as soon as we can get Dan home, I want to get to the bottom of it all, I'll be okay at mine honestly," she answered, "I need to get back to work in the next few days too."

"Alright sweetie. Don't go rushing things though, I'm sure your work will understand, with all that you've been through this week."

"Yes I know and I'm sure they will be fine about it all too, but I've got to get back to some sort of normal life at some point, haven't I? I'll call Leo later and have a chat with him, see what he says."

When they arrived back at Kate's house, Sally prepared a chicken salad for them both, and stayed for a few hours to make sure her niece was okay and did get some rest. It was nearly ten o'clock at night by the time she left and although Kate was shattered, she wanted to read more of the letter from Dan's mother, so she decided to go back through it and work it all out in her mind.

She needed to get things straight in her head before she could even contemplate talking to Dan about it, when he did eventually get home. She wondered how he would react, how he would feel about his mother writing to her and telling her his secrets, their sordid secrets. How was she going to convince him to go back on his medication and why had he lied to her about the fact that his mother was in prison and not in a care home like he had previously told her? Her mind was awash with questions to ask him, and she wouldn't stop until everything was out in the open. No matter how much it hurt or upset her or revealed more about the mysterious guy she'd fallen in love with, she had to prepare herself for this next challenge.

Reading the letter through once more, made her a little bit angry at this point, thinking what she had been through by herself without his support, with him just disappearing on her. He hadn't even known she had fallen down the stairs because he'd left the house in such a hurry, and then not coming back at all for weeks. She had so many things to discuss, she had to make some notes. Grabbing her bag from the kitchen, she reached in to get her recipe idea notebook and pen.

On opening it, she saw the top corner of a page folded over, so she turned to it and found a little scribbled message from Leo. *'Just to say hi, you sexy little thing…Love you K. Leo..xxx'* was all it said but it made her smile, but at the same time, brought a tear to her eye. He was such a sweet guy, and she'd missed working with him and more than that, missed the banter they had at every shift. Maybe he could help make sense of everything right now, he always seemed to know the right things to say in times of crisis. Closing the notebook, she fetched her phone and dialled his number, but it went straight to the answer phone, so she hung up again, not wanting to leave a message, her shoulders dropping in disappointment. She really needed a chat with him right now but maybe he was busy at work, maybe he was at his new job that she was supposed to be joining him with? Questions, questions all the time with the men in her life. The good ones and the bad it seemed.

She opened the notebook again and began writing down in the back of it, all that she wanted to say to Dan, all that she needed to ask him and all that she needed to get sorted out. This was going to take some time, but she felt stronger than ever right now and had to think for the future, their future. If there was to be one with him, that was.

The following afternoon, just after lunch, Kate's phone rang to say Dan was being released at two o'clock. Rob had come over with Sally so they decided he should go and collect him as Kate was still feeling rough. She had hardly slept either, thinking over and over about everything she had been through over the past few days and weeks. The letter had been scoured within an inch of its life as she tried to puzzle it all together in her already frazzled brain. She was determined to be armed with all the details and all the questions for him when they did finally sit down and talk but it had all caught up with her and she now had the headache from hell as well as still being sore from the surgery.

Kate sat on the sofa, her brain aching, her heart pounding.

"I'm not too comfortable leaving you here alone with him if I'm honest Kate, darling" said Sally as they sat patiently together with coffees, waiting for Rob and Dan to arrive back home.

"I'll be fine auntie, honest. He's not going to hurt me, I know he isn't," Kate insisted as she stood up and stared out of the front window glancing up and down the street, "he's just made a mistake and he knows that. I just need to be alone with him and get the whole truth. Then we can work on the next chapter of getting him well again, concentrate on planning the wedding again maybe?"

"Just promise me you will call if you need us to

come back, yes?" Sally asked, standing behind her rubbing her shoulders.

"I will, I promise," Kate replied, holding her aunt's hand still on her shoulder.

"Why don't you sit back down, try and relax, I'll make some more coffee and…" but before she could finish, Kate gasped.

Rob's car appeared, turning into the road; they were back. Dan was home. She watched intently as they parked outside but for a few minutes, nothing happened, no doors opened. They were still in the car, she could see the figures inside, but they weren't moving, they weren't getting out.

"What do you think they're doing?" Kate asked, twitching at the curtains so not to be seen spying.

"Rob is probably having a word with him darling, I thought he might, you know. Man to man talk. Come on, come, and sit down, they'll be in soon."

Under duress, she came away from the window and sat at the kitchen table, spinning her fingers and thumbs around each other waiting. Five minutes later, they heard the door open, then two lots of footsteps were coming down the hallway. Kate held her breath in anticipation to what was about to arrive. She froze suddenly, she couldn't move as their eyes met. Dan was there, he was home standing just a few feet away from her, and she didn't know whether to scream or cry, kiss, or hit him. All she knew was that her heart was racing and thumping through her chest as they stared at one another.

Rob appeared behind Dan's figure and ushered Sally out of the room. For a moment, she felt she couldn't leave but knew Kate had to do this by herself. She squeezed Kate's hand and made her way forward. As she passed Dan in the doorway, she stopped for a second and glared at him, he looked away from her face and hung his head down. Just before they left the room, Sally turned around, mouthed to Kate to ring her, and then left with Rob closely following behind.

With only the sound of the dripping tap from the kitchen sink and the whirring, rumbling din of the fridge, Kate could feel her pulse drumming away. It seemed none of them knew what to do first, what to say and the silence was more awkward, more deafening than ever. There was no hot passionate sex this time round. No flowers, fancy wine, or anything to create a better atmosphere.

"Can I sit down?" he asked quietly.

She nodded back, not leaving the stare of his eyes for a second as he made his way to the chair opposite.

Her eyes were transfixed to his as he cleared his throat. It was so quiet in the room she even heard him swallow down hard, "Kate," he whimpered in a croaky tone, "I…I want to say I'm so sorry," he continued, again clearing his throat, "like a hundred times over. For all this I've put you through over the past few weeks, I really am sorry."

"You can't just keep saying sorry Dan," she snapped back, "just say you're sorry and expect it'll all be grand from here on in. There are so many questions I must ask you to get things clear in my head before we can move on from this," she said, suddenly gaining confidence to utter words to him.

"I know, I know, I have so much to explain to you all," down went his head again, "I'm so ashamed of myself but…" he paused, shaking his head slowly.

"But what?" she asked sternly. She really didn't want to be angry but if she just fell back into his arms like she really wanted to, would he then not tell her the truth that she needed to know? Would he try and fob her off with some feeble excuses or more lies? She had to try and keep strong as weak as she felt right at this moment, "Dan, just tell me the bloody truth, no more lying to me yeah?"

"Okay," he replied, raising his voice slightly in return, "look, give me a minute," he stood up and got a glass from the draining board, filled it with water and then sat back down. Swigging down the final mouthful, he then began leaning and turning the glass around on its edge.

She reached forward and took it from him, calmly repeating, "Dan…just tell me what's going on, please?"

Shuffling on his chair, he cleared his throat once again and looked straight at her. He knew he had to tell her everything now, absolutely all of it, so he took a deep breath and began, "when my dad died...I didn't cope with it too well. I used to have these episodes where I wouldn't go out, wouldn't see anyone, and just sit in my room getting angry and upset." The truth began to spill out of his mouth, much easier than he thought it would ever do so. His fiancé deserved these truths more than anyone else and he needed to get it out in the open once and for all, "my mum, well, she couldn't be there, so I had to rely on myself. I ended up sleeping rough after running away from the foster home where they had sent me. I didn't see mum for weeks after."

"Where was your mum Dan?" she asked knowing already but hoping he would reveal all by himself and proceed to give her more information about that sordid part of all this secrecy.

"Erm…I'll get to that bit in a minute." He stuttered awkwardly, shuffling around on his chair.

Her hopes dashed, she just had to continue listening for now.

"This is so hard for me Kate," his eyes were glazing over now, and his lips were starting to quiver like he was going to break down in tears any moment.

Kate's heart was aching so much, she couldn't help but reach for him. His hands were cold so she cupped them in hers and smiled softly at him, seeing just how hard it was for him to reveal these things to her, "I'm here for you, I just need to understand it all and then we can work it out okay?"

As he held her hands back tightly across the table, he took another deep breath, sniffed back, and said, "you are such an amazing person, you know that?"

She didn't reply, just smiled, and waited.

"You must believe me Kate, all I want is for someone to understand what has happened to me in the past and what I've had to keep to myself all these years," he paused, "no-one else would understand the utter pain and torment I've had to keep hidden, and maybe even you won't understand what it was like for me when I tell you everything. It's still to this day, so hard for me…you know, trying to cope with what I know and what happened, but you must believe me."

"I want to believe you Dan, I really do want to get to the bottom of all this. But it's just, well…" she paused now looking into his pained eyes, "your mum wrote me a letter, a very long letter explaining loads of things…so, I know where she is."

"What?" he froze staring back at her in shock.

"I know she's in prison Dan and to be honest, now, I feel like my life is playing a lead role in a crazy movie or something," she shook her head, "why did you tell me she was in a care home when she's in fact, in jail?"

"I don't know," he shook his head, frowning his eyebrows, "shame I guess," he replied shrugging his shoulders, "no-one else in the family has anything to do with her, or me in fact. Because I've stayed supporting her after what happened, they hate me for it but Kate, she's my mother, I can't just disown her, I can't do that can I?" he pleaded at her.

"No Dan, but if I don't know the full story I can't pass judgement on it all, can I?" Kate was desperate to get it all straight in her head so that they could finally move forward. After losing the baby, all the revelations from his mother and the assault, she didn't feel as if she could take anymore, "the truth, that's all I want from you. I want to know everything Dan, no more lies, no more secrets, please? I don't think I can take any more stress this week, I really don't feel strong enough."

"Alright, I promise. But it's not stuff that you're going to like, that I can be sure of." he replied.

"Try me. We won't know until you explain the whole truth to me will we?"

Dan looked lovingly into her eyes, which were tired, tearful but strong and all his emotions knew that he loved her so much right now, even more than he had done during the short time they had been together, "I love you Kate. I hope you still want to marry me when you find out the truth though," he squeezed her hands firmly, "I must ask you to do one thing. You must promise me something. This information must stay between us Kate. It's so important, more important than you know, and I can't tell you the full story unless you make me that promise right here and now," his voice was intensely serious and he didn't look away from her once, "you can't tell your aunt and uncle or anyone, can you promise me that?"

She nodded back bracing herself for the news that was about to be revealed to her. She couldn't imagine not telling her auntie about it, always relaying her life events to her throughout her years but something deep inside told her this was something different. Falling for Dan had been hard and fast, and she still loved him so much even with what was happening. She couldn't help how she felt and wanted to stand by him, make up her own mind as to if they were to continue their future together.

"Okay. Here goes…" he started.

Chapter Twenty-Three

His Side of The Story...

"From a very young age, maybe since I was about five years old, I watched my mum put up with so much from my dad. He was so violent, so abusive to her physically and mentally. He was a horrible human being Kate, he really was. Years I watched her suffer from his violence and the hurtful things he would shout to her every day almost. In the end, it just became too much for us both," he paused as he looked down to their hands still entwined. He rubbed over her fingers gently and then looked back up at her face, "he used to hit her, every night I would listen as he got drunk and would start yelling and swearing. After an hour or so, I would start hearing him smashing stuff. Most of the time, I would hide under my bed with a pillow over my ears, just to try and block the noise as best I could but it got louder and louder as the years went on," he looked down again as his voice began to crack with emotion.

Kate gave a reassuring squeeze to his hands, and he continued, "it's okay Dan, I'm here for you, carry on when you can," she spoke.

With a deep inhale of breath, he continued, "on my fourteenth birthday, I went downstairs to see my mum once I knew he had gone to the pub. I had hidden behind the door of my bedroom the whole time, and then crept to my window to watch him walk away from the house. When I went down to see her, she was sweeping up some broken glass from the floor, sobbing her heart out and as she turned to see me standing there, I could see blood smeared across her face. Her lip was cut, and her blouse sleeves were torn, just hanging off her arm it was."

"Oh my god, that's terrible," Kate moved forward on her chair and grasped at his hands even tighter, looking into his tearful eyes.

"It was Kate, it was such a horrible sight to see, seeing her hurt and bleeding like that. I'd heard it so many times before and stupidly, not done anything about it but, well...it just gradually kills you inside. My mum was so caring, and I let her down so badly over the years, not protecting her from him."

"You were a child, what the hell was you supposed to do, take him on yourself?"

"Well, that's the thing. I... I did take him on Kate, I took on my father," he took a deep breath and then exhaled deeply, "after I had helped her clean up, we sat down and made the decision that we had to get away from him before he did something worse to her, to both of us. I told her that I would sort it, you know, take care of her, and get away somewhere safe. Anyway, we planned to leave that weekend."

"And did you?" Kate asked quietly.

He sighed, "no. He came home early just as we were about to leave. He saw our two suitcases in the hallway and flipped," he let go of her hands and rubbed his forehead which was now hot and clammy with sweat, "we were literally just seconds away from getting out of the door. If only he hadn't come back early, it would never have happened, mum wouldn't be in prison, and I wouldn't be like I am, messed up and crazy."

"Dan, what happened? What did your mother do?"

Looking up again towards her concerned face, he could feel his heart thumping hard through his chest, "it's what we did Kate, we did it together."

"Did what? What do you mean?" she asked, frowning at him, and becoming increasingly worried about what he was going to say.

"He was yelling at us so loud. He grabbed hold of

my mum and threw her into the wall and I," he paused breathing heavily, "I couldn't take the shouting anymore. I just lost it, it was like something came over me and I couldn't help but,"

"Dan," she asked anxiously, "what did you do?" she repeated.

The silence fell in the room as she waited for him to take a few deep breaths again.

"I killed him," he finally announced the truth, "I killed my dad...it was me that stabbed my father to death that day. I murdered him."

Kate's hands relaxed back from his, "what do you mean? Your mum is the one in prison, not you. Please tell me you are joking?" she pleaded.

"I wish I was but no, it was me. Not her, not my poor mother," tears now escaped from his eyes as he looked at his beautiful lady in front of him whose face had turned an ashen shade of white.

Her eyes now dashing from one side to the other trying to comprehend what his words were saying, "I don't understand," she said, shaking her head, feeling her heart pounding.

"I was fourteen and she didn't want me to be put away in some youth prison detention centre thing, so she decided that we would say that she had done it. Like self-defence. I couldn't help it Kate, I couldn't have him hurt her anymore, but she insisted and that's why she is in prison instead of me. She got manslaughter charges because of the abuse she had suffered. The bruises and previous broken ribs were evidence against him."

"I... I don't know what to say," Kate stammered as she slumped back in her chair.

"She couldn't face knowing that I'd be held in some juvenile detention centre, my teenage life ruined so she took the blame and we have never told any of the family. It's just our secret that we've had to deal with, the two of us," he paused, watching Kate's astounded expression, "well, I guess now it's yours too."

"This is insane Dan," Kate glanced back at him stunned at the revelation.

"I'm a murderer Kate. I'm a rubbish son who let his mother down, killed my father and then let her take the blame and go to prison. I will completely understand if you would rather not see me again, call the engagement off, I can go now, and I'll never bother you again Kate."

She couldn't work it out in her head if she wanted to stay with him or not right now and silence ensued as he just stared at her confused face in the hope she would speak soon. After a few minutes, all she could muster up was, "I need a coffee, a strong coffee."

"I'll make it for you," he replied as he got up quickly and walked over to where the kettle stood. He looked back round to see her leaning forward onto the table with her head in her hands. Was she going to forgive him, was she going to stick by him and how much anxiety had he caused her to tell her this secret? He hated this whole situation so much, seeing the pain in her eyes, knowing that now, she was engaged to some monster that he saw himself as. He flicked the kettle switch and turned away from her.

"Dan…" she said, finally sitting back up after a few minutes, "your mum said you have bi-polar, is that true?"

"Yes," he replied, pouring the boiled water into the mugs, "when I met you, I went to visit her a few days later and told her all about you. I was so taken with you, the fact that you'd made me feel as though I could come off my medication. She warned me not to, but I didn't listen and that's why…well, that's why I went a bit…crazy."

"Is that why you hit that bloke from the restaurant?"

"Yes. I was waiting for you outside," he stirred the coffee and set the spoon on the side, "and I know this sounds a bit creepy, but, well, I was watching you all evening. I just wanted to be near you every minute of the day, and then I saw him slap you," he moved back to the table placing the cups down, "I couldn't handle it Kate, seeing him touch you like that. It brought back memories of my dad when he started hitting my mum. I saw the look on your face, and something snapped inside of me. I'd seen my mum take it for so long and upset for too many years and I didn't want it for you."

She looked at him sternly, "he was just an idiot bloke on a stag-do Dan, I was okay, didn't you see me slap him back? And watching me? Yes, that is a bit…well, slightly stalkerish."

"I know. It's stupid isn't it. I come off the meds and almost immediately, it made me do stupid things but I'm back on them. I promise you, I am," he insisted, "that's why I went to the police to confess about hitting that guy. I wanted to make things right when I realised how friggin stupid I'd been it was the wrong way to react. I'm sorry, I've let you down so badly haven't I?" he sat back down next to her, "do you think you will be able to love me still, forgive me for this?"

She turned to face him, his cheeks were blotchy and red, his eyes puffy and bloodshot but she did still love him, she would forgive him. The tragic events he'd been through during his childhood had been such a traumatic ordeal for anyone to deal with let alone only being a young child at the time too. She needed to be there for him, even if in the long term, it didn't pan out for a future together. She felt honoured in a way, that he had confided in her, no matter how much shock it had caused her. She knew how hard it must have been for him to disclose this awful secret past and she wanted to show him, now more than ever, how much she cared for him.

"Look, Dan. I do love you and I want us to work this out but, well," she paused, cupping her hands around his and his warm coffee mug, "what you've just told me is going to take some time to sink in and compute into my little brain," she smiled jokingly trying to lift the sad atmosphere, "I feel as though I need to know more about what happened that day. I don't need the details, but I just need to know facts if I'm supposed to keep this a secret now, you know, get the story straight?"

He leaned round to face her, looking lovingly and hopeful into her eyes, "I will tell you whatever you want to know Kate, no matter how many memories it brings back or hard it is. I love you so much and I can't lose you, not after telling you all of this for a start. I just can't live without you by my side supporting me."

They moved into the lounge and talked into the small hours about his past and what he had to go through for so many years. Kate showed him the letter from his mother and decided that once they had everything straight in their heads, they would visit her together. Let her know that he was alright, and Kate knew everything. It seemed the only way forward now for everyone.

The following morning, as Dan prepared breakfast and coffee downstairs, Kate sat up in bed and stared out of the window for a few minutes. She was tired from staying up so late talking things over, but she felt refreshed somehow in the fact that their relationship had moved to a whole new level in such an instant way. Her thoughts were suddenly interrupted as her phone began to vibrate on the bedside cabinet. She grabbed it quickly. It was Sally calling.

"How is everything Kate, we've been so worried about you both all night, we've hardly slept a wink you know," she exclaimed, before Kate even had a chance to say hello.

"Oh, I'm so sorry auntie, we just had too much to talk about and get things sorted out. We were chatting until about four this morning, I think it was in the end," Kate replied, instantly feeling guilty for not at least texting them last night to let them know she was okay.

"Oh dear, you poor darling. But how did it all go, or can't you talk at the minute?" she asked, almost whispering.

"As I said, we had a LOT to talk about," she emphasised, "but we have worked stuff out. He just made a mistake auntie with the assault thing, but I'm sticking by him. I want to help. There's so much you don't know about him, he's had a troubled past auntie, he really has been through some crazy stuff but, we are soon to be husband and wife so, I'm going to help him get better. And…We are also going to visit his mum as soon as possible."

"Oh, really?" she said, sounding worried, "that's going to be interesting…yes she's okay darling. Sorry your uncle was asking if you were alright, you know he worries like me. So, you're visiting the prison?"

"Yes. I really want to meet her, and he hasn't seen her in a few weeks what with disappearing like he did. I think it will do him good and like I said, I want to finally meet her as she'll be my mother-in-law soon, criminal, or not?"

"Oh, Katie darling, you are such a lovely human being, you really are just delightful. Your mother would be so proud of you sweetie. Do you know why she's in there though? Any info on what happened there?"

Just then, Dan walked in with a tray full of food and a rose from the front garden in a one of the small shot glasses, "auntie, can we chat later?" Kate spoke down the phone, "Dan's just made a lovely breakfast for me so I'm just going to have a bite to eat. Come round about eleven if you're free?" she smiled at him as he placed the tray onto her lap, giggling at the rose in the glass. He shrugged his shoulders back at her in jest and grinned.

"Alright sweetie," Sally replied, "it may be more like half past as I have someone collecting a parcel at eleven, is that okay?"

"No problem, see you then." Kate said blowing a kiss down the phone and then placing it back on the bedside cabinet.

"I guess they don't much like me at the moment, hey?" Dan asked, sitting next to her.

She grabbed his hand, "they'll stick by me

whatever I decide, if I'm okay, they are happy. Don't worry about them alright?" she leaned forward and kissed him straight on the lips, "aren't you having any breakfast, I can't eat all this Dan?" she said laughing, as she looked down at the bowl of cereal, two slices of toast, two boiled eggs and a croissant. He'd even squeezed some fresh orange juice for her as well as a coffee.

"Unfortunately, I must get to work. I need to try and explain why I've not been in these past few weeks. Probably not got a job anymore but hey, I've got to try and make things right everywhere haven't I?" he rubbed her legs.

"Oh okay, do you want me to come along with you? It won't take me long to get dressed."

"To a dirty building site, no darling. They'll all be drooling over you," he joked, "I'll be back straight after, if I have a job still obviously," he leaned forward and kissed her head before sneaking a slice of toast and taking a big bite.

As she watched him leaving, she remembered last night and how upset he'd been to learn about the baby loss. He had blamed himself for not being there for her and they'd even discussed trying again once things had calmed down. Kate wanted to wait until after the wedding, feeling it would be much better for them to get a few years behind them first after all they've been through already. She also needed to get back to work and see if Leo still had that big job offer for her, so she decided to eat as much as she could, build her energy up and have a quick shower before Sally arrived.

The croissant was lovely and warm, so she munched on that, sipped a big gulp of coffee, and got up out of bed. It certainly seemed to do the trick and as she began to decide which one of her favourite jogging sets to wear, she began to feel ready to tackle anything.

Chapter Twenty-Four

Time Will Heal...

"Hey Leo, that was weird. I was going to call you after I'd dried my hair," Kate had heard her phone ringing as she brushed her teeth in the bathroom and managed to answer it before it rang off. She was so pleased to see Leo's face on the screen as they switched to a video call, and to hear his lovely smooth voice made her smile as per usual.

"Well, there you go. Great minds think alike hey?" he replied chuckling, "how are you babe, you look…refreshed?"

"Why thank you, yes, I'm doing okay, considering, but you won't believe what's been going on."

"Ooh, gossip hey?" he joked, looking closer into the screen.

"Well, sort of yeah. There's stuff I can't talk about but...well I had a letter from Dan's mum, revealing all sorts, Dan is back and you were right, it was him that night of the fight but it's cool," she continued as she saw his face turn shocked and concerned for her, "we've talked about everything, he knows about the baby and that too, he was devastated but, we're working things out Leo and it feels...I dunno, better?"

"Crikey babe...that's certainly enough to deal with hey? Jeez, I need to come and see you properly, but I've got work in about an hour, and it's a late one tonight, sorry."

"Oh, it's okay mate, honestly, we can just chat until you need to get off. I wish I was there with you though. I was so looking forward to the job and working with you, just the two of us as a team."

"You will soon be with me darling and he's really looking forward to meeting you...oh, hang on one sec," he paused as the screen turned to paused and all went quiet for a minute, "look, I'm sorry but I gotta go," he came back on screen saying, "he's just messaged me asking if I can get round a bit earlier. He's got some hot date coming over," he laughed, "I'll call you when I'm home if it's not too late, failing that, tomorrow yeah?"

"Oh, ok mate. Speak soon," and they blew out a kiss to each other before finishing the call.

Kate sighed as she glanced at her reflection in the

tall mirror on her wardrobe and threw her phone onto the bed. Her towel was wrapped around her body, her hair still dripping wet. Suddenly emotions got the better of her as she let the towel drop to the floor and moved her eyes towards her belly. The empty belly that once housed her new life made her shed a tear right there and then and it felt horrible. She felt like life had thrown her a new chapter and then ripped it from underneath her as quick as it had arrived. Scooping the towel up, she had to shake herself out of it. It would never feel any easier, but she had to try and be strong, get her new job with Leo and help Dan with all his troubles and strife. She tousled her hair and quickly towel dried it, leaving it to form the natural wave it always had and made her way downstairs.

Washing up the last of the breakfast mess, she decided to take a short walk to the corner shop and see if they had any wedding magazines. She needed some inspiration and thought also that the walk may clear her head a little. The last few days had clogged it up to the very maximum and at the end of the day, she really had to build her strength up in preparation for the prison visit more than anything. She thought about the contents in the letter again and wondered if she should re-read it and make notes.

As she took her time walking, the neighbours' inflatable snowman peered down at her. The Harrisons family were always the first to put up their decorations for Christmas and they succeeded every year in creating the best display. This year, there was a new addition; a family of three reindeer on the front lawn, with good old Rudolph being head of the gang. It made Kate smile as she passed by nearly bumping into another oncoming admirer.

"Oh, my goodness, I'm so sorry, I was miles away in snowman land," she said apologetically, holding her arms in front of her and giggling.

"No problem at all young lady," he replied, nodding his flat cap towards her reddened face.

"David is that you?" she suddenly realised it was one of the regular diners from the restaurant.

He looked back at her for a second and then smiled, "Ahh, the beautiful Katie. I'm so sorry my love, I think I was away with it too, mesmerised by the new reindeer family," he chuckled, using his walking stick to point toward the garden.

"They are rather lovely aren't they?" Kate replied, "How are you anyway, we've not seen you and Betty for a while?" she asked as they stood admiring the lights flickering away on the garden wall. It didn't matter that it was daytime for the Harrisons, as soon as Christmas arrived in their garden, it was pretty much twenty-four seven lights and decorations until the third week of January.

"Oh, you see my young one, I've not been too...erm...sociable...my Betty passed away I'm afraid," he said, "a few weeks back now."

"David, I'm so sorry," Kate rubbed his arm as he leaned against the wall. The two of them had always come in for lunch and ordered the same menu each time. Ham and cucumber sandwiches with a large slice of Victoria sponge and a pot of tea to share. Kate had loved serving them when she had been on the lunch shift and loved the way they used to hold hands as they supped on their teacups. Betty had always asked for one splodge of clotted cream with her cake slice and Kate used to find the word 'splodge' so funny. They'd often joke 'one splodge or two' when it came to cake time, but it would always only ever be one.

"It's alright my dear girl. She went very peacefully in her sleep, bless her," he continued, "the funeral is yet to come though, just a week before Christmas I might add," he began straightening up his coat and hat, "it's at the big church on Saffron Street…on the eighteenth if you'd like to attend. But I understand if you would rather not, it's all a bit of a grim event isn't it, the funeral lark I mean. When you get to our age dear, it's kind of a regular task we must deal with, you know."

Kate couldn't help but giggle. He was so funny but cute at the same time. She wished she had a grandparent like him. Even discussing the death of his wife didn't faze him or stop his light-hearted attitude towards life in general.

"I would love to come and show my respects

David, if you're sure it's okay for me to come that is. Betty was always so lovely and so nice to me at work. What time is it?"

"Erm, I believe it's eleven thirty sharp my dear but please, you don't have to. It's just a small gathering, there's not many of us oldies left to be fair," he chuckled again, "anyway, you take care dear. I must rush off now, see if there are any more reindeers showing up in the street. I doubt they'll win over these guys though hey," he laughed nudging her arm gently, and with that, he began walking away.

Kate's thoughts turned to her own mother and how much she missed her. She would've loved all the wedding plans and Christmas was such a fun time for them both. The tree would go up on the first of December without fail and they would sit for hours making paperchains to hang from the ceiling. They had always gone to Sally and Rob's for Christmas dinner and then had Boxing Day by themselves visiting her mother's parents' graves in the afternoon. Kate had always made a little wreath to place on them with the holly that grew in their garden. Fiona had talked about them to Kate, showed her photos of them when Fiona was growing up and holidays they'd been on before they died. Kate was only one when her Grandpop, as they called him, had passed away and then six months later, Nanapop had died too, so she never got to know them properly or remembered them very well. She quickly made a note of the funeral date in her phone and set a reminder for the day before, then continued her walk to the shop.

Armed with five of the best wedding magazines with a free wedding planning notebook on one of them, Kate chucked them all onto the kitchen table on her return home. She couldn't wait to delve into them and show Dan when he got home but it was nearly half eleven now and she was also excited to see Sally.

"Hi ya my darling, I'm sorry I'm a tad late, delivery guy was late, then the blooming traffic today," said Sally as she finally arrived just after twelve thirty, "I tell you, sometimes I think I'd get places a lot quicker if I just got off my butt and walked," they laughed as the usual air kissing ensued.

"That's okay, I've been keeping busy with these, look," she showed Sally the array of magazines still strewn across the table, "Auntie, all the dresses, flowers, cakes, how the hell am I supposed to choose what we want and what's best?" she switched the kettle on and took two mugs out of the dishwasher.

"Hah-ha," she chuckled back, "that's what I'm here for sweetie. It's all changed so much already since me and your uncle Rob got married. I mean there are these booth things you and your guests can sit in for photos, you know like passport booths, and some of the cakes don't even look real if you ask me, they are crazy clever with sugar art nowadays. I mean why would you want to ruin that by cutting it up?" she pointed towards a four-tier iced cake that was half white with gorgeous red icing flowers draped down one side, and the other half was dripping chocolate styled with strawberries dipped half in white chocolate, placed on one of the tiers.

"Whoa, that's insane," Kate replied looking over her shoulder, "I have no idea what we would have, I don't even really know what type of cake Dan likes."

"Maybe you should make it darling, it would be more personal, hey?"

"Mmm, it's an idea but, I don't know auntie, it's a big responsibility, the cake is one of the main attractions of the day isn't it? I think I'll talk to Leo and see if he knows someone. Here," she passed Sally her mug of coffee.

"Well, I guess so, but you certainly have the talent for it if you wanted to do it."

For the next few hours, they chatted about all things wedding related and a little bit about what had happened with Dan, the assault, and the police. Kate had promised him she wouldn't tell the full story to anyone, and she wasn't going to let him down, as much as she wanted to tell her aunt absolutely everything. For now, it was her and Dan's secret.

At just after four o'clock, they heard the front door unlocking, time had flown by but now Dan was home.

"I think I'll get off now sweetheart, leave you two to

go through all of these ideas," Sally said as she stood up from the kitchen table, "Hello Daniel," she said as he appeared at the kitchen doorway.

"Hello Sally," he returned, coyly in a lowered tone of voice, shying away from making direct eye contact with her.

"Right then, don't forget," she turned to face Kate giving her a peck on the check, as she made her way down the hallway, "we can have a trip to London to look at some dresses when you are ready, just let me know some days and I will book us in for some champagne lunch at the Ivy while we are there. Have a good old girls' day out okay darling,"

Kate nodded.

"Cheerio then," and landing another quick kiss on Kate's check and a big hug, Sally left.

Dan stood in the doorway of the hall, kicking his work boots off and Kate noticed that he pushed them to one side instead of leaving them in the middle like usual. Inwardly smiling, she walked back over to him.

"How was work? You still got the job?"

"Yes, thankfully. The boss was cool about everything, he's gonna do me a character reference for the police and that just in case anything else comes of it." he replied, shrugging his shoulders.

"Aww, that's good of him. Do you want a coffee or anything to eat yet?" Kate rubbed his arms gently as she got closer.

"Maybe in a bit," he said, wrapping his arms

around her waist, "I need to talk to you first, it's about my mother."

"Oh?" she replied looking worried, "Is she okay?"

"Yeah, yeah, she's fine. It's just…" he glanced down.

"Dan, what is it?" she asked, "is everything alright with her?"

"Yeah, I phoned to arrange a visit, you know, like we said to go and talk to her, so that you could meet her and that?"

"And?"

"Well, she said no. She's refused the meeting; she said no to seeing us."

"What? Why? She said in her letter she wanted to meet me. Why would she now change her mind about that?" Kate pulled back a little in surprise.

"I'm not sure babe. She's a complex woman, my mum. I will try again in a few days just in case she's just feeling a bit under the weather or something," he lifted her hand up and twiddled with her engagement ring, "she'll be alright in a week or so, she does this sometimes."

"Maybe I should put a request in?" Kate asked, entwining her fingers in his.

"No best not. Let's get a takeaway tonight hey, bottle of wine and curl up on the sofa," he changed the subject, "I've missed doing that these past few weeks."

"Okay," Kate replied disappointed at the news.

She really wanted to meet his mother face to face but not wanting to push it, she agreed to an evening in and watched him as he walked off tapping on his phone at various food options. Inwardly, she really hoped that he wasn't lying to her about his mum not wanting to see them. She decided to give it a few days like he said and then approach the subject again if an appointment had not been made. She was determined to meet her future mother-in-law sooner rather than later.

Chapter Twenty-Five

Money Matters...

The following week, Kate returned to work. December seemed to be flying past and the Christmas party rush was in full swing. She had given her notice for her new job with Leo but had promised Max, her manager that she wouldn't leave until January.

"If ever you need some extra work, just let me know yeah," Max said as they finished up for the afternoon shift, "we will be very sorry to see you go but...I can understand the change in wages and the excitement of it all."

"Cheers Max, yes, the money is going to be amazing, and it will help with the wedding a lot." Kate exclaimed, hanging her apron up in her staff locker.

"If we could match it…well, I'd certainly be asking you to stay on."

"Aww thanks Max, you really have been a great boss and if you do need cover and I'm available, I'm happy to help out," she rubbed his arm as they made their way out into the main restaurant, "see you tomorrow."

Kate left and popped into the local shopping centre to find a black dress for the funeral the next day. She'd already raided her wardrobe thinking she had one but must have chucked it out at some point. Unable to find a dress, she opted for some black trousers and a black blouse which had subtle flickers of white butterflies through it. She remembered that Betty always used to tell her about the different types of butterflies that used to fly into their garden during the springtime. She would've liked this blouse; Kate was sure of it.

As she grabbed a coffee from a local mobile van, her phone began to ring, it was Dan.

"Hey beautiful, where are you?"

"I'm just in town, had to get an outfit for the funeral tomorrow, you okay?" she asked sipping on the latte.

"Funeral?" he said, "what funeral babe?"

"I told you last night. A lady who used to come into the restaurant, Betty. It's tomorrow at half eleven, don't you remember me telling you last night after dinner?"

"Erm, oh yeah maybe, sorry. My mind has been a mess since talking to mum earlier."

"Is she alright? Is she agreeing to see us yet?"

"Afraid not darling. I am going to try again in a few days though. I don't understand what's going on with her. Anyway, I've just got in, so I'll start the dinner if you like?"

"That'll be great, thanks honey, I won't be too long, just gonna get the bus so about half hour and I'm all yours." She smiled into the phone.

"Can't wait, see you soon babe, bye." And he hung up.

Kate racked her brains as to why his mother would've changed her mind now about meeting her and, why she didn't even want to see Dan for that matter. Her letter seemed so friendly and inviting, it didn't make sense why she would be refusing visits now. Kate stepped onto the bus as it finally arrived and began thinking to herself that if Anna wouldn't see them in the next week, she would try and write to her and ask why. Maybe then, they would get a better idea of what was going on. Maybe then, finally, they would get to meet.

For the rest of the journey, she scrolled through her Instagram and Facebook, laughing at some of the hilarious videos that some of her friends posted. She was only on the platforms to see their news and hardly ever posted her updates.

When she returned home, Dan had made a meal of salmon, broccoli, and Mash potato so they sat down together with a bottle of wine.

"It's lovely to be back here with you Kate, I really missed you when I was away." He reached across the table and held her hand.

"It's nice to have you back," she replied looking lovingly at him, "have you heard any more from the police?" she asked, taking a mouthful of salmon.

"Not yet. I guess they gotta talk to the guy and see if he's pressing charges or not. They did say that he might not because of the fact he had sort of assaulted you in the first place…frigging idiot."

"Dan…" Kate said in a calming voice.

"Sorry," he apologised, "do you want any desert, I got some strawberries and cream?"

"That'd be lovely, thanks."

Everything seemed to be going so smoothly with them both. He was calm, taking his medication and there was no funny episodes or anger issues. She liked it this way and began to feel safe with him once again. They'd not made love since his return and surprisingly, he was being really good about that fact after she said she needed a bit of time to get used to him being back and all the shocking revelations that had come with him.

The next morning, after trying to get through another huge breakfast that he'd made for her before he went to work, she started to get ready for the funeral. She was going to walk there as it wasn't far from her house. She packed a change of clothes for her work shift afterwards and was on her way.

She arrived at the church and saw David sitting on the bench outside. Sitting beside him, she placed her hand onto his, "How you are doing?" she asked.

"Oh, sweet Kate, you came." he replied looking up.

"I said I would," she smiled sweetly at him. He looked so frail today, but he still managed his lovely grin back.

"You are a sweet girl Kate, you really are. I'm doing alright you know, all things considered. To be honest with you, I'm sort of looking forward to closure and laying my beloved to rest. She never liked waiting around for things you know dear." He chuckled, rubbing her hand, "ah, talk of the devil." He nodded towards the road where the hearse had just arrived.

The coffin seemed so little and was covered with white roses. Kate could see a wreath in the shape of a butterfly too and glanced down at her blouse. Butterflies galore seemed even more fitting for this occasion now and she felt happy in her choice.

"Kate, sweet Kate," David said as he slowly stood up, "when you find your special someone, don't let them go my dear girl, love them as much as you can because," he paused swallowing hard, as his emotion got the better of him, "before you know it, you're an old ancient thing like me and you're forced to say goodbye to your one true love," he straightened his tie, "now, let's go get my beautiful Betty, let's say goodbye shall we?"

Kate felt her throat closing with emotion for him and his grief. She thought to herself what a wonderful man he was and the fact that he was being so brave today. She hoped she would feel like that in many years to come. She hoped she had found her special true love in Dan.

With the funeral service over, she stood outside waiting to say goodbye to David. He had so many people surrounding him, hugging and shaking hands, he looked deeply sad. She couldn't help but think back to her mum's funeral and how terrible she had found it when the coffin had finally disappeared behind the crematorium curtains. Deciding not to attend the wake afterwards, she made her way over to David, "Hey," she said gently, "that was a beautiful service David, Betty got a wonderful send-off didn't she?"

"Oh yes my dear, she planned it to the note you know Kate. She knew exactly how she wanted to go on up to the big guy in the sky," he pointed upwards smiling, "she'll be waiting for me now though, I'd better watch my back hey." He joked.

Kate couldn't help but giggle at his always happy demeanour even at this sad time, "you take care okay. And come and have tea at the restaurant, my treat. I'm leaving in January, so I'd love to visit before I go."

"Oh yes…the new job. Righto, I'll arrange something for next week and Kate," he held out his hand towards hers, "thank you for coming along dear, I know it's not a nice thing for you young'uns to think about."

"David it was lovely of you to ask me, I loved Betty and all her stories."

"She did have some tales didn't she," he chuckled, "she would've adored that blouse too."

"I thought that."

"Right, I'm being summoned," he pointed over to his two sons who were waiting by the funeral car to take them to the wake, "You are welcome to come along dear."

"I won't if it's okay David." She replied.

"Not a problem. I'll see you soon."

They said their goodbyes after walking to the car together and then Kate decided to call her aunt. She wasn't in work until half four today plus she could change into her uniform at her aunts instead of at work. The phone was answered within seconds with Sally's usual friendly manner, "Hi sweetie…"

"Hi. I've got a few hours before my shift, can I come over and see you?" Kate asked, walking briskly across the road to grab a coffee quickly from the shop opposite.

"Of course, my darling. I'll get the kettle on, ooh and could you pick up a pack of those shortbread biscuits you like. Rob ate the last of the stash I tried so hard to hide from him, the cute little piglet that he is."

"Sure, no probs, see you soon." Kate replied chuckling. They said their goodbyes, blew kisses down the phone and then she was on her way.

Arriving ten minutes later, biscuits in one hand and a small bunch of flowers in the other, for her aunt, Kate knocked and waited. Within minutes, Sally was at the door, greeting her with the usual massive cuddle and a kiss to both cheeks.

"Aww, they're beautiful Kate darling, thank you so much, how thoughtful," Sally said as she took the blooms and ushered Kate inside.

"Not as grand as the ones Uncle Rob gets but thought you may like them."

"Darling, you know I love all things flowery, and remember, it's not the size that counts sweetheart…" Sally replied making them both chuckle, "come on in, the coffee is brewing."

Kate made herself comfortable on the sofa while Sally prepared a tray of coffee and biscuits. Glancing up at the fireplace, she noticed the picture of her mother and Sally when they were younger. It made her smile, and she got back up to take a closer look just as Sally walked in.

"This is such a cute picture, how old were you both?" asked Kate holding the frame.

"Oh…I think Fiona was about six maybe which

would mean I would've been eight ish?"

"It's lovely."

"We were at the seaside in Frinton-on-Sea. She had just had a bit of a paddy because mum wouldn't let her have chocolate sauce on her ice-cream," she laughed, "I think dad took her back over to the van and sneaked some on though, look," she pointed towards Fiona's mouth, "you can definitely see chocolate round her mouth, bless her. She could wrap dad round her little finger she could. Bit like you and Uncle Rob darling." She nudged Kate's arm jokingly, "coffee will be two secs."

Kate returned the photo and stroked her mum's face, whispering, "miss you mum," kissed her finger and placed it on the photo once more.

"So, what have you been up to this morning?" called Sally from the kitchen.

"Had a funeral, hence the black clothes. A lovely lady who used to come into the restaurant with her husband, Betty, and David," Kate paused as Sally placed the tray on the coffee table, "have I told you about them before?"

"Erm, Betty rings a bell yes, I think you've told me some of their funny love stories."

"They were such a cute couple. I bumped into David the other day and he asked me to go along so, yeah, that's where I've been this morning."

"I hate funerals, ever since your mothers, I've not been able to attend anymore. I dread to think about, well," she lowered her voice, "if Rob goes before me."

"Let's not talk about it hey." Kate interrupted.

"Yes, good idea. Anyway, I'm glad you popped over. I wanted to give you this." Sally handed Kate an envelope.

"What is it?"

"Open it and see silly billy." Sally began opening the pack of biscuits and placing them onto the side plate from the tray.

Kate ripped open the envelope and pulled out a rectangular piece of paper. It was a cheque, written out to her for ten thousand pounds, "What?"

Before she could say or ask anything further, Sally put her fingers to Kate's mouth, "it's our wedding present to you darling…do not tell me you won't accept it alright. Spend it on the wedding plans, your dress, the honeymoon, whatever."

"But auntie, are you sure?"

"Kate, darling. Your mum left five thousand pounds for you in an account with strict instructions that it would be used for your wedding so…Rob and I agreed to match it so you had a nice bit of money to get those wedding plans in place and…" she paused sipping her coffee, "it means your mum has been part of the wedding planning too so, please, pop it away, use it and enjoy."

"I don't know what to say," Kate stared down at the cheque, then flung her arms around Sally nearly causing a coffee spillage, "Thank you, thank you so much. I love you all so much." Tears had welled up in both their eyes and as they sat enjoying their drinks and biscuits, Kate scrolled through her phone showing her aunt all the wedding ideas.

She was even more excited about all the extras she could now provide for their big day without having to worry Dan. He'd been working extra hours at another building site so that he could add to the wedding fund but now, with this boost, maybe he wouldn't work so much, and they could plan this together a little bit more. Since the engagement, it had been her gathering all the information about cakes, flowers, dresses, suits; she felt sure he would be more involved now that he didn't need to work so many extra hours to pay for it.

Chapter Twenty-Six

Together Plans…

Kate's work shift went by quickly, and she was so excited to get home to tell Dan about the wedding fund money. Instead of waiting for the bus, she called a taxi, texting Dan on the way that she would be home soon and had some news.

Stumbling up to the front door, laden with bags, she fumbled to get her keys from her pocket and shoved them into the lock. Just as she began to turn the key, the door opened. Dan was standing there in blue denim shorts and no top, she smiled up at him and he winked back, grasping hold of the shopping by her feet. She had got the taxi to drop her at the corner shop before arriving home to grab something for dinner. It was only a five-minute walk back and she now wished she had not bought so much.

"So, my mum has agreed to have a meeting, but it's just with me for now," he said as they began to unload one bag of groceries.

"Oh?" replied Kate, disappointed, "why doesn't she want to meet me Dan? Why did she say in the letter that she did and now…?"

"I told you before babe, she's a complicated woman my mother. Let me go see her and then I can tell her how much you wanna meet her yeah?" he rubbed the small of her back as she stretched up to put the pasta into the cupboard above.

"I guess so…just please tell her, well…that I really want to meet her. She's going to be my mother-in-law soon for goodness' sake," she paused, "do you think she would be allowed out for the day to attend as a guest. You know, like they do in the movies, day release or something they call it don't they?" She chuckled as did he.

"I'm not sure, movies are very different from real life babe. Especially where prison is concerned," he replied, arching his eyebrows, and turning to the packs of meat on the side, "anyway, I'm starving, let's get dinner sorted hey? What we got here?"

Reluctantly, she decided to give up pushing any further with the discussion hoping that once he had been to see his mum, a visit could be arranged with her going along finally. She was getting desperate to meet this intriguing woman and get to ask her about

Dan some more. For tonight though, she wanted to chill out with him and hopefully cheer him up with her financial news.

Turning the oven on, she then grabbed hold of her handbag. "Before we eat, I have some exciting news actually," pulling out the envelope that her aunt had given her earlier, she held the cheque in front of her face, "check this out," she said, emphasising the word check, and laughing at her own joke, "excuse the pun, but look what we got."

"What's this for?" he asked taking the cheque and reading it.

"My aunt gave it to me this afternoon. Apparently, my mum left me some money for when I had wedding plans and then my aunt matched the amount as a gift to us, so," wrapping her arms around his waist, glancing down at the piece of paper in his hands, she continued, "ten thousand pounds Dan, ten thousand bloody pounds!" she repeated just a tad bit louder, "we can splash out a bit more now, have a better honeymoon too. What about having that big car you liked, to take us to the reception venue, you know," she carried on excitedly, leaving his side and reaching for a wedding magazine that was perched on the sideboard, "was it a Rolls Royce or the white Bentley you fell in love with?" her fingers flicked as fast as she could get them to, through the pages until she came to the wedding cars section, waving the article in front of him, "look at that, it's beautiful, we can have one of those to take us to the church as well now with that money."

He looked blankly back at her and then towards the cheque again.

"What do you think?" she asked, hoping he would grab hold of her, swing her round and they could celebrate.

"I'm not sure I like the idea," he bluntly replied, placing the cheque face down onto the table and sliding it toward her.

Kate was confused, yet again by his weird reaction. They'd talked about the cars in all the exciting days after the initial engagement and now he seemed like he didn't want any of it. She watched in a stunned silence for a minute as he fetched himself a beer from the fridge and began walking away from the kitchen, "I thought you'd love one of those cars. Didn't you want a nice journey in one for our big day?" she probed, still puzzled as to why he wouldn't want to accept the money and get the dream wedding they had both talked about. She knew he loved big fancy cars, and this could be his chance to travel in one and for such a special occasion too.

"Kate," he turned in the doorway, "I just want a small wedding you know that. We don't need anything fancy or plush, it's not your rich relatives wedding, it's just us. I don't want their bloody money to pay for my wedding stuff. I wanna be the one who pays for it okay?"

"I know but…"

"Why don't we put it towards a new car instead of that old banger you drive round in?" he interrupted, slurping another big gulp of beer down his throat.

"I don't want a new car and…because my mum wanted it used for my wedding, that's why?" she sternly replied pumping her chest out slightly and crossing her arms.

He shook his head at her, "I'm tired alright Can we drop the subject yeah?" His deep eyes looked straight into hers as if to let her know that this conversation was over, finished. There was nothing else she could answer back, and she did not want to start an argument with him. Her head tilted down, and he walked off into the lounge, plonking himself on the sofa with his feet aloft on the coffee table. Grabbing the TV controls, he switched it onto the sports channel to watch a rugby match that had already started.

Kate stood in the doorway of the lounge watching on. She couldn't understand why he'd just cut off their conversation like he had and now was oblivious to her standing there wanting an answer or at least an explanation as to why he'd changed his mind regarding the wedding car he'd gone on about so much, just weeks before today. She remembered how excited he had seemed days after the engagement but now, he was distant, and it seemed like he never wanted to discuss the big day. As much as she wanted to continue talking it over, or at least try to, she didn't want to annoy him, so she turned back into the kitchen and started preparing the vegetables to go into the steamer.

Once the veg was pealed and the family size chicken and mushroom pie was in the oven, she went to check the post, supplying Dan with a fresh cold beer on the way.

"Oh, cheers darling," he said, slapping her behind as she passed in front of him, "you're a gem, you know that though right?" but before she could say anything, he promptly went on shouting something at a player on the television.

Standing in the hall, she flicked through the various junk mail leaflets, optician invitations and pointless window and doors offers. The last thing in the pile she noticed was another envelope like Anna's previous letter. Nervously, she glanced into the lounge to ensure Dan was still sitting there engrossed in the match. He was happily swigging his beer, legs crossed on the table, so she called out to him, "Dan, I'm just gonna run a bath while the dinner is cooking, can you keep an eye on the veg?...Dan...?"

Some sort of grunt of agreement came back so she made her way upstairs and locked herself in the bathroom, staring down at the envelope. She wasn't sure if she should open it or not but then again, why would Anna have written again so soon. She hastily ripped open the envelope and carefully unfolded the letter. It was only one page long this time so frantically, she began to read.

'Hello again Kate. I just wanted to write to you once more because Daniel has been in to see me. He seems better in himself so you must have convinced him to get back on his medication. This is good news and so, I just wanted to thank you really. I've not told him that I have written this and it's probably best that you keep it to yourself too. You must know by now how unpredictable he can be with secrets. Anyway, thank you Kate; and I do hope you will change your mind about not coming to see me. Dan said you are nervous but honestly, I won't bite. Xxx Anna. Xx

Kate's eyebrows frowned and she had to read it through one more time to make sure. He'd been to see her, although he told her he hadn't. She didn't understand any reason why he would lie to her especially about this subject. Especially when he knew how much she wanted to meet her future mother-in-law. But now, another letter had come, and she couldn't tell him about it. She decided there and then, to write back to her without him knowing. She needed some clarity on what was going on between them and more importantly, who was lying to her. Once the Christmas rush was over, she was determined to get a letter penned and arrange to visit her in prison. Get some final answers to the mysteries that were surrounding her fiancé and his mother. She only had a few weeks to wait and then she would do it, find out some truths finally, hopefully.

*

The final week of December came, and Kate had her last shift working at the restaurant. It had been an emotional evening and she'd enjoyed having a few drinks afterwards with the team. Leo had even come along as a surprise, which had made her cry even more. Max had a cake made for her and the other girls had bought her flowers and a personalised apron with 'Kate, Bad Ass Baker' embroidered across the front. Although she was sad to be leaving this place, she knew she would visit them all often and her new job was going to be so exciting and different.

Christmas day was spent at her place with Dan and then boxing day at her aunts. Dan hadn't wanted to stay for too long and made an excuse to leave after a few hours saying he had a headache. Not wanting him to be alone at home, Kate left with him.

"You sure everything's okay darling," Sally asked as Kate walked toward the door following Dan who'd already got into his car.

"Yes auntie, all fine. I think he may have had too much to drink yesterday. Our first Christmas together and we get sloshed on Gin shots." She laughed hoping her voice would sound reassuring enough for Sally not to ask any further questions.

Kate knew deep down; he didn't have a headache. He just didn't want to spend all day and night there. They'd already had that conversation a month ago when Kate had told him the plans for the festive period.

"They are going to be your in-laws soon Dan." She'd remarked to him, "and I've never not seen them at Christmas, it will be so weird for me."

"It's just that it's our first one together, I wanted it to be a bit, well, you know, special," he'd replied, using his seductive eyes to convince her this time, "and after everything that has happened these past few months, the baby and that…" he paused, holding her hand as they stood in the kitchen.

Her heart hurt so much whenever the baby was mentioned, and she knew he was hurting too. He'd not even had the chance to know about it so, they had finally agreed with the plans and although Kate really wanted to be at her aunts, she knew she had to play it safe and spend it with him this year. She thought back to her imagining the next few years to come, in two or three years, they'd have had some married life together and there could even be a new baby in the picture. She would then be able to have a big family Christmas of their own. For now, they would build their future and look forward to new beginnings and of course the wedding in the new year.

Chapter Twenty-Seven

Anna…

January crept up and Kate was excited to begin her new job finally, working alongside Leo. Within a few days, she had made herself familiar around the kitchen, wine cellar and outside dining area. The place was more amazing in real life, the photos that Leo had shown her so many weeks ago didn't do this place justice, and every day, she felt extremely proud to be working for such a high-end client.

This evening, they had catered a four-course meal for twenty people and by the end of the night, her, and Leo, felt shattered and pleased to finally get in the car and make their way home.

Leo had driven tonight wanting to show off his new car. They got in, he pushed a few buttons and then set off for the half hour drive to drop Kate place.

"So, any news on the mother-in-law-to-be yet? Has she agreed to see you?" Leo asked as he turned the music down after having a singalong together.

"No," Kate replied, trying to work out how to switch the air con on, "I sent the letter so it's a waiting game now, I suppose. I need to know what's going on, you know. It's all got so…weird. I don't know who to believe. And I can't really talk to Dan about it, not yet anyway. I just need my mind put at rest; it's been driving me insane."

"I can imagine. I think you're doing the right thing though mate, go see her, get some answers, and then confront him, just…" he paused, leaning forward to switch the right button, immediately directing the fans to blow cold air onto their faces.

"What is it Leo? Say it." She glanced across at him.

"Just be careful yeah. I worry about you mate. He's so…"

"He's so what..?" Kate replied quickly. In her heart she knew Leo had never really been sure of Dan, from the first time they met but he wouldn't admit that to her, "Leo…?" she pressed, as he avoided eye contact with her.

He cared way too much about their friendship and working relationship to say that he didn't trust the man one little bit. "Unpredictable," he finally answered.

Kate looked away from him, saddened by hearing

what she knew was the truth about her fiancé. He was unpredictable but she loved him, she loved that about him for some unknown reason.

"You know what his moods can be like, suddenly changing at the drop of a hat," Leo continued, reaching across, reassuringly squeezing her hand, "especially when it's to do with his mother."

Kate glanced down into her lap at their hands entwined now and took a deep breath.

"Don't be sad Kate. I'm sorry, I'm here for you whatever you decide, I just don't wanna see you hurt and upset."

Looking back at him, she smiled, "I know Leo and thanks but…well, I'm gonna find out what the hell is going on, one way or another, I'm gonna get the truth at some point, from someone."

"You will. And I can't wait to see what the mother says to you."

"Me too. Anyway, let's drop the subject hey, could we stop off at the garage before you drop me off. I'm gonna get a bottle of wine."

"Sure." He replied beaming a massive smile across at her, then turning the radio back up so they could enjoy his tuneless singing performance again.

When she eventually arrived home, she found Dan fast asleep in bed already, so she crept back downstairs, poured herself a glass of wine and re-read the letters from his mother once more. She really hoped the list of questions she had made in her notebook, would help her get the answers she craved for soon. Hiding them back in the cupboard drawer, she sipped her wine up, pulled a blanket over her tired body, and fell asleep.

The next morning, Kate got a letter with an appointment to visit Anna on the following Sunday afternoon. The week seemed to go on forever waiting for Sunday to arrive, but she'd had plenty to keep her busy. She had booked to attend a local wedding show with Sally and Leo mid-morning and would make her way to the prison afterwards. Dan had promised to come to the wedding show after his rugby game but as they finished tasting cake samples, smelling flowers, and watching the bridal catwalk parade, he was a no show. A short text message came through as they were leaving the venue to say he had to work an extra few hours, and that he was sorry.

Leo and Sally just gave each other a concerned look as they watched Kate read the message. Her face changed from an excited bride-to-be in that instant, but she wasn't going to admit her disappointment. She didn't want them thinking bad of him and there would be plenty of other wedding fairs he could be at. "He's had to work through." She told them.

But in a way, maybe him not turning up today was for the best anyway. It now saved her from making some false story up regarding where she was going afterwards.

"Are you sure you don't want me to come along?" Leo asked as they said their goodbyes outside the venue.

"No honestly, I'll be fine. It's only booked for me anyway. It's all very strict," she grimaced a nervous face at them both, "are you okay to drop auntie off?"

"Yep sure, no problem."

"Let us know how you get on sweetie?" Sally asked, kissing her on the cheek.

"Will do. Speak later, love you both." Kate blew another kiss before getting into her car. It was an hour drive away and her tummy was doing somersaults thinking that she would finally be seeing Anna and be able to talk to her about everything. Would she remember all the questions to ask her and what would she think of her future daughter-in-law? Time would soon tell, and she felt sick with nerves.

On arrival, Kate realised the seriousness of where she was and what she was doing. The massive walls surrounding the main building, the heavy barbed wire rolled across the tops of the walls and the vast amounts of security cameras and guards glaring down at her, making her feel terrified and that was just to get in the place. Her mind was racing as she made her way through all the checks and finally sat in a large bland room with twenty plus other visitors. Small tables with a plastic jug of water, a few plastic cups and with chairs opposite one lone chair for the prisoner. Husband's, boyfriends, mums, dads, sisters, brothers, even a few small children visiting their mums. It was like a scene in a movie, and it was something Kate did not fancy seeing in real life on a regular basis.

After ten minutes of all the visitors being seated, the inmates started arriving. Kate didn't even know what Anna looked like but as a woman began making headway towards her, she realised she was about to finally meet her mother-in-law.

"Anna?" she said, checking, standing up.

"That's me," the woman replied, "and you must be the beautiful Kate, wow," she paused as she glanced up and down at Kate's slightly trembling body, "The picture Dan showed me doesn't do you justice my dear, you are stunning." She smiled with her eyes wide still.

Kate blushed as they both sat back down.

Anna was slightly taller than Kate with mostly grey hair in a short cut style. Her skin was tanned, and Kate thought she looked remarkably good for her age and for being in this place too. Some of the women that had passed by Kate before Anna, looked terrible. Tired, weak, thin and some had cuts and bruises on their faces. It was like a scene from the new Netflix series about a woman's prison.

Kate knew she only had under an hour to get her notebook questions answered and Anna could see by her facial expression that she was eager to get started.

"So," Anna said, "you've come for some answers I

guess?"

Kate nodded, "Yes please, if you don't mind telling me that is?"

"Of course not my dear, you deserve to know why you're here visiting me in this wretched predicament of a place hey?" Anna replied and from that second, she didn't hold back, telling Kate the short version of her story. "You see," she continued, "I'd been hit one too many times by that fateful day. There's only so much a woman can take you know dear. He slapped me so hard Kate, my face was hurting like never before. At first, I thought he might have broken my jaw, it was such a hard slap that time," she rubbed her jaw gently as though to soothe the pain that she had felt, "Something inside me flipped. I turned round, grabbed his head, and just screamed with all my might at him," she paused looking at Kate's astounded expression, "do you want me to carry on?"

Kate just nodded again in a stunned silence, her pen poised against the notebook to write down what Anna was saying but, it wasn't writing anything, frozen on the spot, a blank page. Kate just continued listening intently instead. She couldn't bring herself to look away from this woman who was now opening her heart up with this story.

"My heart was racing, I could hardly breath at one point, but I knew...I just knew that if I didn't stop him, it would not end well for me or for my beautiful son, Daniel. I had to protect my child," she paused glancing down for a moment before meeting Kate's eyes once more. "The times he cried in my arms at nights. Once his father had left after one of his episodes, you know. I hated seeing my boy so upset. I knew that he heard everything, and I felt terrible for that Kate, I really did."

"I'm so sorry for you Anna." Kate replied feeling tearful herself, imagining how helpless they both must have felt during those times.

"Thank you. Anyway, as I said, something flipped on this night and I knew I had to do something serious; to save us both," she sipped on her glass of water, refreshed her lips with her tongue, and carried on, "after I grabbed his face, he fell back. I think he was shocked that I'd reacted to be honest, but as he fell, he hit his head on the edge of the dining table. I immediately saw the blood coming from his head and the rage in his eyes Kate, I tell you…you never want to see that rage looking back at you, not ever." She said sternly.

"What happened next?" Kate whispered softly.

"That's when I reached for the knife."

Kate glanced around the room briefly. She felt like she was in a movie listening to someone's confession, or being set up with some outrageous prank, but it wasn't a joke, this was real and scary. This was it; the truth was spilling out right there in front of her. This woman who was about to become family to Kate was revealing, admitting her crime. She placed the pen down and closed the notebook. She didn't need to record this, she wouldn't be forgetting these details any time soon, "you stabbed him?" she asked.

"Yes. I stabbed him. He wasn't going to stay down there; he was coming for me you see. He would've killed me given the chance; I just had a feeling that this moment was it, I know he would have that time. So, yes, I'm afraid that's what happened. I stabbed my husband…again and again until…" she paused again taking a mouthful of water this time and swallowing hard, "it all stopped, he was on the floor, bleeding, dying and…well, he couldn't hurt me or upset our son anymore. So then, I ran, I just ran outside hoping someone would help me. I was so frantic, scared and horrified with myself and then…"

"What…?" Kate's eyes were wide open, and she was now leaning forward on the table. The look of sadness on Anna's eyes were crushing her heart. This poor woman had defended herself against that cruel man. All she wanted to do was go round the other side of the table and hug her, "what happened?" she asked again.

"Daniel." She paused, "Little Daniel came out into the road and grabbed onto my hand," she glanced down at her hands, turning them over, "his little hand was there, holding mine, covered in blood. He knew what I'd done there and then, bless him."

Kate sat back in her chair, exhausted almost at

what she had heard and remembering the discussion she'd had with Dan, saying he had done all this, the exact story but with him being the one with the knife. But why? Why would someone make that up?

"Are you okay Kate, oh dear, I've gone and upset you haven't I?"

"No, it's just...well," she paused and glanced round the room once more.

"What is it Kate?"

"Well…It's just…" she stammered wondering if she should even be telling Anna what he'd said.

"Did he tell you another story?" she asked, sitting back, and folding her arms across her body.

"Yes. Dan told me he did it, he said he was the one who stabbed his father, and you took the blame, because he was young and so he didn't get put away in some detention centre or something."

"Oh, that poor boy, my precious little Daniel." Anna smiled back at Kate, "this is exactly why I said he needs to be on his medication."

"I don't understand why he would say it was him though, why would he want me to think he was a murderer?" Kate shook her head, glancing around the room but not taking anything in at the same time.

Before anything else could be said, the bell rang to mark the end of visiting time.

Anna stood up to leave, "Kate, please be careful with him. I fear he's maybe got some of his father's traits."

"Thank you for your time today Anna, I'll be in touch." Kate replied quickly before all the inmates were shipped back out to their cells once more.

As they waited to leave the prison, a shell-shocked Kate now had a brain working overtime once more. She didn't even know what to make of it all and why he had lied about being a murderer. It may have made him seem even more mysterious, but she wasn't sure she liked that kind of story. Pretending to be a murderer when all the time his mother had been sent to jail because of it? There was only one thing for it, she had to confront him, she had to tell him where she had been this afternoon, that she'd met his mother in secret and more over; the fact was, she knew the truth. In some way, she couldn't wait to get home and see him, speak to him, and get her head straight. In another, she felt scared about what he would say, or how he might react. Her only hope was that he would be there and tell her why he'd lied, be honest so they could sort things out for good this time.

Chapter Twenty-Eight

The Final Straw…

Approaching her garden gate, Kate dug down, searching for her door key out of her increasingly heavy handbag. It had been filled to the brim, with product samples, business cards, and various special offer leaflets from the wedding show. As she swung her hip to close the gate behind her, the front door suddenly opened and flung back, making Kate look up. She wasn't prepared for the sight that was now coming before her. A tall, curly haired, blonde woman with sparkling platform high heels, fishnet tights and something vaguely resembling a dress of some sort in a hideous pale yellow hue shade, began tottering down the steps. She made her way towards Kate who now stood frozen on the spot, her hand still deep down and motionless, in her bag, but everything seemed to fall silent. Kate was stunned by the image that had suddenly appeared in front of her, coming out of her house, walking down her front steps, down her pathway.

In an instant, she contemplated in her brain what was going on. It was as though her mind was working ten to the dozen in the quickest of milliseconds, creating stories about the scene. He'd had some tart of a stranger back to her house while she had been slugging away with her job for the past five hours straight, earning top money so they could have an amazing wedding, traipsing round getting wedding information for their big day. And then not even turning up as promised to go to the fair with her. Then to make matters worse, she had now found out, from his mother, that he had lied to her again and in the sickest of ways too. He'd pretended to her that he was the one who murdered his own father, and she didn't have the slightest idea why? To make her scared of him, to try and manipulate her into keeping secrets from those who loved her? Questions ran through her mind like formula one racing cars, it was all happening so fast. She really hoped that this was one of his pathetic jokes and he'd come out to explain any second. He would appear behind this girl and make everything Kate was thinking, wrong. Surely he would prove that she was going mad thinking all this rubbish scenario that was playing out.

As the girl swished her slender body, passed Kate, she grinned widely, showing off a set of perfectly straight and extremely stark white teeth. Her plumped-up lips donning some awful shiny bright red lipstick accentuated the gnashers even more. Kate did not smile back just watching this person now walking away, flicking her head from side to side like she was in a famous shampoo or hair colour commercial on the TV. For a moment, Kate couldn't help but think that she looked remarkably like one of the girls she had seen at the sordid strip club that horrible evening weeks ago. But what was she doing in her house? Why was there a goddamn stripper in her home? What was Dan playing at now?

"Dan," she called, as she shook herself out of the shock stance and went indoors, "Dan!" she repeated, a little louder, angrily throwing her jacket over the banister followed by chucking her handbag against the bottom step of the staircase. A few of the leaflets fell out onto the floor as it toppled over, angering her further but she left them where they laid. She wanted answers first before getting frustrated even more with now seemingly not very important, or relevant wedding stuff.

She heard music playing upstairs, it was coming from their bedroom, so she kicked her shoes off trying to get them under the hall shelf cabinet and made her way up towards the noise. A minute later and she was at the bedroom doorway, watching him naked, singing along to the radio.

"Daniel!" she yelled over the music, finally grabbing his attention.

"Oh, hello lover," he shouted back, turning to see her angry face, "Alexa, turn off," he called out, making the music stop suddenly, "you're back early babe?" He pulled on a t-shirt and some jogging shorts covering the lower parts of his body.

Kate instantly noticed he hadn't bothered to put any boxer shorts on as he pulled the shorts up, glimpsing his white butt again as he turned to grab his hoody.

"You had a good shift, cook anything fabulous or fancy tonight for the old footy boss bloke?" he continued, acting all sarcastic.

She stepped further into the room looking towards the bed which was not made as she had left it this morning. "Who was that girl just leaving?" she pointed back towards the door not entertaining his question. It was her turn to question him, not the other way round. She needed to know what he was doing, and now.

Sniggering back, smirking a sarcastic grin, he replied, "oh, that was Lucy, my massage lady, she's hardly a girl babe," he said rolling his eyes as he continued, "met up with her last night after work, told her I'd had a bit of an injury at Rugby practice, so she offered to come over and give me a free massage. Who am I to turn that sort of offer down, hey? She has amazing hands you know." He made a gesture with his own hands as if rubbing the air, then arched his back, and held his hips, "oh yeahhh," he moaned, "feels so much better now."

"Massage? Seriously Dan?" she shrieked back, puzzled by the fact that he expected her to believe that a girl who looked like that, dressed like that, would be here just to give him a massage. She thought about the stark image she'd just witnessed outside her front door again. The so-called lady, as he referred to her, didn't have a treatment bag or anything, hadn't even had a massage table with her. Just a tacky little clutch bag under her arm, "where was her massage table then?" she questioned giving back a tone of sarcasm to him this time.

He nonchalantly shrugged his shoulders as he stood ruffling his hair in the mirror, "she's a professional, she doesn't need a poxy table babe, we just used the bed, it's softer anyhow."

"Really Dan? What do you take me for?" she replied as she shook her head at him, "I'm not an idiot. You really think I am going to believe that sort of bull crap story."

A few seconds silence ensued as he continued to try and calm his messy hair, then suddenly, he turned and came toward her, "Well, yes Katie darling, I do actually. It's the truth babe, you know I don't lie to you," he answered back, "look darling little Katie, give it up okay?"

"No," she shouted back, "I won't give it up. I'm fed up with your stupid, pathetic lies and games you think are alright to play. Who was she Dan? Who was that woman coming out of my house!"

"I told you," He snarled back now, gritting his teeth, "give it up already, just shut up about her, she's nothing alright!" his voice grew louder, "it's none of your bloody business who I have round." He turned back walking towards the bedroom door.

Kate felt as though her veins were bursting through her skin with anger and the adrenaline was flowing fast and furiously up her entire body, making her hot and sweaty. "It's my house Dan so it is my business actually and stop calling me Katie for Christ's sake."

"It's your bloody name love." He shouted back as he pulled the bedroom door ajar and began walking out.

Suddenly, Kate felt more enraged than she had ever done before. She didn't understand his cruel and sarky attitude towards her, and he was making her feel belittled and worthless. She did not feel special as she should, as she had done so many times with him. As his fiancé, this was angering her in a way she didn't even recognise in herself. She reached for her hairbrush which was on the dressing table beside her and without thinking, she threw it at him, striking his back as he went through onto the landing.

For a few seconds, he just stood motionless, facing away from her. The silence was deadly deafening, and she felt her breathing begin to quicken. When he did finally turn round, she could only see his eyes glaring darker than ever and deeply into hers. She had never seen him look so menacing, and immediately recalled what Anna had mentioned to her earlier, *'you never want to see that rage looking back at you'*. And there it was, pure rage in those once beautifully seductive eyes. Now, it seemed her turn to run away, just like Anna had run from her husband, she now had a growing urge to run as fast as she could away from her future husband, and that awful angry and scary stare. But he was blocking her way, she had no escape out of that room for the moment. With her chest heaving, and no other option in her mind, she held out both of her hands in submission, "I'm sorry Dan, I didn't mean to do that. I didn't mean to hit you with it, I…" she stammered with fear encroaching her earlier brave and bold voice. All she wanted was to turn back the clock, to not have tried to be so brave, to not have thrown the brush, and especially to not have stricken him. His eyes said it all, he was furious, "I, I…I'm sorry," she repeated, voice trembling, body shaking, "I."

But before she could say anything else, he interrupted her, "you'd better be sorry, you really shouldn't have done that," he looked at the brush on the floor, "you could've really hurt me with that thing you know," his stare was getting more intense by the second and his tone was frightening but he remained strangely calm, "all this fuss, just because I want to have a bit of fun with another girl, I've told you before, men have certain needs, we need excitement. You're so bloody busy with this new job, won't go to the clubs I wanna go to…so hey, she was up for a bit of fun with me, so I took it okay."

She gasped in shock as his admission verified what she had thought already. He had cheated on her, sleeping with that tramp of a woman. She knew deep down in her heart; it was probably not the only time. But what made her feel so much worse was that it was in her house, and it looked like, in her bedroom, her bed, their bed, which made it ten times as bad. If she hadn't come home early, she might never have found out either and it made her skin crawl thinking of him and that stripper in her bed together doing God knows what. It certainly wasn't a massage like he'd made it out to be.

"It's just sex babe, nothing serious," he blatantly muttered.

"Why Dan?" she asked, beginning to cry.

He shrugged his shoulders.

"Why are you doing this, behaving like this again? After everything we've been through," she shook her head in disbelief, "have you stopped taking your meds again?" she begged for a valid answer to come back out of his mouth, hoping to cling onto this relationship in some way.

"Oh, for Christ's sake Kate. You're obsessed with

my bloody meds and the bloody illness. I get sick of it you know, you're my girlfriend not my bloody mother!" he shouted, waving his arms up.

"I'm your fiancé," she corrected him, "I'm going to be your wife Dan. I care about you, is that wrong?" she pleaded.

"I don't need this." He said, returning into the room, "do you know what," he reached down and grabbed a pair of jeans and a hoody that had been dis guarded on the floor, "I've had it. I'll make it easier on both of us, shall I?" he came into the room further and began opening the chest of drawers.

"What do you mean," she cried at him, her eyes filling with tears, "Dan, what are you doing?" her eyes frantically scanned the room, watching his body moving around the room, collecting clothing, bags, and items in his arms.

"I'm leaving, that's what I'm doing. I need some space from this shit. You're too much and do you know something else?" he paused, turning to face her, "maybe I'm just not ready to settle down with one woman yet. I've admitted what you've been thinking for months haven't I? I've been having sex regularly with other women, strippers who meet my needs, and it's what I intend to carry on doing," he paused again, throwing all his items into his holdall bag from inside the wardrobe, "if you can't handle that, then I'm off. We're finished. Is that what you want? For all this to be over, be on your own again, with no-one except your precious aunt and uncle keeping you with their money?" His voice was overpowering, and she almost felt as though he was someone else right now. Someone she didn't like at all; someone she didn't recognise. She couldn't believe what she was hearing, and she hated the way his behaviour had turned bad again. As much and as hard as she had fallen in love with him, this wasn't how she dreamt it would be all those months back, she deserved better than this, so much better and she knew that. She stood motionless and silent, just looking at the person, the figure in front of her.

"Well?" he shouted, coming closer, making her jump.

Startled, she began shaking her head at him, tears streaming down her cheeks, falling to the floor like heavy raindrops in a massive puddle. Her heart was beating so hard, she thought it may come out of her chest and explode any minute. With the echoes of Anna's words of warning in her head, she decided to remain still, remain quiet so not to anger him any further. She couldn't even bring herself to look into those eyes anymore, so she just looked down.

"Fine," he replied to her silence and stormed past her, knocking her sideways.

Within a few minutes, his rushed footsteps stomped down the stairs, mumbling something to himself that she couldn't quite understand and then, slamming the front door hard behind him, he was gone, and the house fell silent once more.

Standing for a minute, shocked to the core, Kate tried to calm her breathing down as fast as she could. Her heartbeat was thumping still through her chest, and she had to place her hand on it trying to compress the feeling of it bursting out of her body any minute. Again, there he was, just walking out suddenly. Why and where did he keep running off to? Her brain ached as much as her heart, wishing she had asked him long before now about where he'd gone all the episodes before.

'Maybe', she thought to herself, *'it was better she hadn't asked, better she didn't know the truth behind his strange tantrums and mysterious ways.'*

As soon as she was sure that he had left the house, she slid her saddened body down the wall, clutching her arms around her knees and placing her head down into them.

She began sobbing quietly at the realisation of what had just happened. He'd walked out on her again, leaving her crying her eyes out on the bedroom floor this time, and she was confused as to what to do next. Although she had felt petrified that he could in fact, return at any given moment, something deep inside told her that it was the end, it was over. More than anything, she hadn't deserved to be treated this way. She didn't want and couldn't take this type of toxic relationship one more day, let alone marrying him, being his wife. His mother had revealed her story proving he was a complete liar, and the awful truth was that he'd been sleeping around on her all this time. He was a cheat, a liar, a conniving, selfish and blatant player. He had turned out to be someone who didn't care about her and her feelings in the slightest.

After a few minutes, she looked up and around the mess of a bedroom, noticing the few forgotten clothes strewn across the floor that had obviously fallen out of his arms in his haste to leave. There was a pair of boxer shorts hanging over her dressing room chair, a few socks laying by the doorway, his team rugby hoody hung on the back of the door. So much remained in her house of him and it began to wile up frustration and anger inside of her once more.

Getting to her feet, she tried to remain calm, gathered everything up and threw it into a heap onto the bed, tears silently but freely flowing as she did so. The last thing to go was the crystal vase he'd bought on their first official date together. She held it tightly in her hands, glancing over its glimmering beauty. She couldn't destroy this item; it was just too beautiful so she decided she would donate it to her favourite charity shop instead. A short walk into town in a few days' time would be suffice and let someone else enjoy putting their flowers in it. Placing it back on her shelf, she realised this was in fact the end. This was the end of her once very sparkly and exciting relationship. It was the end of Kate and Dan; she wasn't going to have this life with him and listen to him deceiving her anymore. Their promised future was in tatters, their dreams of a cute intimate wedding was over, and she didn't want any more reminders of him anywhere near her.

Opening the window as wide as it would go, with trembling hands, she scooped up all the contents from the bed, including the bed covers, and threw it all out into the garden below. For now, that's where they could stay, she didn't want his things, his scent, or his memory near her. His lies were over, for her anyway. Wherever he'd gone to this time round, it, she, they, whoever's path he was now crossing were welcome to him.

For the first time in the rapid and sometimes very strange, controlling relationship, she had fought back, stood her ground, and she felt relieved. Not that the relationship itself had ended but, that she had tried her best to stand up for herself. If only she had been strong enough to realise his cruel and disturbed personality sooner.

Her tears would dry eventually but she knew this was the end for her and Dan, it was finished. It was the final straw. And all she wanted to do now was see and talk with one person. That one person who she loved more than anything in the world. Leo, she had to be with Leo.

Chapter Twenty-Nine

I Love You Leo...

They'd spent the past few days closer than ever. Leo had invited her to stay at his place while Rob got all the locks changed and took all the remaining items of Dan's to the local charity shops and clothing banks. They'd even set her up with security cameras to ensure she was safe whatever time of day or night. Sally had hired cleaners in for a thorough top to toe once over of the house. Kate felt as though she wanted and needed every scent of her ex-fiancé gone for good.

She was still heartbroken and the moment she had taken off her lavish engagement ring brought on the final tears that she shed over him and the whole relationship. But in another way, it had also settled her mind, she was free of him and the sadness he had brought to her in the end. She was now cleared, cleansed, and refreshed. She'd decided to try and pawn the ring to get some of the money she'd lost back from the wedding plans. But that was one task that would have to wait for now. Locking it in the small safe under her bed, at least it was out of sight for the moment. As beautiful as it was, she didn't need that reminder.

Dan hadn't made any attempts to contact her at all, no messages, no calls, or anything. It was almost like before when he had disappeared for weeks, but she was thankful he hadn't, as were all who knew what had happened. She heard on the grapevine that he'd shacked up with an older woman and they'd moved to Scotland, of all places. Seemingly the furthest place away from her. How much of that was true, she didn't know, and she didn't care. So long as he was away from her. Good riddance to him.

"So, that's me single again hey?" Kate said as they sat at the bar in town the following weekend, "I'm bloody single again Leo." She repeated shaking her head at herself.

"Oh babe," replied Leo, "I'm so sorry it turned out that way but, well you know…"

"Please don't say you told me so Leo," she interrupted, "I can't handle that sort of judgement, especially from you of all people."

"Hey, sweetheart, I'd never say that you know that

surely?" he placed his hand over hers, looking into her pleading eyes, "look," he continued, "all I was gonna say was…well, it's probably better that you found out what he was really like before the big wedding day," he was trying his best to make her feel a little bit better, "I mean, you could've married the git you know and then have all the divorce crap to deal with on top, imagine going through all that? It's much better finding out now isn't it?"

"I suppose so. Urghh," she huffed, taking a large swig of wine, and wincing as the strength of it hit her throat, "all the wedding stuff Leo. It's been so horrible contacting the suppliers and telling them it's cancelled," she leaned on the bar, placed her head in her hand, and swirled her glass around in front of them, "to be fair though, they've all been so nice about it. I've lost all the deposits and luckily I hadn't found the dress yet either," she raised her eyebrows to him as she glanced over, "but…yes, I guess at least the whole wedding fund money wasn't wasted on it. My mum and aunt gave me that money, I'd hate to have spent it all on a crappy future with that twat!"

"Good, that's the spirit girl," he rubbed her hand again and smiled, "loads of weddings get cancelled for one reason or another, it's sad but it does happen, hopefully not too much for the suppliers obviously but that's life I suppose you just never know what's round the corner do you?" he shrugged.

"No, you sure don't. I'm going to take the ring to

the pawn shop, although now I'm wondering if it's even of any worth," she said trying to laugh at that fact, "I've written to his mum, you know, Anna, just to fill her in really in case he goes to see her and tells her his side of things, the bull of a story that is."

"I think she'll know who to believe from what you told me about her. Surely she knows him better than anyone hey? Anyway, want another one?" he said, lifting his nearly empty glass up, swallowing a last sip. He needed to get off the subject and try and cheer his best friend up now. They hadn't come out tonight to wallow in the sadness, he wanted to make sure she smiled tonight.

"Oh why not," she agreed, finishing hers and sliding it forward to the bar tender, "I hope she writes back to me though. Whatever has gone on, she went through some awful stuff and…"

"Sweetheart," he interrupted, "you must concentrate on yourself now, heal that precious little heart of yours and maybe, well, maybe just forget them both. It's for the best, I'm sure she will understand."

Kate looked back up to her friend, he was right, she did need to forget them and this whole episode or chapter in her life now. Anna would understand completely. She wasn't a monster like Dan was, she had acted in self-defence, not planned a whole murder scenario, killing her husband, the father of her beloved child. The child that had now done so much damage and caused so much stress. She nodded back and gave Leo a knowing smile. Somehow, she knew a reply probably wouldn't come back from Anna. They protected each other so she wasn't going to expect to hear from her again. Leo was right once again.

"Two more of those please mate." He asked the barman, swiping his credit card.

"Maybe we could grab a takeaway and another bottle or two and go back to mine?" she said, fiddling, nervously with the loose button on her shirt sleeve, "maybe it's time I went back there?"

"Yeah sure, that's fine with me. I'll have to chip off a bit earlier though, big dinner party tomorrow for the footballer remember?"

"Oh crikey, yes. Hey, why don't we stay at yours then, its closer and we can go together in the morning?" she asked taking her fresh glass of wine.

"Ooh, Kate...people will gossip you know, inviting yourself to stay at mine hey?" he joked back nudging her.

"Erm...do I look like I care what people think at the minute?" she pointed to her 'not bothered' face and they both started laughing. The wine was kicking in now, tipsy, or not, she didn't want to be alone tonight. The first night back might feel weird and she knew she would feel more than safe with him by her side.

"So, what do you fancy to eat then gorgeous

chops?" Leo asked as they walked arm in arm out of the pub and down the high street towards the vast amounts of fast-food outlets and restaurants.

Kate was feeling a bit wobbly on her feet and was glad that she'd decided to only wear flats this evening, "erm…" she stammered glancing around the street. The lights seemed extra dazzling and she squinted slightly as she tried to focus.

"Are you sure you're okay mate?" Leo said concerned as she tripped momentarily and began giggling at herself.

"Yes, yes, yes Leo," she drunkenly answered, "just need some grub in me to soak up all that naughty wine you made me slurp tonight." She waved her arm up, pointing towards a burger joint, "let's get cheeseburgers and cheesy chips, come on." Letting go of his arm, she swayed across the pathway and practically fell into the doorway of the food takeaway.

Leo rushed to keep up with her, and sat her down on a bench inside, "I'll order the food, you just sit there, alright? Don't go moving." He was beginning to feel bad for letting her drink too much and after placing their order at the counter, he glanced round watching her sitting there, slightly swaying in her seat. She was attempting to fold the napkins into what he thought looked like planes. Reaching for each one from the container on the table, then swiftly screwing them up into crumpled balls of nothingness. Pure frustration in her face but quietly giggling to herself at the same time. She looked sad, her usual sparkling eyes were full of the woes of hurt from the relationship breaking down, from the excitement of having the dream wedding, everything getting cancelled and moreover, the heartache that Dan had caused her. Then there was the mother-in-law revelation that had shocked all of them. In the large scheme of things, she'd coped well up until tonight where she seemed to be falling apart a tiny bit as the alcohol sunk in. She'd told him earlier how she hadn't eaten since yesterday morning, making him feel worse for filling her glass with the wine that she'd insisted on having. The only thing he could think about was keeping her safe. This was his top priority and responsibility tonight, trying to make her a weeny bit happier and ensuring that their new job together was her new life focus. He decided it would be best to eat the food there and then, maybe this would give her the chance to sober up a bit. Soaking up the wine with a nice big greasy burger and fries.

When they had finished, he called a taxi to take them back to his.

"Can we go to mine instead Leo, sorry to be a pain but…well, I think I wanna sleep in my bed tonight after all." She asked resting her head on his shoulder as they waited outside the food joint.

"Sure, no probs babe." He replied as he checked his uber app to see how long the ride was going to be, "I'll get the cab to drop you off first and then I'll come get you in the morning about half ten, eleven? Is that cool?"

Kate just nodded back.

"Are you sure you're okay staying at yours?" Leo asked noticing she was still a little bit shaky on her feet.

"Erm, I guess so...yeah, I'll be tickety-boo I think. But…" she glanced up to his face, "can't you stay Leo, can't you stay with me?" Smiling up at him, she thought in that split second how incredibly handsome he was. His loving denim blue eyes staring back down into hers, full of warmth and love for her and the friendship bond they had created over the years. His strong but gentle arms were holding her body close, keeping her safe. As she stroked her fingers down the front of his shirt, smelling his scent, something came over her. She stretched her neck up and kissed him full on the lips. As he pulled back, she realised from the body language that she had crossed a line, she'd made a mistake kissing him and instantly felt regret.

Just then, the taxi pulled up in front of them and she quickly climbed in, immediately feeling embarrassed with herself, wanting the ground to swallow her up to avoid the awkwardness that she had now created in one stupid moment.

Leo walked round the other side of the car and got in beside her, "Kate…" he started, fastening her seatbelt then clipping in his own.

"Leo, don't," she stopped him, "I'm so sorry...I shouldn't have done that. I shouldn't have kissed you, it's the bloody wine. Forgive me, please? It won't happen again. Oh, bloody hell, I'm so embarrassed." Turning her face to the window, she could feel her entire face blushing a nice shade of flushed red. Her body felt clammy with sweat and panic over the kiss that never should have occurred.

He reached across and held onto her hand which was now trembling, fiddling with the hem of her dress, "it's okay. It was just a bloody kiss, a friendly little kiss, no biggie alright? Kate?"

She didn't reply, just continued to try and escape through the car window reflection.

"Kate..." he repeated, squeezing her hand.

She turned to face him again, her cheeks a nice blush of rose red but he smiled back with a knowing expression, making her feel just a little bit less anxious and mortified that she had even thought to kiss him like that. After everything she had been through over the past few months, all she wanted was to love again but Leo was her friend, her best friend at that. Never would she risk losing this friendship, she just couldn't imagine not having him in her life. She was not going to ruin this and vouched in her mind not to drink wine like that again. She never would have attempted to kiss him if she hadn't been so tipsy.

The silence continued during the ten-minute car

journey. She didn't know what to talk about and by the time they arrived at her place, she now felt instantly sober.

"I'll walk you in." Leo said as he began to open his door.

"No, honestly, I'm fine," she replied, turning to him, "I'll meet you at work tomorrow yeah," she asked as she stepped out of the car, holding the door slightly ajar for a moment, "thanks for tonight Leo."

He smiled and nodded back, "I'll pick you up at half ten. You sure you're okay alone?"

"Yep, honest. See you in the morning." She closed the door carefully, standing straight up and watching as the car pulled away. Leo was looking out of the back window and just as it was going out of the road, he blew a kiss to her with his fingers. Her heart melted. It had been so torn up just lately by Dan's actions and sharp departure, but Leo was fixing it, slowly but surely. Even if it was just as a friendship, she loved him and she knew he loved and respected her too. A true friend, a true gentleman.

Taking a deep breath, she made her way up the pathway and inside. The house felt cold and empty, no flowers adorning the windowsills anymore, no scent of a man waiting for her to arrive. She leaned back against the front door, staring down the hallway remembering all the times she would come home to those muddy boots laying on the floor. In one way, she did feel a sense of relief that it was over but in another breath, all she wanted was someone to come home to. A body to cuddle up with at night. Someone to share her home with.

"Urghh," she grumbled to herself, throwing her keys onto the sideboard, kicking her shoes off in different directions and making her way upstairs to her bedroom. The evening had been so much fun, if not a tad embarrassing for the last part, but she was home now and exhausted.

As she climbed into bed still fully clothed, she grabbed her favourite blanket from the foot of the bed and lay down staring at the ceiling. Her instant sobering up was appreciated, the room wasn't spinning as the burger place had been. It felt nice to be back in her own bed, even if she was alone. Looking across at the shelf, she remembered that she had to get rid of the vase that still sat there peering down. Holding back the tears, she slowly got up, grasping it angrily and then dropped it into the bin below. Seeing it break as it hit the hard surface was another heart-breaking jerk for her but in some way too, she felt better for finally binning it. As much as she had aimed to give to the charity shop, now it would be gone sooner. She grabbed some wet wipes from her dressing table and threw them on top of it so she couldn't see it anymore and then slipped back into bed, contented that the only thing left to go, was the ring. *'A job for auntie, she'll know what to do with it.'* She thought to herself laying on her side, feeling exhausted at the sudden adrenaline rush. Just as she began to finally relax and close her eyes, her phone pinged a text message.

It was Leo. *'Hey…xxx'* was all it said.

'Hey…xxx' she replied after quickly grabbing the handset.

'Love you…xxx' came back, making her beam down at the screen with a wide smile.

'Love you too...xxx' she typed and waited while she watched the message bubble, wondering what he was going to say next. Or maybe he wasn't going to answer anything else. What else was there to say?

'Need a cuddle…???' it pinged back finally.

She gasped. She did need a cuddle, a cuddle that would last hours and heal what was left of her little broken heart. Her eyes welled up as she tried to see through them to type a message back to him as fast as her fingers would allow, *'I need that more than ever…xxx'* and the tears escaped, trickling down her cheeks. He always knew what to say so she waited to get some sort of emoji cuddle message back.

'Come and open the door then, I have a BIG hug out here and it's getting cold. Brrrr…. Leo..xxx'

She threw the blanket off her body and quickly made her way back down the stairs seeing her reflection through the door. Unlocking and opening it, she flung her arms around his waist. She couldn't help but cry, sobbing into his chest as he held closed the door behind them and held her tightly. It was as if the final tears needed to be released tonight, all the emotions of the previous weeks had surfaced to the top and hopefully, they would be the last tears she would waste on Dan and his lies.

*

The following morning, Leo was up at eight o'clock making her breakfast in bed. They had a few hours before going to work together and he was determined to get her to eat something beforehand after last night's alcohol intake. A decent 'Leo' full English was just the ticket.

"Leo, this is amazing," she commented seeing the tray of food being placed onto her lap, "you didn't have to do this though, silly."

"You need to eat a good hearty brekkie, start taking proper care of yourself babe. Get your strength back up and that. If you won't do it, then I'm going to make sure I'm here to shove it down your mooey." He joked, smiling at her, pointing to his own mouth.

"What have I done to deserve you Leo?" she asked, picking up the cutlery.

"Oh, stop it and eat," he waved his hand at her, "I'm gonna jump in the shower if that's alright with you, then we can pop back to mine, pick up my work clothes, and get the food bonanza show on the road, okay?"

She didn't answer, just made a 'mmm' noise back at him as she was too busy delving into the mushrooms and slurping her coffee in-between mouthfuls. He stood at the doorway for a second to watch her. This morning, she had a whole different aura around her and one he preferred seeing around his friend. Smiling and feeling proud of himself, he made his way into the bathroom, leaving her to enjoy her food feast and then get dressed.

When they were both ready to leave, he called another cab and they made their way to his, then to work. It was a lunchtime soiree today with a handful of guests attending and once they had eaten, the client and his friends made their way to the football club to watch a match in the VIP box, leaving Kate and Leo to finish clearing everything up.

Kate sat down at the kitchen island while they had a quick latte from the very expensive coffee machine. Leo had recently mastered the art of creating a heart with the frothy milk, something Kate was not so good at. She was better at using the stencils while sprinkling chocolate powder over the tops of the drinks.

"Phew, that was pretty full on for a lunch wasn't it?" she wiped her brow, "I don't know how they eat so much in the middle of the day? I think I'd be sick if I ate all that or have to have a three-hour power nap afterwards or something." She laughed.

"Big appetites I guess," Leo joked back.

"Grab me one of those cupcakes babe," Kate pointed to a plate of cakes that had been left and bit into the light sponge, getting butter icing on her nose.

"Messy pup," he said throwing her a tea towel to wipe it, "anyway, listen. I have some news."

"Ooh yeah, you always seem to have something to tell me lately Leo babe."

"I know but it's something we've not done before and I don't want to seem, oh I don't know, give you the wrong idea or…"

"For god's sake man, spit it out, the suspense is killing me already." Kate blurted out, munching on another bite of the cake.

Leo chuckled and sat down next to her, "ok, well, listen up girl. My brother has this place in Spain that he rents out most of the year. It's a little two bed apartment in Murcia. Anyway," he stopped again as he gestured for her to wipe more buttercream from around her mouth, "you're like a child when you eat you know." He laughed.

"Haha…carry on." She urged cleaning her face once again.

"He's had a cancellation and said I can have if I want a last-minute holiday. I've cleared it with the boss man, so…if you're up for a bit of Spanish sun and Sangria, wanna come with your old buddy for a week's holibobs? Saves me going alone and to be fair, I think it would do you good to get away. Only if you're up for it though?"

Kate jumped off her stool and threw her arms around him, squealing in delight, "of course I'm up for a free holiday, yes Leo," she shrieked at him, "you are amazing you know that?"

"Well…" he paused, "yeah I know." He joked back, trying to stay stable on his chair as she rocked him from side to side.

His heart was beating as fast as hers and he knew they would have the best holiday together even with the next big revelation he had in store.

Chapter Thirty

New Surprises…

"Hello, you," said Sally answering the door the following week.

"Hey." Kate replied.

"You can use your key my darling, we don't mind you know. You're not likely to walk in and find us running around naked or anything sinister like that." She joked, ushering Kate through the doorway.

"Haha, God forbid hey? That's a sight I wouldn't get over in a hurry" returned Kate, air kissing her aunt as soon as they got close enough.

"Look at the tan on you girl" Sally exclaimed standing back and admiring the warm glow to Kate's normally fair skin.

"I know, the old Spanish sun seemed to like me this

time round." She joked back.

"Beautiful darling, you are simply glowing, it suits you."

"Thanks, the weather was awesome."

"Anyway…how is my favourite niece?"

"I'm your only niece, auntie." Kate giggled back, switching the kettle on as they stepped into the kitchen. There was a wonderful baking aroma in there today and she noticed some large chocolate muffins that must have just come out of the oven, as they were still sitting on the wire rack.

Sally laughed back, "oh you know what I mean sweetie. Help yourself to one of those. Chocolate chip ones this time, although I can't promise what they'll taste like. It's a new Jamie Oliver recipe, jeez that bloke can't half cook some delicious looking things can't he?"

"He certainly can. You know he's my favourite chef. Anyway, they smell gorgeous," She leaned over the side and took a deep inhale of the chocolate aroma, "it's not like you to bake cakes auntie."

"Well, no it isn't but…honestly…I got bored. On another subject and more importantly, how are you doing, are you alright darling? Are you coping better now?"

"Yes, I'm okay. Still keep feeling incredibly tired and, well...slightly overwhelmed with everything that's been going on but, no, I'm good," she nodded, placing one of the warm muffins in front of her, "I'm thinking more positively now and just wanna get on with my new job and life in general really I guess, you know, crack on with my future, make new plans."

"Superb! It sounds like you have everything in order darling. We've been so concerned about you, we really have been worried, sweetheart," she reached for two mugs from the cabinet behind her, "here you go, let's christen these new ones," she said as she placed them by the kettle. Kate could see immediately how expensive they were from the design. She remembered they'd seen them in Harrods a few months back on a trip to London and Sally had taken photos of them on her phone. She hardly ever bought things in store, she liked to order online and have new ones delivered. She'd always said to Kate that she didn't like the fact that so many people may have touched the ones in the shop, and it had always made Kate chuckle.

"Very nice," Kate commented admiring the design again. "What on earth have you got in that big bag anyway?" she asked pointing to a bag which was placed at the end of the kitchen table.

"Oh, erm…" Sally stammered, "we will talk about that in a moment. Now these muffins, shall I get a plate for you? How many would you like to indulge in? You look like you need feeding up a bit."

"To be honest, Leo stayed over last night and cooked me one of his special almighty breakfasts this morning, so I don't think I could eat too many right now," she replied, rubbing her still full belly, "I'll munch on this one and maybe take a couple to work though if that's okay. Leo and I can have them later after our shift, we can just pop them in some foil before I go."

"Leo stayed over again?" asked Sally, raising her eyebrows jokingly and smiling sweetly as she picked two muffins to wrap.

"Yes, but don't get excited auntie. It's purely friendship. I learnt the hard way by coming on to him while we were away and…"

"And…?" Sally pressed leaning in to face her niece, "don't tell me he turned my gorgeous niece down?"

Kate laughed, "I'm afraid he did."

Her aunt grunted.

"We were both a bit tipsy, you know how sun and alcohol can do funny things to people…"

Sally nodded.

"We'd had a fabulous day. Went to these mud baths in the morning."

"Mud baths?" Sally questioned looking puzzled.

"Yeah, you get in this lake; there's flamingos in there and everything. They're funny looking things but when they take off, incredible sight. Anyway, you get the mud from the bottom of this lake, rub it all over yourself, bask in the sun to let it dry. It goes like a pale light grey kind of colour, and then you get back into the Salt Lake and wash it all off."

"Urgh, sounds disgusting darling." Sally turned her nose up and grimaced slightly.

"I know, I thought the same when Leo suggested it, but it was so much fun and something very different. It took a while to get it all off but, our skin was ultra-soft afterwards. I think it exfoliates, you know, like the mud face masks we used to do with mum. Anyway," she continued, "after we had dried off, we went on a boat trip over to La Manga; it's the Miami of Spain apparently, have you heard about it?"

Sally nodded once more, "yes I have, I think Rob said about going there next year. It looks an incredible place. There are some huge hotels on it isn't there?"

"Yes. It's gorgeous, even with all the building work going on…so, after a bit of exploring on the main strip, and of course, souvenir shopping, we had an amazing dinner watching the sunset at this restaurant looking over the sea, it was all very romantic auntie."

"Mmm, mmm," Sally urged.

"Before our boat back, we spent an hour just sitting chatting on the beach. It felt…well, it felt right, so, I just went for it and…" she paused, tilting her head back and taking a deep breath.

"And what sweetie…" Sally urged again enthralled with her story.

"And nothing," Kate replied, finally making eye contact with her aunties whose were wide open intrigued to hear the gossip, "he erm.."

"Sweetheart, come on, tell me…you are killing your old auntie here with the suspense. He what, what happened next?"

"Well. I should've guessed something was amiss from the last time I drunkenly flung myself at him, going in for a full-on kiss on the lips but, well…" she paused, "The thing is he told me a secret. He's not into women…" she finally replied arching her eyebrows now and making a disappointed expression with her mouth.

"Oh…oh," stammered Sally, "now that's not at all what I expected to hear coming out of your mouth today." She continued, sitting back in her chair, "Wow…after the way you two have been so inseparable lately, I had you and him married in a few years' time, darn it!" she shrugged, pouting her face back at Kate, "bless him, I do love Leo, he'll make a wonderful catch for some lucky bloke though hey?"

"He is auntie. And yes he will. I love him so much, he's been the bestest friend I could've hoped for just lately," she glanced down at her phone and pressed the home button to reveal the screen saver of the two of them. The said sunset cruise on a boat trip, both smiling from ear to ear, embraced in each other's arms like all the other couples on the ferry. Not a care in the world right at that moment, not for anything or anyone else, it was their time and just glancing down at it made Kate's heart warm.

The memories they had made together in Murcia were precious and unforgettable. The moment she'd kissed him and declared her love for him had been even more awkward than the last time, but at the same time made their friendship even more special. Yes he had stopped her but for good reason and the fact that he opened his heart to her about his sexuality meant the world. He hadn't confided in anyone up until then and she felt honoured to have been the first to know. It was almost as if they had a renewal of their friendship. A new and everlasting friendship bond between them had been created and they both knew it could never be broken, no matter what was thrown at them next.

"Apart from that little set back on the romance side of things, the holiday was good yes?" Sally asked, pouring the boiled water into the cafetiere, and giving it a gentle stir before placing the top part on.

"Perfect, it was just what I needed, at just the right time too. We can't wait to get back to work though, crazy isn't it? Missing working."

"Well, not really, the passion you both have for cooking and the way you two work together, it's no wonder you love it and miss doing it. Oh, you do make a wonderful couple darling, even if it's just in a professional capacity."

"Thanks auntie. We do work amazingly well together. He told me about his five-year plan to open his own little wedding catering business and he wants me to manage the admin side of things as well as be his business partner. He's so good with the planning side of things so it sort of makes sense."

"Oh that's wonderful news. Maybe you could practice by doing our wedding anniversary food next year? It's a special one you know. Quite the milestone too," she moved the cafetiere onto a tray with the mugs and ushered Kate toward the back doors, "let's sit outside hey? Make the most of this dry weather and this blooming pagoda thingy-me-bob Rob had installed at the weekend." She nodded up towards the grey coloured, aluminium structure now covering their already gorgeous patio area as they got to the doorway.

"It's lovely auntie, very fancy looking." Kate took the tray from her aunt and started making her way outside while Sally grabbed the mystery bag from the table.

Kate had always admired Rob's taste in garden decor, whatever ideas he came up with always turned out so stylish and this new fixture fit in with the existing garden just perfectly. She remembered back when they first moved there and the garden was so overgrown, they didn't even know there was a shed at the end. The octagonal paving slabs had scrubbed up well with the pressure washer that Kate had been allowed to use on them. They led all the way to the end of the sixty-foot garden and remained there to this day. He'd designed the whole area on his computer and in a matter of weeks, had it all landscaped with a home office and home gym room at the end of the garden, perfect green stripy lawn and copious amounts of planting that looked like it had been there forever. He'd even bought Kate a wicker chair which hung in the only surviving tree so she could sit and read or just chill out. She remembered being allowed to choose the fabric to cover the cushions with. She now realised how horrendous they were and was glad to see that they now housed a lovely mint green covering instead. The hours she would spend in that swinging chair after her mum's death were special times, time to reflect, time to mourn and moreover, time to think.

"Apparently," Sally went on, interrupting Kate's thoughts, "we can use this area whatever the weather now, it has these blinds or shutter things I think they're called. You use a remote control to open and close them, very technical hey. It also has built-in; or 'integrated' lights, as your uncle says, a heating bar thingy and everything." She pointed as she grabbed the controls that were neatly attached to the inner wall, "I don't know…men and their gadgets hey sweetie. Too many fiddly buttons for silly old auntie to work out. It keeps him entertained anyhow." They both giggled, "oh and before I forget," she passed her an envelope, "I got a good price for the dreaded ring, it seems it was real diamonds after all?" she exclaimed as Kate's eyes widened at the wad of cash inside.

"Whoa! Thanks for sorting that out. That's everything gone now. I'll put this towards a new bed I think." Kate replied, slipping the money back and putting the envelope into her trouser pocket.

"Great idea. I love that new bed smell." Sally replied inhaling as if she could smell one.

It made Kate laugh again.

Once the coffees were nicely brewed and they'd got sat down and settled, Sally reached for the mystery bag once more from under her chair. Out of it, she produced a box, placing it gently on the glass top table and then sat back in her chair, looking nervous. They both just stared at it for a moment.

"What's this?" asked Kate, putting her mug down and leaning forward to get a clearer look at it.

"It's your memory box. Do you remember decorating it when you were very little?" Sally said as she ran her hand across the top.

It had 'Katie-Jane' painted across the lid with small doodles of stick figures and butterflies with overly large and very sparkly, thick glitter wings. It made Kate smile.

"I think you were about five or six when Fiona, sorry, your mum, had a creative art session with you. I remember the glitter went everywhere," she glanced at her hand which was covered with glitter just from picking the box up, "still gets everywhere, blooming stuff." She laughed shaking her hands over the side of the chair, dusting the patio with shade sparkles of pink and silver.

"I think I do recall something yeah, but what's inside the box? I don't really remember putting things in it."

"Kate, I've been meaning to tell you for many years but," she paused as she made eye contact directly, and sat up straighter, "I guess, there's just not been the right time or something has come up and just lately especially, there's just been too much going on for you but…"

"Auntie, what is it?" Kate was growing increasingly intrigued by her aunt's now overanxious tone of voice. She reached forward and pulled the box towards her.

"Sorry sweetie," Sally apologized, "Fiona wanted to put this box together so that you would be able to piece together your childhood a little bit better and like I said, I've tried to tell you before, but life happens and…oh ok, here goes," she paused again, and took a breath of air, composing herself in preparation for what she was about to reveal, "Kate darling, my sister adopted you. She adopted you when you were a tiny wee baby, just a day old in fact."

Kate looked up in complete shock, her eyebrows high and her eyes widened, "adopted?" she questioned, shunting her chin forward.

"Yes darling," Sally continued, "Fi used to foster

babies and young children from as soon as she was able to, but eventually she wanted to settle down and have her own family. Unfortunately, what with never meeting the right person to start a family with, and then the doctors confirming that she couldn't conceive herself, which devastated her, well, I think that's what made her start looking into adoption. She was so desperate to be a full-time mum you know," she stopped to take another breath, looking into Kate's stunned and confused face, "she wanted to have one she could call her own and keep forever instead of having to keep giving them back or watching them go from home to home. The fostering system can be tough on everyone involved sometimes. She wanted a baby to call hers. You were that baby Kate, you were Katie-Jane, her forever baby."

"I, I don't understand auntie..." she stuttered, her hands now shaking, "hang on, let me get this straight? So, my mum, Fiona, wasn't really my mum?"

"She was your mum sweetheart, just not your mother, does that make sense?"

Kate tilted her head, trying to comprehend it all, "so she wasn't my birth mother you mean? And I was adopted? I was born to someone else?" she asked. Her brain was spinning frantically, trying to comprehend this big news, and she had no idea how to feel or express the right words to utter. So many questions raced through her mind.

"That's correct, yes. Your biological mother couldn't take care of you. She was only a teenager when she fell pregnant so, her and her family agreed to have you adopted as soon as you were born. So Fiona became the lucky lady to have you. She became your mum. We became your new family; you became an Ellington."

"This is insane auntie. I had no idea." Kate exclaimed, taking her glances in turn to the box then back to her auntie.

"I know it must be confusing, well, more mind blowing than anything I suppose."

"Well, that's one description for it. I can't believe it, that I'm adopted," She placed her hands gently on the lid of the box, "can I look inside now?"

"Yes, yes. It should answer any questions that you may have that I can't answer maybe?" Sally reached for Kate's hands, holding them tightly but softly, she quietly said, "I hope you can forgive me for not telling you sooner, but especially forgive my beautiful sister, Fi, your mum," she looked straight into Kate's eyes, "she was a very special person, we both know that don't we? What she did for you, no matter how short a time it turned out to be, she was your mum and she loved and cared for you so very dearly, just like your uncle and I still do. We gained the most precious niece when she brought you home that day, it's a day I will never forget. You were such a tiny bundle. She was utterly in awe of you Kate, as were I. As I still am to this day lovely. Please forgive us?"

Kate didn't have any words at this moment, she just looked back as Sally squeezed her hands and then released them, nodding and smiling confidently, knowing that she could never hold a grudge against any of them. She just needed some answers, some clarification of what this all meant for her and her future. Who she was and where she came from.

It was time to look inside the box.

Chapter Thirty-One

Finding Herself...

As Kate slowly lifted the cardboard lid, her heart thumped hard like a drum beating against her rib cage, but memories instantly started flooding back as she grasped hold of each item in turn. Sifting through the old baby photos and the messy scribbles of drawings that had been carefully tied together with delicate ribbons and placed inside this fantastic array of thoughts and days gone by for the family that was so precious. These moments in time had been frozen in this box, every single one being that extra special touch to Kate and her past. The brittle seashells from the beach down in Cornwall two months before Fiona had died, the dizzy eyed octopus fridge magnet that Kate had thrown a tantrum to have from the

Sealife centre in Yarmouth. The tiny yellow umbrella that she'd had in her first pretend cocktail in London after watching The Lion King musical with Fiona and Sally. The first picture of Rob cradling Kate with her mother and auntie proudly standing beside him, all beaming with joy on their faces.

So many lovely trinkets of her childhood now stared back up at her. Nearing the bottom of the treasure, she spotted a small red box with the tiniest and cutest little black bow glued to its top. Lifting it out, Kate held it in her hand, remembering it in an instant and thinking now how big her hands had gotten since the last time she had held it. Her mind travelled back to when she was just six years old, and her mum had presented her with this exact box. It creaked as she opened it and there it was, exactly how she remembered. There laid her special necklace that Fiona had designed and made for her during her creative jewellery business. A single little daisy set in resin on a length of leather-effect string. Kate thought back to the vast number of times they used to visit the park and make daisy chains together after discovering the love of the little flower. She would make Fiona and Sally wear the necklaces until the daisy withered and broke, then would have to try and persuade them to go back to the park to make more. Kate remembered too how she had cried her eyes out when Fiona told her that the daisy blooming season was over at the start of Autumn. This was another reason why the necklace had been created, so that she could have a daisy all year round while they waited for Spring to arrive once more.

Those last few months when Fiona was feeling so weak but wouldn't let her daughter go to the park alone. Such precious moments flooded back right now and as they did, her eyes began to leak happy tears as the emotion became overwhelming. A cascade fell as she held her hand over her mouth, trying her best not to sob.

"Oh sweetheart, are you alright?" asked Sally, changing chairs to sit next to her, "oh my darling, come here." She said wiping the wetness from her nieces' cheeks.

"I'm okay really," Kate answered softly, sniffing back her emotions as best she could, "I loved her so much auntie, I think about her every single day that she's been gone and I miss her every day too," she paused as she took a deep breath, "I don't care that she wasn't my birth mother. I don't care how she got me; she was a truly amazing mother to me, and she will always be my mum."

"That's beautiful Kate, just bloody beautiful. Excuse my French. I miss her too, we all miss her and her cackly little laugh, one thing I miss so much." She reached around Kate's shoulders to comfort her. It was heart-warming to share this moment and she'd taken it so much better than she had thought. Sally felt relieved that the secret was finally out, finally told.

They spent the next two hours going through the box items, over and over, and all its wonderful contents brought them a variety of mixed emotions; joy, laughter, tears, and sadness but in a happy way. Kate now had her birth certificate, the adoption papers, her first ever little knitted bonnet, and pink hospital bracelet, all the special trinkets that mothers keep for their new-borns. They laughed as they read notes that Fiona had left for the special occasions she would never get to witness like Kate's prom, special milestone birthdays and finally one meant for her to read on her wedding day.

It read, '*To my utterly, gorgeous, pretty, talented, clever girl…yes you silly billy, although now I suppose you're a grown woman. Anyway…let's try that again…To my beautiful daughter Kate on your wedding day. I will be watching the whole special day, don't you worry yourself and I know you will be the most stunning bride ever to walk the earth, just make sure you pick a gooden, well…I suppose if it's your wedding day when you are reading this then…you must have. Oh you know what I mean sweetheart. Congratulations on being a Mrs. From the proudest mum of the bride ever. Mummy Ellington. xx*'

"Oh bless her," Kate said taking a moment to realise that she must've written these beautiful, meaningful notes knowing how sick she was, "Let's hope I get this special wedding she's talking about one day hey," she chuckled in jest.

"You will my darling, you will. And she's right, she usually was…you will be the most stunning bride ever."

As they both glanced down at all the things in front of them, the loving, caring face that was Miss Fiona Ellington beamed back her beautiful smile in all the old photographs. Tears of joy, tears of sadness and many fits of laughter were created during that afternoon, and something they both knew that they would treasure together from now on as a very special place and time in their lives.

*

A few hours later and Kate was full on busy, back at work enjoying her new job once more with her best mate Leo. They were creating an extravagant finger food buffet ready for their client to entertain guests that evening. As they baked and prepped, she filled him in on all the details regarding the shocking revelation of a conversation she'd just had with her auntie earlier. As soon as she had left Sally's house, he'd been the first person she wanted to text about it but in a hurry to get to him, she'd left a cryptic message leaving him anxious and in suspense.

When he finally got all the juicy information, he'd relaxed a little and was excited to hear everything, "well, that is certainly not what I expected to hear this afternoon babe. Your life is getting ever more interesting by the blooming week isn't it?" he said nudging her as he grabbed some herbs and spices from the rack on the wall next to her, "what are you going to do with all this information then?"

"First of all, I wasn't going to do anything but then, well then I changed my mind. I'm going to find them; my real parents, well my biological parents, oh you know what I'm trying to get at," she flustered, "I want to meet my real mum more than anything Leo."

"I bet you do. Wow, this truly is incredible news though. I mean, how do you feel about it all, finding out you were adopted and that?"

"Well as you can imagine, I was pretty damn shocked initially. I never had a clue. My mum, Fiona, she was my mum. She still is my mum. She'll never be replaced as the person who took care of me, she's the one who brought me up until…" she paused, glancing up at him.

"I know darling." He replied. He knew she hated saying that her mum had died, no matter how many times it had come up in conversation.

She smiled back, "but I'm sort of, I don't know, I guess I'm kind of excited in a way," she continued as Leo listened intently, "after all the crap I've had to deal with just lately with Dan, it's like a whole new chapter has now emerged and evolved my life into something interesting, something unexpectedly good in a weird way. It's crazy but I really feel like something exciting is about to happen, you know, when I meet them; when I get to meet and see my real mother?"

"Awesome, it's excitingly awesome Kate, it's going to be fun delving into it all."

"Let's hope this chapter comes without too much drama this time though"

"Oh man yeah, Jeez, don't need any more of that in your life," he replied, frowning his eyebrows at her, "this is proper exciting though. You could have a whole new family out there Kate. You could have siblings; sisters, brothers, imagine it?"

"I didn't actually think about that part of it all you know." Kate stopped slicing the red pepper on the board and glanced up across at Leo on the other side of the worktop, munching on a carrot stick.

"I wonder if you look like your real mum?" he said, popping some mini bacon quiches into the oven.

"Most daughters look like their mums don't they?" she replied, starting to slice again.

"I guess so. My sister used to look more like my dad as a baby but now, well, she's the image of my mum, they look more like sisters when you see them together, don't you think?"

"Yeah they are Leo, like twins. Maybe it's an age thing. Anyway, I just want to meet her the once really to begin with."

"Do you know much about her?" he asked, wiping his hands dry after washing them in the sink.

"Not a lot to be honest. Just her name, where she was from and how old she was when she gave me up for adoption. I think it was all very secretive from what my aunt told me. She might not even want to meet me; she might have a new family and not want the past showing up." Kate said suddenly feeling anxious about it all.

"That could happen I guess. I suppose you need to prepare yourself for that predicament. If she was only a teenager, it must have been so hard, you know, going through giving birth and then just handing her baby; you, over to a complete stranger and that's that, goodbye, wow." He said, blowing out a puff of air in disbelief.

"How many films and documentaries have we watched together with this exact situation happening hey? And now it's panning out for real, it's now my life becoming a sort of movie." She said using her knife to swipe all the sliced peppers into a large bowl.

"Madness." Leo replied, passing her the salad tongs to toss it all over as he added some olive oil into it, "and of course, if you need any help, just shout, I'd love to be part of your journey of new family self-discovery."

"Obviously," Kate agreed, grinning back at him, "I have no idea where to start but I'm going to get on it as soon as I can. Do some research and that first, see what I have to do, who I have to call etc. I know it's not going to be easy but I'm going to give it my all and try and find them." She wiped her hands onto her apron and began untying the back, "Anyway, are we nearly done here?"

"Yeah, I think so. Just gotta wait for these bad boys to finish baking and then it's the normal setting up, making it all look posh and highly expensive for the boss and his super rich footy friends." He joked.

"Cool, wanna grab a drink after?"

"Sure, the old work girls messaged me earlier actually. They wanna meet up at the Dog and Duck so shall we catch up with them?"

"Yeah, that'll be nice."

"Actually, I think Jessica is dating someone who was adopted as a toddler...yeah, I'm sure she mentioned it the other night, maybe she could help you find out some stuff?"

"Ooh, interesting," Kate replied covering the final dish of food with foil and hanging up her apron in the larder cupboard.

"We need to check him out anyway so it's a good excuse to get him there," Leo joked, "Alexander, I think she said, very posh name hey?" he said closing the larder door after hanging his apron up next to hers.

"No way as cool as yours Leo." Kate replied nudging him as they made their way outside.

"Well of course not. I have the coolest name in the world you know," he strutted along pointing the key at the car to unlock it, "Anyway, enough about me and my ultra-fabulous coolness, let's go get some chillaxing time." he exclaimed as they got into his car and made their way to the pub to meet their mutual friends.

It had been way too long for them all to meet up and Kate was especially looking forward to it. She had missed too many parties and events with them, cancelling nights out due to her wanting to spend any free time out of work with Dan. Now he was gone, she wanted to apologise and rebuild those friendships, not that anyone had taken it personally. They all understood the new romance thing. Now, all Kate could think about was trying to enjoy life again as a twenty something young woman.

Leo sent a quick message to Jessica before they set off, to ensure that she brought her new boyfriend along. They were all excited to meet him anyway so made sense to combine the two projects.

Kate practically spent the whole evening chatting away to Alex, jotting down everything he had with helpline links, websites, and people to contact regarding finding adoption information. She had vowed not to drink too much this evening, not after the last time she'd been out with Leo and made the move on him. She was on a mission now; she had her future to discover so getting drunk wasn't an option tonight.

*

On the short journey back to Kate's place afterwards, she recalled all the information she could back to Leo. Her notebook was full of scribbled ink, ideas, and points for her to look up. She felt so excited with it all and couldn't convey it fast enough.

"I think you may have a serious amount of work to do over the next few months or so?" he said, finally getting a word in edgeways as he pulled up outside her house.

"Yes. More than I imagined there would be but I'm up for the challenge," she winked at him, "Are you?"

"Oh you know how much I love challenges like this honey bunny, sign me up, right this minute." He winked back with a knowing smile as he leaned over to kiss her cheek.

"It's time for me to find out why. I just want to find out the truth; you know the reasons behind my real mother giving me away like she did, like she felt she had to. I just want some answers to all these random questions running around in my crazy mulch of a brain." She replied, wobbling her head to and fro.

Leo just gave her hand a gentle squeeze in return, and they said their goodbyes.

As she watched him driving out of her street, she thought even more about her real mother and how this could now affect her life. This was her time to put closure to her past few months that had been a nightmare, and to add a new chapter, a new story to her future. She'd had enough lying and deceit over the past year with Dan and his games. That awful episode was over, and she now needed this truth more than anything ever before. It was time to discover who she really was, where she came from and why she was given up in the first place. One way or another, she was determined to find out more about her past and her real mothers' life, no matter how long it took.

Chapter Thirty-Two

Ben & Sarah…

For the next year, Kate worked as many hours with Leo as she possibly could. Their wedding catering business was full steam ahead in a matter of weeks and they were busy most weekends with lavish food creations. She had even started to bake again, fulfilling the needs of the brides who wanted cupcake towers instead of the more traditional three tier stand-alone cakes. In the evenings and any spare moments she had time to relax, she would spend it tirelessly searching the internet, carrying out all the research she needed to do to try and locate where her birth parents were and how best to contact them. She then took on an evening volunteering job at a local youth club that helped young mums who had become pregnant. She wanted to try and understand what they went through, emotionally more than anything. Trying to understand how they were feeling somehow made her feel closer to her own situation and gave more of an insight into her own birth mother's thought processes and what she must have felt.

Finally, she made progress finding her real father. It was easier to discover the whereabouts of him to begin with as her birth mother had recently got married so the surname change put a delay on her search. Her dad's name was Ben and remarkably, he lived only a few towns away. She had found her biological father and after meeting with him and his mother whom he still lived with, after a few months, they finally located Sarah in Cambridge.

Kate had taken on yet another part time job to pay for her new car that she was saving up for and deliberately took that position because of the proximity and location. It was right near where her mystery mother had her own beauty salon. Kate felt confident, once she made some sort of contact, things would fall into place automatically. Unfortunately, the plan didn't quite tally up.

After her shift, she phoned Leo to tell him all about it, "I'm gutted Leo. I had this crazy idea that she'd just welcome me with open arms, and we'd be reunited after all these years, I feel so silly now and I think I might have scared her off."

"Oh dear, maybe she was just in shock. I mean, wouldn't you be if someone just turned up at your local coffee store claiming to be your long-lost child?" he said trying to reassure her, "what did you say to her anyway?"

"I asked her if I had the right name. She said yes first of all but then said she'd got married, which we sort of knew and then…"

"Then what sweetheart, what happened?"

"Well, she practically run out of the shop. I've never seen anyone leave the shop the way she did Leo. What should I do?"

"It sounds to me, like she was in complete shock darling. You can't really blame her can you?"

"I guess not," she sighed, "Ben is going to try and talk to her. I daren't tell him about today though in case he gets mad with me for trying to go it alone and find her. I think he feels so responsible about the whole adoption, teenage baby thing."

"I don't think he'd be mad Kate. By what you've told me already, he seems generally happy and amazed that you even want to know him, he's not gonna risk losing you again is he?"

"Oh Leo. How come you always know what to say to me in a crisis?"

"Just a swell type of guy I guess," he chuckled down the phone, "look, try not to fret. She's gonna need some time to figure out that you are back in her life."

"But I'm not back yet am I?" Kate replied in a downward tone of voice.

"Time Kate, give it time," he told her, "Look I'll be round shortly okay, grab a couple of bottles of wine and we can chat some more yeah?"

"Okay," she agreed, "sorry for being a pain in the neck again."

"I'm going to pretend I didn't hear that missus, now get to the shop. I'll see you in twenty minutes."

After they'd said their goodbyes and hung up, she sat on the bench outside the coffee shop, glancing down the street. In her heart, she hoped that Sarah would come waltzing back towards her and then she could apologize for being so abrupt, but she didn't appear, so Kate made her way to the corner shop to get two bottles of wine, a large share bag of snaps, which were Leo's favourite brand of crisps, some salted nuts and chocolate buttons for them to snack on later.

The weekend flew past with two wedding breakfasts and an order of fifty pink and blue cupcakes for a baby reveal party. Leo had come round to help Kate with the baking and after the order was collected, they decided to watch a movie at his place.

As they sat settled together on the sofa, her phone pinged with a message from Ben.

"Oh my god." Kate exclaimed as she read it.

"What's up chick?" Leo asked leaning closer to see the message.

"It's Ben, he's found her. Look...she's agreed to meet me." She showed him the phone message stunned in silence, "Tomorrow!" she said louder almost shrieking with excitement.

Leo wrapped his arm around her shoulders, pulling her in closer with a gentle shaking action, "I told you it would be okay didn't I?" and kissed the side of her head, "Yay, you're gonna meet your mum Kate. This is cause for a re-fill on the old wine girly."

Kate watched on as he jumped out of his seat, grabbing hold of the wine bottle in front of them and pouring the fruity blush liquid into their glasses.

"Here's to new beginnings." He said, passing her glass and chinking them together.

She remained quiet for a few seconds, beaming a smile down at the message, then sat back, took a large swig of her drink, breathing a sigh of relief. This was her new beginning, and she couldn't wait to see what it would bring her.

The next morning felt strange for Kate. She hadn't slept more than a few hours, too excited and too many questions ready and waiting in her mind to ask. Leo had stayed over to try and keep her calm, helping her make some notes. They'd both booked the day off work, and he was going to wait at her place to hear all the exciting news when she returned from their meeting. Kate felt more nervous to meet Sarah than she had to meet Ben and didn't understand why. She'd chatted to Ben for hours regarding what had happened between the two of them all those years ago, and soon realised how difficult it must've been for Sarah to cope in those circumstances.

"I feel like my whole body is shaking." She said to Ben as they made their way into the small outside patio area at the back of the farm shop.

"You'll be fine," he tried to reassure her.

"What if she doesn't show up? What if she doesn't like me?"

"She will love you Kate, what's not to love about you? And she will turn up, she promised. Look, Sarah is lovely, you've nothing to worry about with her, I promise okay?" he held her hands to try and steady them. They were cold and they were in fact, trembling.

Kate just nodded back, then followed the waitress to their table in the far corner where they awaited the arrival of the final piece of their little jigsaw. Ben ordered them some strong coffee to ease the tense atmosphere and Kate tried to relax.

It seemed like an hour before she suddenly arrived. There was a deafening silence as Sarah approached their table with the waitress chatting away to her. Kate froze as she realised it was her mother coming towards her and she looked even more nervous than she had on that awkward day at the coffee shop. Her face was flushed a nice blush of pink as Ben asked her if she wanted a drink.

"Oh, just a water for now please," she replied, sitting down opposite Kate who was still in a stunned silence.

Strangely, for a few minutes, she didn't feel as confident as she had before when they'd met briefly but she knew something had to be said soon. The silence had to be broken by one of them.

"I'm sorry if I startled you in the coffee shop the other day. It's lovely to finally meet you," Kate blurted out trying to sound more confident than she actually felt. Kate noticed how blue Sarah's eyes were, they were exactly the same colour as hers, but the gaze didn't last long.

Sarah smiled back but didn't say anything. She was clearly nervous, and Kate's heart went out to her.

As Ben made a sharp exit, pretending to nip off to the toilet, the tense atmosphere increased slightly as Sarah watched him leave the table but then finally spoke, "Katie...I...I need to say something."

Kate noticed Sarah's hands trembling so much she had to get them out of sight. Now she felt sorry for her and needed to try and calm her down. She knew what she was going to say, she knew she was sorry, but Kate didn't want to hear an apology. Sarah didn't have to apologise for trying to do the right thing by her daughter in a time when it wasn't the done thing to have a child as a teenager.

"Please don't say it Sarah," she replied, "you don't have to say sorry. Ben told me everything. I know the story and I understand the reasons you did what you did, honestly, it's okay." Kate reached her hand across the table in the hope that Sarah would grasp hold of it, and they could somehow bond, help each other in this moment but she didn't move towards it, she just looked. Her eyes filling with water, Kate could see how emotional she was getting so she slid her hand back and continued trying to make the situation a little bit easier on both of them. "Please just call me Kate, no-one has called me Katie for many years now. I don't want to cause you any stress Sarah. I just wanted to meet you, to see you properly, meet my birth mother finally, even if you can only do it this once."

They looked at each other, their eyes darting about trying to take in details of each of their faces. It was like they were the only ones there in that place right now.

Sarah finally mustered up a sentence, "It's just been a shock you know. I never expected to see you again, not ever."

Kate could hear Sarah's voice breaking with emotion. She then tried to reassure her by telling her about her volunteer job with young mums, explaining how different it is now to how it was when Sarah was a teenage mum. All she wanted to do was chat with her real mother and ensure that she understood that there was no blame, no animosity towards her for the choices she had to make, and eventually, they got there.

Ben stayed out of the way for most of the afternoon, leaving mother and daughter getting to know one another. It was now turning into a magical meeting for them both and Kate was loving life once more with her newfound parents, especially Sarah.

They both relaxed and just enjoyed it until it was time to leave. Kate had to get back to work so Ben offered her a lift.

As they all emerged outside into the car park, Kate said her goodbyes to Sarah who was now unable to keep her tears back.

Noticing the droplet trickling down her cheek, Kate reached over and wiped it, "Sarah don't be sad," she said calmly, "like I said to you earlier, I don't hold any grudges and I forgive you, it wasn't your fault," their eyes met as she continued, "Ben was too young as well. I see it all the time in my job, but girls get so much more support these days. It's very different for them, but these things happen, and you did what was best for you at the time. And the main thing is you did what was best for me. I appreciate that, I really do. I had a great childhood because of the difficult choices that you had to make, so you don't have to feel guilty about any of it, not at all, okay?" she held Sarah's hands like she was the adult, "look, if you want to meet up again, that's absolutely fine but if you don't, that's fine too. I know all about your life now and I don't want to cause any trouble or interfere with that. I just wanted to meet you, just once to see if we looked alike which now sounds weird," she chuckled, "so I'm more than happy you were brave enough and came today, it's been awesome."

Sarah's tearful eyes glistened in the sunlight as she just said one word, "Wow." And it made Kate smile, "Kate, you are such a beautiful person, I feel proud to call you my…" then she stopped, "sorry." She apologised.

"Your daughter?" Kate finished the sentence for her, knowing it was what she really wanted to say. She wiped another tear from her face and sniffed back hers too this time, "I've really gotta rush now otherwise I'm going to be late but text me okay, whenever you want to."

With that, they had one final hug and Kate climbed into Ben's car excitedly waving out the back window as they slowly drove down the long driveway. She wanted to capture every moment of Sarah, her mum, standing there waving goodbye, smiling so happily back.

"Happy?" asked Ben as Kate finally turned to face the front of the car again.

"Very." She replied, "Thank you so much for convincing her to meet me Ben. And you were so right, she's just soooo lovely, such a sweet person."

"Exactly like her daughter then hey?" He smirked back.

"Oh stop with the flattery, Mr Charm almighty," she playfully punched his arm, "just get me to work hey?" then they just laughed as Kate switched the radio on and turned the volume up.

She was so happy to have them in her life now and the future seemed to be growing ever brighter once more. She hoped this was the start of something exciting for everyone and couldn't wait to tell Leo all about it.

Chapter Thirty-Three

Sally…

"Man this road is always a nightmare; they need a crossing putting in or something." Ben said as he glanced up and down the road for a clearing to pull out. The traffic was heaving today, pedal bikes were swerving in-between the cars and lorries frighteningly fast going about their business. They mainly consisted of vast amount of food delivery riders that had now become even more popular in the town.

"Oh, I know," Kate answered, tapping away another quick text message to Leo. She'd briefed over the afternoon meeting as soon as she'd got into the car, knowing he'd be anxious to know how it went. She finished up by telling him to pick up an expensive bottle of champagne to celebrate later.

He'd quickly replied with a massive 'YES TO THAT!!!' with the added three champagne bottles icon, a line of laughing emojis, and six red balloons making her chuckle. He did love his emojis.

"It's fine Ben, don't fret, I'll get out here. It's only five minutes' walk down there, and it'll save you getting into all the town traffic, one-way craziness."

"You sure?"

"Yeah course, honestly, it's no problem, look, you can see the shop sign from here." She pointed, grabbing her bag, and unclipping her seatbelt as they pulled into the nearest layby.

As she went to open the door, her phone began to ring. It was Sally.

"Hey auntie, one second…" Kate said excitedly as she said goodbye to Ben, stepping out of the car, "See you later yeah…I finish at about ten ish if you wanna pick me up?"

"Yes sure, I'll try and get nearer though, don't want you crossing this road at that time of night hey?" he blew her a kiss with his hand.

Kate just smiled back, gave him the thumbs up, and shut the door, juggling her phone into the side of head, and throwing her handbag over her shoulder.

"You still there Kate darling?" Sally asked.

"Yes, I'm just trying to get over the road to work, it's so blooming busy today."

"Do you want to call me back then?"

"No it's cool. Here's a quick lowdown. I've had

such a fab afternoon. Sarah is so lovely, and she looks just like me auntie. We have the exact same colour eyes, it was like looking in a mirror, we have the same hair and everything and we're going to see each other again. We've swapped numbers and that. She's gonna introduce me to her husband and his family. I'm so excited auntie."

Sally hesitated in answering. Although she knew this was exactly what Kate wanted, what she needed to answer all her questions, it was still hard to imagine her not being the major part in her life. It had just been the three of them for so many years now, but Kate had worked so hard to find her birth parents and Sally was going to be there for her whatever happened. This was no time for her to feel selfish. After everything she'd been through with Dan, and the shocking secret regarding his mother, Kate needed this excitement and this new chapter of happiness and she was pleased for her niece, "That's great news darling." Was all she could say for now.

"Ben on the other hand," Kate continued, sounding breathless, "well, he's a bit of a wild one still to be fair but Sarah, well, she's amazing and I can't wait to get to know her more...I cannot wait to fill you and Uncle Rob in a bit more when I see you next. Leo is going to be anxiously awaiting with a bottle to celebrate tonight, I've already text him to make sure. It's a good thing to celebrate hey?"

"Oh most definitely darling. We look forward to

catching up with it all."

"One sec, I think I can finally cross…"

Sally could hear the heavy drone of the busy traffic through the line, the loud beeping of car horns every few seconds and Kate's excited breathing down the phone. She could just imagine her beaming smile on her face.

Kate was juggling her phone, changing to the other side of her head to carry on with the call, still frantically looking to cross the road. She couldn't wait until tonight where she'd get back to her place seeing Leo after her coffee shop shift. She hadn't needed to get this extra job at the local store, but she enjoyed the social side of it too as it was so different from the private footballer's home catering job. Plus it was where she had first captured a glimpse of Sarah; albeit a rather strange meeting that didn't quite go to plan.

"Right listen auntie, I'm going to have to go, it's manic out here today, traffic blooming everywhere,"

"Ok sweetie, you be careful out there." Sally replied.

"I will. Sorry, but I'm going to be late if I don't get a jiggle on, I'll call you in…" Then her voice stopped abruptly.

Suddenly, all Sally heard was the daunting sounds of banging, crashing, and smashing of glass, then the phone line cut off, the conversation fell deathly silent. "Kate," she called down the phone, "Kate!" she repeated moving the phone from her ear to see that the call had been disconnected. She quickly pressed the button to call her back, but it went straight to Kate's answer message. She hung up and tried three more times but still nothing. It wouldn't even connect to the answer service now. As many times as she dialled the number back, there was no answer. Distraught with concern, she decided to try and phone the coffee shop where Kate should've been. There was an obvious sound of commotion going on as she finally managed to get through, so the manager apologised and said he would call her back shortly.

She yelled upstairs to Rob for him to come down and then, after an anxious few minutes waiting as patiently as they could, her phone rang, making her jump.

"Sorry about that Sally," the voice said, and Sally knew it wasn't good news by the tone he was now using. There had been a terrible road accident just yards up from the shop.

As he uttered the next few words, Sally's heart sunk, her stomach churned, and her eyes began to fill with tears.

"It's Kate." he said, his voice cracking with sadness as he spoke.

As if in slow motion, she listened intently as he relayed what had happened. Her mind blank, her heart torn into millions of pieces, crushed with pain, and smashed beyond repair.

Kate had been hit by a swerving car that had mounted the pavement trying to avoid a lorry which had gone out of control for some reason. The driver was already dead and the car passenger, badly hurt and being cut from the wreckage as fast as possible. But Kate lay unresponsive in the road where she had been thrown by the car.

"The ambulance crew are with her now Sally, but I think they've called the air ambulance," he paused, "yes, I can hear the helicopter trying to land in the school field opposite." His voice grew louder.

Everything was whizzing around Sally's head, ten to the dozen. She felt as though she was in some dream state and couldn't think properly. It must be serious if the helicopter had been called out. Her face grew whiter by the second with shock. Rob took the phone from his wife as it dropped to her side. Within a few short hours, it was all over.

*

"My darling Kate" Sally begun, "Why did you have to leave? Why did it have to be you? Why did I keep you chatting on the phone, not concentrating on those bloody roads? Why, why, why? I'm asking myself these questions repeatedly every day since you left us." Sally sat on the bench beside the grave, tears silently running down her face.

Just a month earlier, she was happily chatting to her niece on the phone, her niece who was so excited to have met her birth parents, excited to have a new lease of life after all the problems with Dan. But now she was gone. Buried, no more beautiful Kate to lighten up all their lives and it hurt Sally like crazy. "I still can't believe you are gone from our lives. I didn't do my job to protect you like I promised I would, I'm so sorry my darling Kate." She paused as she glanced across at her sister's gravestone. Kate had been placed next to hers, "I'm so sorry Fiona, my beloved sister, and the best mother to Kate. Forgive me sister, please, do forgive me for not protecting her." Her eyes were so welled up with tears, she could hardly see the flowers that Rob had placed down.

"You have to try and stop punishing yourself darling, it was a terrible accident." He said as he held her tightly in his arms.

Sobbing her heart out, all she could think was how cruel life could be sometimes. Not only had life taken her wonderful caring sister from cancer, but now it had taken her sister's daughter, her niece in another tragic circumstance.

"You know what hurts me the most Rob?" she whimpered, "most of all, I will never forgive myself for not revealing the truth about her adoption sooner."

"Sally please don't.."

"No Rob," she interrupted, "she could have had so many more years to discover her past if I'd just got that bloody box out a bit earlier. She should have had so many more years ahead of her to thrive, to love, to live. Now look," She paused, pointing towards the ground, "I just hope she forgives me. Please forgive me for Telling Lies."

***

If you enjoyed this book, please take a few minutes
to post a review on Amazon as that will help
even more readers enjoy it.

Simply go to Amazon, search for
'T.A. Rosewood', choose which book you'd like to
review and type away. Just a 'loved it', 'would
recommend this book' sort of thing is great.

It really does help self-published authors to get our
books out there to many more readers.
Thank you so much x

OTHER BOOKS BY ME...

Reasonable Lies
Jane's Journal
Secrets & Lies
Sarah's Secrets

More Coming Soon...

Thanks...

To my gorgeous children – you've been more than just children this past year, you've been my support, my friends, my rocks, and I'm so proud to be your mum. Thank you. xxx

To my ever-loving hubby and his creative skills – there are no words to express what I feel for you. Soul mates don't come round that often and you're a keeper! Glad I gave nice a try. xxx

To my beta readers - I would like to thank you amazing people who have gone through this book for me and given me the courage and strength to get it finished and out there. Your constant support and advice have helped me no end and I'm truly thankful to have met you all, online and a few in person now.

And to you, the one holding this book right now – for buying, downloading, and reading this book. Thank you for taking the chance on it and taking the time to read my stuff.

You all make me one happy author.

About Me...

Hi, I'm Traci, and I write under the pen name of T.A. Rosewood because I've always thought my real name was too boring. It's a combination of my first initials, my favourite flower and surname.

I have had a passion for writing ever since I can remember, and I penned my first short story when I was just thirteen years old. It was written in one of my spare school textbooks and was called, *Looks Aren't Everything*. It was about teenage love and all the drama that comes along with that side of things.

In my GCSE English exam, I had to write a two-page story, but I couldn't stop once I'd started writing, so it ended up being thirty pages long – and yep, I failed English for that! The story, called *The Runaway*, was again about teenagers, love and running away.

During my twenties, I began writing and publishing poetry plucking out events in my own life to express emotional poems. (Collection to come).

As life grew busy getting married, having children, and working, my writing stopped until 2015 when I met Jojo Moyes. She was opening our local bookstore, Harts Books, and it inspired me to start writing again. That very evening, I came up with a storyline and after nearly four years, *'Reasonable Lies'* was published as my debut novel.

In 2021, I released a short novella called Jane's Journal which is the personal diary of the main character from Reasonable Lies. This came about after an Instagram virtual tour of Reasonable Lies. People had questions for Jane as to why she lied, so as the reviews came in, I wrote the journal to answer those questions.

Readers also fell in love with the secondary character from the debut, Sarah, so her story was released in January of 2022, and is called, Secrets & Lies.

Intrigued by this character, again, my readers wanted to know more about her and so another short novella diary was created later that year. This one is from Sarah's point of view spanning three stages of her life.

My two novels have since gone global and are available all over the world now. I also have many more books to come so watch this space!

I live in North Essex with my husband, two children and two West Highland Terriers, Daisi & Robbie.

Keep In Touch...

I would love to hear from you,
so please find me on all the social media platforms.

Find me on
Instagram, Facebook, TikTok,
Twitter, & Goodreads:
Tag me using - @TARosewood and use the
hashtag
#tarosewood.

For more news, updates,
book signing events,
and competitions,
please visit my website:
www.tarosewood.com

Reading Journal...

Do you like to record the books you read in your own personal notebook and write up your reviews?

How about your very own reading log?
Traci has designed and created her very own one for you and it's available on Amazon.

Just search Amazon for this number
B0B7QLDGHF

Printed in Great Britain
by Amazon

86298188R00233